Praise for Chr
The Best of Our Past, t

'Christi Nogle is one of my favorite new voices in
horror. Her fiction is by turns devastating, horrifying,
and beyond beautiful.'
Gwendolyn Kiste, Bram Stoker Award-winning author

'Just as you think you have a handle on what a Christi
Nogle story might be, you turn a page and are surprised
anew. Enigmatic, surreal yet shockingly visceral, often
rooted in a deceptively familiar domesticity turned
nightmarish, these strange and unsettling tales unfold in
lyrical prose that belies their savagery.'
Lynda E. Rucker, Shirley Jackson Award-winning author

'An astonishingly original collection of dark tales –
mysterious, haunting, challenging and disturbing,
written in crystalline prose as compressed as poetry.
Read and then reread and be doubly rewarded!'
Ramsey Campbell, author of *Fellstones*

'Christi Nogle takes readers on a dark yet wondrous
journey through perils, horror, and thrills in this
extraordinary debut collection. Behold the timelessness
of these lives, these tales!'
Eric J. Guignard, award-winning author
and editor, including *That Which Grows Wild*
and *Doorways to the Deadeye*

CHRISTI NOGLE

ONE EYE OPENED IN THAT OTHER PLACE

This is a **FLAME TREE PRESS** book

Text copyright © 2024 Christi Nogle

FLAME TREE PRESS
6 Melbray Mews, London, SW6 3NS, UK
flametreepress.com

US sales, distribution and warehouse:
Simon & Schuster
simonandschuster.biz

UK distribution and warehouse:
Hachette UK Distribution
hukdcustomerservice@hachette.co.uk

Thanks to the Flame Tree Press team.

The cover is created by Flame Tree Studio with thanks to Shutterstock.com.
The font families used are Avenir and Bembo.

Flame Tree Press is an imprint of Flame Tree Publishing Ltd
flametreepublishing.com

A copy of the CIP data for this book is available from the British Library and the Library of Congress.

PB ISBN: 978-1-78758-836-3
ebook ISBN: 978-1-78758-838-7

Printed and bound in Great Britain by Clays Ltd, Elcograf S.p.A.

CHRISTI NOGLE

ONE EYE OPENED IN THAT OTHER PLACE

FLAME TREE PRESS
London & New York

To the editors and staff of the magazines, journals, small presses, and podcasts that make up our thriving literary scene. You are appreciated.

CONTENTS

PLAYMATE

We stayed in the Uber during the ferry ride. The driver sweated and kept looking at me and Grace in the rearview – but he didn't try to banter. My daughter and I give off an air of self-containment, I suppose. Something about us does not invite conversation.

Her shorts were too short. She kept lifting herself and pulling down the hem. We'd been in cars and planes all day and I hadn't noticed until now.

"How'd you get so tall all of a sudden?" I said.

Grace looked down, her thick hair shifting onto her face. I tucked it back behind her ear and she smiled, but it was that long-suffering smile I cannot bear.

I sighed and looked out the window. All the nearby cars were empty, the passengers gone to the deck or the little concessions area, trying to make the most of the ride.

"This ferry used to stop at the *little* island too," I said and caught the driver's eyes in the rearview.

Did he know anything more than I did? He only squinted.

I said, "There's a bridge, but it might be down for good by now. But there used to be a man who rented little boats...."

"What are you saying?" said Grace.

"That there might not be a way to get where you're going," said the driver. He let out a tortured sigh.

There was a way, though. We drove through town and out in the country ten miles or more, circled around a bit, and finally found the bridge. A crooked line of orange cones blocked one lane, but there were no workers and no signs. I watched sweat roll down the driver's forehead and felt the vinyl seat slick under my legs. Grace had stopped fussing with her shorts. She was limp, done for.

A rocky, curving road came next and then a smoother road overhung with trees. The air felt cooler.

"I always thought this part was so beautiful," I said. I'd never taken Grace home to see my people, not once, and I was ashamed of that. There was no great falling-out. We'd just been busy.

And my mother had never called me home before.

I think Grace wanted to ask if we were almost there. Instead, she said, "It's pretty." What did she think of this place? All the fanciful tales I'd told of it, she must have felt she'd come through a portal into fairyland.

The road pitched up again. We saw water below us – and the stark pale beach.

"The house is right down there," I said.

But it wasn't.

We drove the low road parallel to the beach, drove it twice. The two dozen houses that had stood there were missing. They hadn't left holes like you see when houses are moved, not rubble like you'd see after a tsunami. Fences still stood, trees and bushes stood. The places where houses had stood were just low piles of dirt, or mounds of uprooted beachgrass, cast gravel, or nothing at all.

I was crying. I had a feeling of fate, of doom.

I was thinking of a hand made out of sand, a child's hand reaching up out of the ground and taking my beach toys away. Was that one of the stories I'd told Grace? It was hard to say, now, what I'd made up and what I'd lived.

"What happened? Was it a storm?" the driver said.

"Maybe you lived on a different road," Grace said. She touched my shoulder, and I leaned away.

"There are no other roads," said the driver, who was looking at his phone.

"But she called me," I said.

"Who?" said the driver.

"My mother. She said the power was out, but she called from the big island, from town."

He pulled over, finally. "What do you want me to do?"

I tipped him well. All the time I was getting our bags together, Grace was up in my face saying, "Let's go back with him. Let's just...."

Go back to our little life?

My mother called me *home* after all these years. I wasn't turning back.

The car waited a long time as we walked the beach road, then he left. Yes, it was hot. I hid our bags in a blackberry thicket and went on, feeling unhinged. Grace was wailing by then.

We walked the road again and again. Our legs began to ache.

I stood in the spot where I swore the house had been. I'd described it to Grace so many times. I didn't have it wrong.

Without warning, all the memories came back. Playing outside with the other children who lived on this street. An image of a little dust devil sprang to mind, and I pushed it back. A sharper image of a child's hand cast in sand, gripping on to a red plastic spade.

Most of my time here was just playing on the beach and hiking up into the...I looked up toward the green hills and caught the glint of glass in the trees.

"Is there a *house* up there?" I said.

"I don't think..." said Grace. Her eyes were better than mine, but she was a skeptic. She always said no first. Maybe one day she would be sorry she'd lived her life that way.

"It is," I said.

"No," she said, and then after a moment, "yes."

★   ★   ★

I knew it once we'd gotten to the base of the hill. Not *a* house but *my* house – the house where I was born. It had been repainted sometime, a mossy green with raspberry trim. I remembered it yellow and white. Well, it had fit with the beach and now it fit with the hills.

Our clothes snagged on berry thickets and shoes scuffed against the rocks. By the time we met the door, we were drenched and raving with thirst. I couldn't speak for Grace, but my head throbbed. Even then I saw the signs of wrongness. The house had been moved – impossible enough on this island – but how had the house been moved?

It was recent. The shreds of vine that had pulled up with the deck had not yet lost all their green. I tapped at the door.

It all felt too surreal, like a death can feel, like a noonday dream.

I tapped the door, and it swung right in. The house was that far off level. The floor was sloped and broken.

"Hello?" Grace called.

I couldn't speak. "Mother?" I tried to say, but no sound or air came out.

We saw straight through the house – it was that small – straight through to the kitchen windows. The forest moved beyond them like a quick breeze on fur. Something shifted against the wallpaper inside, but it was too dark, and it was all beyond me anyway. By then, I'd fainted.

★   ★   ★

I lay on the bed, my mother sitting on one side of me and my daughter on the other.

Mother bent down to hug me and kiss my cheek. A strange waft of vinegar, or was it wine? Standing, she said, "I shouldn't have called."

Her face was more haggard than I'd expected, but the light made her seem warm and welcoming. I focused past her to the dresser, where perfume bottles and beaded necklaces were displayed along with my baby picture and Grace's most recent school photo. Everything was so real and mundane. There was nothing outside the window, only sky. We might have been back at the beach except for the sounds. No music of surf. Different birds too, and something more.

I clutched my head.

My mother smiled and left the room.

"There's something wrong with her," Grace whispered to me.

I rose. "Mother?" I called, suddenly panicked that she'd disappeared, but she rushed back from the kitchen with an aspirin and a warm can of beer.

"No water. I'm sorry," she said.

A rumble came like an earthquake, and Mother eased us down to the floor. A deep, dark shadow fell across us and then passed. Mother hushed us with her finger, and when she took her hand away from her face, she was smiling broadly.

"What the fuck was that?" said Grace. She was flat to the floor, and Mother helped her ease up. The ground still rumbled, though it no longer felt so urgent to stay low.

"It's a…giant, I suppose," said Mother.

And I knew before she said.

"Your little playmate, you remember?" said Mother. "She grew all at once. A week ago, maybe? It was all a big mess. I didn't even know what was happening. But she asked for you, in her way. She wanted you back."

The rumbling hadn't stopped. It was slighter now.

"You'll see her soon. Look out the window," said Mother.

Grace began crawling toward the window.

"No, don't," I said.

"I want to see."

Mother said, "I thought she wiped them all out. I didn't mind. But last night, after she put the house up here, I got out on the roof, and all along the hills I saw candlelight in windows. I think a lot of people were spared."

"Oh my god," said Grace.

"Get away from the window," I said. I couldn't move.

"Remember you used to talk about her? No one believed," said Mother.

"I see her, all of her," said Grace.

"Please," I tried to say, but my throat was too tight. I barely breathed, and so all I could do was hear:

Gunshots, a deeper rumble.

Distant screams, the sound of a house dashed against rocks.

My mother – quite drunk, I realized now – was saying, "She's like the wind, I think, but magnetic. She calls things to her. Makes herself. Sometimes she's sand, and sometimes she's trees and rocks, like now. But never water." Mother laughed, an awful drunken cackle. "We thought she was afraid of the water. Isn't that funny? We thought how good she'd never leave, because she wouldn't—"

"But you were wrong," said Grace.

Mother only laughed. Maybe she would never speak again.

The window where Grace watched filled up – and it was beautiful – it filled with an eye. The tree forms of the hazel-colored iris were made of uprooted trees and earth and strands of moss and beachgrass, the narrowing pupil the black rocks of the cliffs, the whites were our soft pale sand, and over it all hung a glassy orb of water. Enough to fill a pool.

"She controls the water just the same as anything else now," said Grace.

Paralyzed as I was, terrified as I was, I marveled a moment at Grace's calm and her swift intelligence.

The eye was gone, and Mother still laughed. She began to sound like she might vomit.

"Come," Grace said, beckoning toward me. "Come see."

And I did. I crawled, uphill it seemed – the floor had shifted again. I crawled to the window and saw the giant still full-bodied, very far from us, only for a moment. Like a statue chiseled from the cliffs and grown over with ferns, she stood still. It seemed she stared at me.

I caught the rubble of the cast-down house and looked away quickly, back at her.

She'd turned. Her steps were light now. We didn't feel them.

"I know what she's doing," said Grace.

I didn't, and then I did. She was heading into the water. Her toes came apart when they touched it. We saw the rocks and trees and earth crumble and float.

Her ankles came apart as they met the water, her calves, her knees.

"I can't believe this," said Grace.

Mother had stopped laughing. I didn't turn to see her. I had to watch the giant.

When her hips fell away, she paused. She dived forward, and yes, there was a great splash that should have killed everyone. It didn't quite reach us, though, so far up in the hills we were.

EVERY DAY'S A PARTY (WITH YOU)

Morning goes like a dream, just a nice hunk of quiche and a coffee with my favorite person. Frost and Christmas lights wreath the diner's dark window. We lean in and whisper because the handsome mystery man is stealing glances at us again from his booth in the back of the room.

"Looking at you," she whispers, her breath all warm and coffee-bitter.

"No, you," I say.

It took a long time to find my best friend, but I've found her. Gloria. She's divorced like me. She has a teen daughter like me, though her Mira is away at school.

Her song plays – that Laura Branigan song – so low you can't make out the words. I always thought Gloria was a name for a blonde, but my Gloria's colors are Snow White's. Her perfect little nose is red from her walk over here.

The handsome man stares again and we whisper, we giggle.

The song's changed to that one that goes, "Every day's a party with you, with you."

"So how's Char been?" Gloria asks.

I sigh. "Not so bad last night, really. The other day she called me a monster, though. 'Mom, you're a fucking monster.' That's what she said."

"Don't swear, dear Sara," Gloria says, leaning back with a smirk.

"You're unattractive when you swear, dear," I say. Gloria's mother said that to her one time when I was over. We laugh now, remembering that, and then the tabletop vibrates.

"Got to go," Gloria says, checking her big black pager and rising from the booth.

"Your dad?"

"Who else?"

I stay a while longer nursing my coffee, but it's still dark when I leave Jack's Diner.

★ ★ ★

Moss Park. The town is shaped like a Venn diagram. The park is the shape of a cat's pupil, a long, pointed ellipse carpeted in an odd verdant moss. The pointy ends of the park are treed, but at the center is just the moss crossed by walking paths and a tall, white-painted gazebo in the center.

I pass through the gazebo. The Christmas lights inside it are cherry and teal and lemony-green just like everything else in Moss Park.

So beautiful, the big bulbs and tiny ones, all throwing their colors onto the white ceiling and the beams. Everything's bathed in these colors.

The town wasn't always this way. When Char and I moved here, it was all brown and gray and…poor. I remember the first day here, walking lost, looking for the post office. Rain and dullness. I stopped for directions in a cruddy little convenience store in what amounted to a garden barn. I don't even think that store is still here now.

I cut across the park to the bookstore where I work. The owner, Mrs. Sylvester, is my landlady too – Char and I stay in the guesthouse behind her big Victorian. The old lady's so absent from my days I seem to have taken over her place. It's like I am the owner of the bookstore now. Everyone treats me that way, just as everyone treats Gloria like she, and not her father, is the owner of Glories, the swanky jewelry store across the park.

And whenever I go into the big Victorian to make dinner or to take a long candlelit soak in the big downstairs tub? I feel *I* am the sprawling house's mistress, not Mrs. Sylvester. The feeling I get from that is complicated, a little guilty and a little blessed. I suppose the young do overtake the old at a certain point and that's natural.

★ ★ ★

Mrs. Sylvester and Gloria's broad-shouldered old dad are having words across the street. I can't hear what they are saying. She's just parked, must be coming into the bookstore to do an hour or two of paperwork, and he's caught her. Their stances are stiff like cats. I imagine growling.

And then Char comes up behind me. She must have sneaked in the back way, but she was so silent.

"Get a room," she yowls, looking out at the old folks, and we laugh.

"Why aren't you in school?" I say, but she only scoffs and sprawls on the settee, taking out her sketch pad. The inside of this place is all warm wood and book smell, and the windows are wreathed with frost and colored lights like all the windows in Moss Park.

The handsome mystery man walks past the bookstore just then. It seems he's deciding whether to open the door, but Mrs. Sylvester pushes by him muttering like a crazy thing; he flinches back away from her, and he turns and walks past. I catch just a flash of his baffled, sweet face.

"That was close," says Char, but I don't have time to ask her what she means.

The doorbells are jingling. Mrs. Sylvester's sweeping in on a cold breeze, already complaining. She'll want tea.

★   ★   ★

The days go harder then. It's almost Christmas, but we can't seem to find fellow feeling. It's *because* of Christmas – all this mess. The people on their side of the park want white lights, the people on our side want to keep the cherry and teal and lemony-green lights that we've always had, and that is the root of the strife.

Gloria and I shop our way around the park, catching glimpses of the mystery man here and there. Tourists have invaded Moss Park. There's no seat to be had at Jack's. We look in at the strangers all cozy in their sparkly red vinyl booths until Jack brings us travel cups of coffee.

Last night Char said, "You *are* a monster." She rolled her eyes when I told her I'd called my mother a bitch once or twice, too—

"Not a bitch, a *monster*," she said.

The point was that she hadn't invented being a horrible teen. It's natural, normal.

But is it, though? Maybe that's why I'm not telling Gloria. Her daughter rides horses at boarding school and goes overseas on vacations.

My daughter, I see her doing something normal for a change, I see her coming in from a run and say, "It's so nice you like running, dear."

She says, "I wouldn't say I *like* running. It's more that I want to keep this body functional for as long as I can. Don't you?"

Is there something really wrong with Char?

And why am I not sharing any of this with Gloria? It feels like the Christmas light argument has spilled over to us somehow. I notice when we're on her side of the park, the shopkeepers aren't as nice to me as they used to be.

We're looking at sweaters for the girls when we bump into him. The handsome man from the diner's back corner. He's just on the other side of the table, touching the sweaters. I look up straight into his face, and I think there will be a spark, but there's nothing.

"Oh hello," says Gloria, and he only looks baffled again, or I am getting a feeling of bafflement from him; I don't actually see his face.

"We see you in Jack's all the time. We've never met," I say, holding out a hand to shake, but he's moving back. He's stumbling back and is gone into the crowd, just like that.

"Shy," says Gloria. "It's cute. You should follow him."

"*You* should," I say, but I get a little chill. His reaction, like he'd seen a ghost.

We don't follow him. We get matching Fair Isle sweaters for Char and for Gloria's daughter, who will be flying home in a matter of days. I imagine bright-eyed Mira clutching hers to her chest, saying, *It's perfect, I love it, I love you, Mom.*

Char, I know, will just throw hers in the closet and never take it out. She wears black, always, and this sweater is all marled in teal, cherry, and lemony-green like the lights they're taking down all over Moss Park.

And the white lights are going up, whiter than white, dazzling like sparklers in summer.

Gloria and I are headed toward the center of the park when she stops. "I'll catch up," she says, and when she does catch up to where I'm watching men change out the lights on the gazebo, she has two tall cups. Coffee, I think, but it's not. It's a strange syrup. I cock an eyebrow.

"Cinnamon cocoa," she says, and we sip while we watch more of the lights come down.

"Out with the old," she says.

Far past the gazebo, out near a treed end of the park, I see an old man and a woman arguing, gesturing wildly. Is he beating his chest? Did she just slap him?

I am glad that Gloria doesn't see.

★　　★　　★

"Skip work this afternoon," Gloria says over breakfast. "We're having a wrapping party at my house."

We're in Sylvia's Café, all silver sparkly vinyl and white lights and frost wreathing the windows. More cinnamon cocoa with berry tarts. No handsome men stealing glances in here.

"I can't skip. Mrs. Sylvester barely comes in anymore," I say.

"Just ask," she says.

So I call and ask for the afternoon.

"Take the whole day," Mrs. Sylvester says. The old lady's a little breathless, almost giggling.

"Is someone there?" I say, but she only says it's fine, go have fun. She'll get the store opened later or she won't; it hardly matters either way.

★　　★　　★

Gloria's living room is staged with a tree and candles and the fireplace lit. Silvers and blues, violet and white lights, a stink of wine and cocoa spiked with butterscotch schnapps. Gloria's pretty sisters and cousins, her mom, a couple of young dads as well, all wrapping presents on card tables.

I clutch my meager bag of gifts and find myself a place to wrap.

Gloria's youngest sister isn't here. She's getting married soon, and then she'll move far away from here. Gloria's mother's going on about the blend of pain in losing her very last baby and the joy in seeing her settled.

Gloria stiffens a bit. She must see it as a commentary on her solitary life.

When Gloria's husband left her – just about eighteen months ago, I suppose – it was like in a movie. She was depressed, sure. For months she was all puffy around the eyes and wore pajamas when she wasn't at work. But she snapped back. She snapped right back.

"Michael is the best. We just grew apart. It happens," she says.

They're wrapping the presents all together because that makes sure everything's color coordinated. The colors are silver, blue and violet like the room.

When I've wrapped my presents, I stand out of the way.

The white-lit Christmas tree is like a wall, like a hedge inside the house. Being up near it gives me a feeling of dread. And it smells so strong, like a dark green candle.

The music video plays low on the television: *Every day's a party with you, with you. Wanna have a blowout with you, with you.* Claymation supermodels crawl out of a wedding cake. They dance and merge. I feel a little exhilarated like I always do when that song plays, but I feel sad, too, like I'm looking back on a happier memory.

Gloria's mom says, "You're really settling in now. What's it been, two years?"

Almost.

"Moss Park is so great," I say. "You know, in the town we lived in before, there was a lot of crime. A woman and her daughter...."

"I don't know this is the right story for company," Gloria says.

I nod. "You're right."

A woman and her daughter were butchered. They disappeared, and the investigation ran on the news every night. They found them in the woman's neighbor's backyard, just a slurry of blood and guts in a shallow hole.

The neighbor had been away on vacation.

The dead woman's own tub was where it happened. They found blood evidence there even though it had been bleached.

"How's Mira?" says one of Gloria's sisters.

"Thriving. I miss her something terrible, though," says Gloria. "Just knocking around this big old house all alone."

All eyes go to me again, and I say, "I wish I could have done something like that with Char – not boarding school – I could never have afforded that, but I wish I would have pushed her to do sports. All she wants to do is read and sketch and mope, mope, mope."

"She's artsy," says Gloria.

"She hasn't grown – not an inch or a pound – since we moved here," I say.

"She's a great kid," says Gloria's mom, who barely knows Char at all.

She says the most horrible things to me, I don't say.

"Char has the most beautiful hair," says someone else who barely knows her.

The thing is, no image comes to mind. Is Char's hair black, like her clothes? Brown? Blonde like Mira's? I can't say. I can't call up her face.

I'm turning toward the fireplace, toward the mirror, but I can't see anything in it. I face back toward the tree.

"This is really *something*," I say. They look away. I guess it's lower class to point out how nice things are.

★   ★   ★

It's dark and all are tipsy when I leave. On the way home, I pass the bookstore. Lights are dim inside, but I see Mrs. Sylvester's shape on the settee. On the very end of the settee, legs crossed. I imagine a pensive look on her face. Someone broad-shouldered looms behind her, closer and closer. His hand comes down.

I'm stopped, now, lit by Christmas lights. If anyone were looking, they'd recognize me. No one's looking. His hand comes down, over the breastbone, stroking up her neck. Her neck is arched and her arm is raising. She's pulling him down into a messy, groping kiss.

The wind feels hot on my face as I turn away. The Christmas lights are all like sparklers, forked spikes coming off them.

Passionate anger breeds passionate love, I think. But not real love. Real love is smoother.

Every day's a party. It plays in the street. Gloria's perfect nose, her little cold-reddened ears, her beautiful eyes all come to me in flashes.

I have time to walk, time to think and have a little romantic-comedy-style epiphany.

★ ★ ★

"Where were you?" says Char at the door to our guesthouse.

"So sorry, I should have tried to find a pay phone," I say. I'm beaming and flushed, but I can't see her face. I'm not sure if it's a shadow, some strange shadow striking only her face, but I can't see her at all. The hair could be any color.

"You're not well. I can see it – hell, I *smell* it," says Char.

I have my hands on her shoulders now and am turning us, trying to turn her into the light, but I still can't see her. All I get from her is the mood – amusement, scorn maybe. I begin to move away, but she holds me there. Her hands are on my temples. Like strange waltzers, we hold each other out at arms' length.

She says, "Listen, I hinted to Mrs. Sylvester that we might be going on vacation. Just in case."

"I don't know what you mean." I don't. It doesn't matter.

"You think you're in love with her? You're so deluded," says Char.

Am I crying? Char can see what I've been thinking? I say, "I walked and I thought tonight, Char, honey, and I think I know what I want."

And maybe this is why Char's been so evil lately, why we aren't getting along – because she's jealous. She doesn't want Mommy's attention going anywhere else. Kids are always this way when a parent falls in love.

"You want to *be* her," Char says, and maybe that's true, too.

I think of our neighbor, back in that other town. I think of her screaming in the bathtub.

"You're poisoning yourself from the inside," Char says. "You're wearing out the brain."

She's on drugs, is all I can think. I break away from her and all goes dark.

★   ★   ★

Some long time later – dawn glowing through the sheers – I wake at the table. My mouth's packed with rotisserie chicken. My hands are deep in the jelly of the cold carcass. Char sits gazing like a judgmental cat from the other side of the table.

"What are you looking at?" I say.

"Just making sure you don't choke on a bone," she says gently.

"I'm going. I'm going to Gloria, just as soon as I take a bath," I say.

"I think you better do just that," says Char.

But I'm too full. A queasy few steps is all I manage, and with all the lights blazing, inside and outside, I drop.

I dream a double wedding, then, out in a lemony-green field of teal and cherry flowers, white dresses hot like sparklers – each of us with a copy of the man from the diner's back booth – but that is false and the men fade away and then Gloria and I seem to merge. Shudder apart, merge again like clay figures.

I see a Venn diagram. I see a massive many-winged bat, each eye the shape of a Venn diagram.

I start awake into darkness. Char has spread a rough blanket on me. I think she's washed my face.

I go out the door with mouthwash in my bloated cheeks. I spit it into the snow on the way to the street. Christmas lights are swirling and sparking. It's all coming apart.

It's just…my eyes are wearing out. Or my brain is wearing out, like Char said.

The brain is wearing out. I'm wearing out *the* brain. That's what she said.

★   ★   ★

Gloria's wearing off-white satin pajamas, the top open with a lace-trimmed cami underneath. She layers even for bed. I've never seen her without her makeup before, and she's even more beautiful.

I wait for her to invite me in.

"It's just as well you came over. I can't sleep, I'm so anxious, you know, for the holidays to get going," she says, but her eyes are weary.

Music plays somewhere. "Gloria," it was, and now it's changed. *Every day's a party, with you, with you, with you.*

I'm not sure if I'm going to kiss her. The desire to do that, if it was ever there, is gone. It seems like something big has to happen, though, to explain why I'm here.

The oven timer goes off, and we move that direction, passing the Christmas tree, which is now just a regular-sized tree with dim white lights.

Why'd you change it? I'm about to say, but I know, I know. I think of Gloria's family's stares as I praised the tree and almost laugh.

I've been wearing out the brain, placing colors on everything, glamouring myself somehow.

She takes sugar cookies out of the oven. Perfect pale angels and trees. The glass bowls of icing (cherry, teal, lemon-lime) sit ready alongside jars of nonpareils and cinnamon dots.

Pouring a cocoa, Gloria says, "I made the marshmallows. They might not be quite right."

It's the velvetiest thing I've ever had in my mouth, toffee and chocolate and something else, creme brûlée? But the walls seem to be melting. I'm not feeling well.

I go to kiss her finally, and she flinches back. I feel her pulse like a drum on the ground.

"It's fucking hot in here," she says.

I wish you wouldn't swear, dear.

"We should go to your bedroom. It'll be cooler," I say, all low and flat.

"I can crack the window here," she says.

"I need to lie down. I'm not feeling well, all of a sudden."

So we walk down the hall, slowly. She's looking back at me. I enter her bedroom and go straight for her bathroom door.

"Oh, it's a mess in there," she says, but I shut the door. "Oh, okay."

I look in the mirror. Too thin, too old, no face at all. My dry hair's dyed black like a parody of Gloria's.

The bathroom is nice – no doubt, but it's all gray and dull. There's a pubic hair on the toilet seat and a ring of hard water stain inside the bowl.

Back in the bedroom, I lie down. She's sitting on the hope chest at the foot of the bed, looking through photo albums.

"This is what I was doing when you knocked," she says.

She passes me a picture of Char and Mira.

"That could be yesterday," I say.

"Oh no, Mira's a foot taller now, I bet," she says.

But Char's still the same. Because she takes care of the body.

★   ★   ★

I'm not seeing things right, but here's what I see: in the mirrored closet doors, the room is small and gray, the carpet plush but worn, the damask on the bed dated, not a suitable bedspread for Moss Park at all. I see me standing, her cross-legged on the hope chest lid. I see me take her by the scruff of the neck, lift her. In my hands she becomes a husk, just…like an outfit, like a costume. In the mirror, I'm turning her in the light. I find the zipper, a fine hidden zipper like on a wedding dress. I unzip her, step inside.

I am not seeing things right, but it doesn't matter. Char was correct. I wanted in; that's all.

I look in the mirror; my hand on her throat, Gloria leaned back for a passionate kiss. Body tense and arched, the satin falls against her, outlining her curves. I aim for her lips and take her neck instead.

★   ★   ★

It's all over, all memory. The air is hot as it was in the kitchen now and a smell is coming in from the bathroom. A gentle knock on the door.

"Mira?" I say.

"Char," she says. "Is it all over?"

The satin is cool on my skin. The room is gray and empty. I look to the mirror, but it isn't there anymore. The shards are piled against the door tracks and scattered all over the carpet, where there are rusty stains. The soles of my feet are dark.

"Open the door please, dear. I'm...decent," I say.

Char's wearing her Fair Isle sweater like the one I bought Mira.

I say, "Your mom was just here, dear. I don't know where she—"

"Please," says Char. "Just don't."

She comes into the room, bolder now. She steps over broken glass and looks in the closet.

"Now, honey, I don't think you should—"

Char moves into the bathroom. The shower curtain makes its quick sweeping sound.

"What's this in the bathtub, Mom?" she says.

My heart races and a feeling of guilt sweeps over me.

"What's in the bathtub?" I say, going to the door, but she meets me there. The curtain is back in place already.

"I'll get it cleaned up later," she says. "Just rest now. Take it easy." She shakes her head. "I guess if you could take it easy, we wouldn't have this trouble in the first place."

"I don't know what you mean."

She takes my head in her hands. Her bony little fingers poke around.

"You do something to the brain. You wear it out too fast. You don't use the memory, I don't think, but you use something else, the visualization part or something. I don't know that much about brains, sadly. Just let it be. Just close your eyes and lie down here awhile."

She sits down on the hope chest next to me.

"Do you smell the blood on your pajamas? Can you feel it?" She takes my hand and touches it to the cuff of my other sleeve, which is damp. I squeeze the fabric and the moisture pools around my fingertips.

Before she can stop me, I'm up and in the bathroom. I shut the door behind me.

"You don't have to look," she says.

But I've already swept aside the curtain, taking in the tangle of blood and guts, the tortured dyed-black hair.

Char is beside me. "You always choose the same general type, don't you? Maybe your own body looked like that long ago, do you think?"

"We should go," I say, thinking of the man who used to always watch us. He wasn't handsome, really. Maybe he thought he knew this Sara woman. Maybe he did know her.

"You need a shower," says Char.

"Yes, and then we need to go, get out of Moss Park," I say, a lump in my throat because I can't imagine leaving this place, though I've already left it, haven't I? When I go outside, won't everything be soggy and poor?

In the mirror, my face is already not quite the face I coveted. The eyes are still big and blue, but the skin has lost its glow. I shudder to think what I'm doing to the brain.

Char strokes my hair, says, "We need to go get Mira. We have to pick her up at the airport."

"And then?"

"And then we have company coming. We get through Christmas, and then we go."

"You and me?"

"Gloria and Mira, yes…. God, Mom. Try to stay with it just a little while," she says.

I *am* trying.

She strips me, shoves my feet into slippers, walks me to Mira's bathroom for a quick shower. I dry myself, and she wraps me in a fluffy gray robe. She sits me on the living room floor near the fire, leaves and comes back with a fancy tray of hors d'oeuvres from one of Moss Park's pretty little shops. I was with Gloria when she bought it.

"That's for the party," I say, but Char's already messed it all up.

"I know, I don't normally eat this stuff, but it doesn't matter now, does it?" she says.

It doesn't.

I breathe in the meat smell, watching her feed like an animal. I can't really be her mother, can I? She's a relative, anyway, and she may be my only one.

"Go get the photo albums. I saw them in the bedroom," she says.

"Why?"

"So you can tell me who the people are. We're going to have a lot to do, to get through Christmas. It will help if I can pass as Mira, don't you think?"

But the thought crosses my mind – this girl isn't anything like my Mira.

"When's her flight coming in?" I ask.

Char frowns, finds the pink datebook on the kitchen counter and starts scanning. "One p.m. The Christmas Eve party starts at…seven. We're in a tight spot, you know. We have to keep them out of the master suite. They'll want to pile their coats on the bed and use the bathroom. Jesus. It's going to be rough."

She's getting greasy prints all over my datebook. I reach for it, and she puts it in her back pocket. I whimper when she wipes her fingers on the Fair Isle.

"I know you'll want to sleep until it's time, but you can't," she says. "If you sleep, you're going to forget. You're going to delude yourself. It's something you do with the brain, Mom. It always happens."

Char sits down again. She takes her sketchbook out of her bag and starts drawing. I feel like I've never been close enough to see her drawing before. It's just endless abstract shapes and patterns all finely detailed, going right up to the edges of the page.

I scoot around so we're sitting side by side. There are figures in it now, bats and weasels and slimy things. Her pencil moves so fast.

"Why do you do that all the time?" I ask, but she just keeps going. I watch, and the watching brings back a little something all vague, like déjà vu, a little half-memory of some moment somewhere else, when I was something else.

"We're monsters, Mom," she says, and I see her, clear and full. For an instant I see who she really is. I rest my head on her shoulder and try hard to stay awake and aware. The hair she wears now is gorgeous, long auburn waves. I wonder if she'll miss this hair, and there's another pang of guilt. She took such care of this body and now she'll lose it because of me.

The song is playing somewhere: *Every day's a party, every day's a party with you.*

The page is finished. She turns it and starts anew.

Soon we'll go to the airport. The two girls will go into the master bath. There will be a mess, but Mira will take care of it.

"Mrs. Sylvester?" I say.

"I left her a note. I don't think she's thinking of us right now, anyway." What a funny expression this girl has. I find her quite dear.

We'll get through Christmas. We'll go someplace new. I won't remember any of this later, but it's nice right now to have my head on her shoulder. It's nice to drop into the drawing with her.

"Oh, we still need to go over the photo albums," I say.

"It's fine. I'll just call everyone *dear*. They won't notice."

I touch the page. "You'll keep doing this when you're Mira, won't you?"

"I'll be just the same. I don't change. Neither do you," she says, and I smile.

WATERFALL

The big couple promenading through the cafeteria had an aura of royalty, the boy in his long tweed coat and the girl – who I noticed right away was heavier than me – in a floor-length sleeveless dress showing off pale tattooed arms. Her hair was silvery blonde and spiral-coiled; his lay in long black feathers hiding his face until he tossed it back to reveal a handsome round jaw and large dark eyes. People called out to them, stopped them for a moment to talk and laugh, then they walked on to the next table.

"We call them Branjelica," said my cousin Allie when she noticed me staring.

"Brad and Anjelica?"

"No, Krissy, *Bran* and Anjelica," Allie corrected, not quite rolling her eyes.

It was my first day at her school. We sat with her friends, every one of them thin and nervous. The word *meticulous* came to mind. I felt out of place with them, as I so often did.

"Those two are popular, yeah?" I asked.

"The most popular couple in school," said Allie.

I didn't see how that could be. They were seniors for sure. That helped, and maybe Bran played football or something, but I'd never known a popular girl as big as Anjelica. I couldn't imagine wearing a dress like that, and my arms were nowhere near as large.

Soon the couple had come to the table next to ours, and I could make out her tattoos. Beautiful, intricate graywash butterflies, moths, and other insects, each with a tiny human face. They were the kinds of images I'd have loved to be able to draw, to imagine. She laughed and talked, her voice gravelly and bubbly at once. The kids kept touching Bran on the hands and arms and casting loving eyes on him, yet something about his stance told me he was no football player. His manner was sweet and shy.

For a second, as Anjelica spoke to some girls, his interest lagged. He looked at the sketches on the front of my notebook and then straight at me. He smiled. They moved on, and soon they'd left the cafeteria.

"Why are they so popular?" I said, realizing just then that I was interrupting a conversation between Allie and her friends.

"They're rich," said one of the friends.

"Or he is," said another.

"I think they can get things for people," said another.

"I mean, all of that I'm sure, but they're *hot*," said Allie, as though that was all that mattered. The others nodded.

I was about to feel offended – I very nearly bolted up and made a scene – but looking in their eyes, I could see they weren't joking. Not at all.

★ ★ ★

It was my first day of school, but not my first night at home with the uncle and aunt, Allie, and her little brothers. It was dinner number nine, in fact, no more interesting or comfortable than the previous eight. Chicken breast, rice, and cooked spinach with a side of raw spinach salad. Talk of accounting (both of them worked in the same firm), talk of sports, and now that the summer was over, talk of school.

It was the first night I didn't call Grandma straight after dinner. We'd cried on the phone eight nights, and that was enough. She was as sorry as I was about the move. She wished she had kept me, would come get me if I said the word, though she didn't like to drive so far. I'd resolved to let her be.

This move was supposed to be good for me, and all the aunts and uncles felt it was the first step in getting Grandma out of her little broken-down house. Maybe she'd follow me here, or to another of her sons' houses, or to a retirement community of some sort (though if there was money for that, why not money to fix up her place?). Without me she would move, and she would be happier too.

Happy like me.

I lay on the bed watching storm clouds and letting my mind go blank. There was homework, but it wasn't anything. My phone was already buzzing less and less often. I was going to let all those friendships fade as quickly as they could. I was going to make something new of myself. The thought brought up images of those human-headed butterflies on Anjelica's arms.

My window looked out onto the street, which was filling with puddles. Cars splashed along in and out of the subdivision. It was that time of the day when everything's dark blue, except the sky was all black and silver with storm clouds. I found it lovely, and after a while, pulled out a sketch pad and markers. I didn't care about capturing how the sky looked so much as the feeling of doom and promise I got from it.

I was supposed to be firming up some vision for my future. Drawing was all I could think of, maybe cartoons or graphic design. The aunt and uncle were going to *love* that idea, no doubt. Plus, I wasn't all that good at it. Back home, maybe, but here, everything I did would be less than it had been. I threw away the first sketch and started again.

I thought of calling Grandma after all, but just then, a tall pewter-colored Jeep-type thing crawled by. It was like they were looking for an address. I saw four or five heads through tinted windows. Then the front passenger window rolled down enough to show a glimpse of Anjelica's silvery curls.

The car behind them honked, and they moved along.

★　★　★

After gym, at the mirror, Anjelica came close. She looked paler and even larger than I remembered, in nothing but Doc Martens, a black bra, and boy shorts. I looked away quickly.

"Bran noticed you yesterday," she said.

"Oh, I…." I had nothing to say. I wasn't sure what I was looking at now, just a blur of red in the mirror.

"Don't worry, I'm not the jealous type," she said, but then she must have realized how frozen I was. "I'm sorry. I'm just weird."

"You're not weird at all," I said quickly.

She bumped my shoulder with hers. "Just trying to make friends. Anyway, come with me."

"Come where?"

She pulled on a pink eyelet minidress. "Lunch," she said, tossing her curls over her shoulder on her way out of the locker room. I noticed how short the dress was and how her underwear showed through.

Once she was out the door, I distinctly heard someone say, "Wish I could get away with that."

★   ★   ★

When Anjelica drove us to lunch, it was in the little convertible she paid for with her job at the ice-cream shop. When Bran took us, it was in the Land Rover his parents had bought him. We'd stop by a drive-through on the way to the park, or we'd sit in a restaurant when Anjelica drove us. Bran always took us to his place. He'd have stacks of sandwiches or charcuterie or something else appealing in the fridge, and beer if anyone wanted it. He lived in a poolhouse, no kidding, behind a mansion I never set foot in. We never went to Anjelica's, but she stopped there once to get a change of clothes. It was in bad shape, smaller and worse than the house Grandma raised me in, which everyone said was so far gone.

Bran did get things for people – drugs and kegs and things like that, though nothing hard. I don't think he made any money. I think he just did it so people liked him even more.

It was never just the three of us. It sometimes felt that way, but there were several other couples who were around a lot, and a few hangers-on. I felt at times these single ones had crushes on Bran or Anjelica or both. I suppose people thought I did, too.

It was different with me, though. If I got right down to it, I fantasized that they were my parents, or an older brother and sister – or a more ideal uncle and aunt.

My real uncle and aunt were delighted about all the friends I was making and how well I was doing in school. Teachers had never been mean to me – most of them anyway – but now there was a brighter, more delighted way they looked and spoke to me. As though they really did expect great things. My art teacher fawned over me so often and so convincingly I felt vaguely high around her. It felt like I was brilliant in every way. Not only brilliant but irreproachably good.

I didn't quite trust that feeling.

One day while we were washing dinner dishes, the aunt said, "That Anjelica dresses in a figure-flattering way, doesn't she? I wonder if you might like to go shopping and get some things like that."

I knew by then that she wasn't joking or being mean. Even if this particular aunt had not been humorless, I'd seen enough to know that to everyone – kids and adults alike – Bran and Angelica were unquestionably, objectively beautiful. I was getting the sense that they saw me the same, but I wasn't sure yet.

I had been starting to feel less comfortable in the oversized hoodies and sweats I'd always favored. "Maybe you're right. I wore a swimsuit over at Bran's," I said.

"Oh?" said the aunt.

"School was out at noon on Friday, remember? We went to his house, and it turned into a pool party. I didn't have anything, so Anjelica loaned me a…bikini." I guess I still thought she would frown, advise against it.

Instead, she brightened. "Oh of course. We'll get you another one, or maybe a few? You don't want to be seen wearing the same thing every time. I'd love to see you in some little dresses too. I can't wait."

I thought of calling Grandma about the shopping trip. I thought of sending her sketches I'd done, too, but instead I just texted my usual: *miss you*, and a big red heart.

*   *   *

My makeover made quite a stir. Anjelica started calling me Kissy because of my new dark lipstick. When we strode through the cafeteria one day, schmoozing on our way out to lunch, I heard someone say, "Branjeli-Krissy." Another corrected him, "No, Branjeli*kissy*."

Once, I watched Anjelica work in the ice-cream shop when the family stopped in for Allie's birthday. It seemed as though all the other workers were extensions of her body. They orbited around her, did her bidding. An awkward boy in line ahead of us tried to flirt with her. She flirted back, and again with the next customer, again with the uncle. The plastic cup overflowed with tips, and at a glance from Anjelica, one of the others dumped it out behind the counter.

"Why would such a fine young woman need to work at a place like that?" the uncle said when we were in the car.

"I think it's admirable," said the aunt. With a sweeping look at us children, she said, "Her strong work ethic will serve her well."

And yet there was something missing from our friendship. Some closeness. At the bottom of it was the fact that we did not talk about whatever magic surrounded them. How could we, with these others always around? Try as I did to be the last one at a party, there were always people sleeping over, people offering me a ride home.

I began to fantasize about times with just the three of us. Something would be revealed – a ritual? A séance? Candles on jewel-toned velvet, chalk, thick books of spells. A dark attic with a round stained-glass window. After, Bran would pull me up on his soft lap and stroke my head until I slept. Maybe Anjelica would feed me, pour a bath for me, help me into my new clothes.

I was never any smaller in these fantasies; I was just as big as I was, and still deserving of care, adoration, indulgence.

★   ★   ★

My wish came true with no warning, just before Halloween. I was lying on my bed watching the street and sky, and Bran's Range Rover crawled up. I glimpsed only the two heads in front. The passenger window rolled down, and there was Anjelica, beckoning.

It was cold for October. In my new clothes, I was always cold. I hurried out and hopped in before the traffic could back up behind them. The inside was warm. I pulled a silky blanket over my bare legs.

"Our sweet Kissy," said Anjelica.

Bran held my eyes in the rearview. "It's time we talked," he said, but then he didn't say anything else.

Bran was a mystery to me still. The two of them were clearly charmed, but while she beamed and shone, he never seemed quite happy. Maybe it was from living alone in the poolhouse behind the mansion where his parents rarely visited, where his little sisters and their nanny kept house. Maybe – more likely – it was because he never found a way to engage with the world so fully as she did.

I didn't know where we were going. We hadn't been to many places at all, just the strip of restaurants, the high school, the subdivisions. I felt slightly anxious, remembering one time my friend and I got into a car with some boys back home, and they stopped out on a country road. The driver said, "You read the bumper sticker, right? 'Ass, gas, or grass. Nobody rides for free.' And I'm not thinking you have any grass."

"Shut up," my friend had said. She'd laughed, kicked the seat.

And I had frozen. I knew, on one level, that they were just joking, that I ought to laugh, but I couldn't.

I loved Bran and Anjelica. I didn't want to feel like I couldn't ask things of them, so I asked, "Where are we headed?"

"It's okay," said Anjelica.

"It's fine," said Bran. "We love you. We wouldn't ever hurt you."

"We're doing this because we love you and it's what you need," Anjelica said. She looked back at me, stroked the blanket over my knee, and I believed her. I trusted her.

"You've been living in the glow around us, but you need to have something of your own," Bran said.

"You're going to show me something now, aren't you?" I said, feeling very small and fragile.

"It's time," said Anjelica.

We drove a long way through smaller, sadder towns, and then we missed most of the sunset as we headed into the mountains. I could barely make out a creek along the left side of the road. I texted Allie, told her I was sleeping over at Anjelica's. Poor Allie, always so jealous now. I texted the heart and the *miss you* to Grandma.

We drove.

We came to a forest service sign and turned in just as it was getting dark. We drove past an empty campground to a parking lot with two other cars. A trailhead.

"Don't forget the blanket," Anjelica said. "I brought it for you." When we got out, she helped me drape it so my head and legs were covered.

As we walked the trail, Bran outpaced us. Anjelica took my hand, leaned in close. "It's his parents who know about this place and what's here. That's why they're so successful."

Were they successful, really? Maybe she only meant they were rich. A feeling of anticipation flooded over me.

We stepped aside for a couple with a flashlight, going back to one of the cars no doubt. We did not have anything to light the way, but there was moonlight glinting through trees. The trail was good and solid. I hadn't pictured Grandma in a while, not really, but it occurred to me that she could take this trail, so smooth and level it was. I imagined her walking slowly beside me, imagined her falling back.

I heard the waterfall before I saw it. Louder and louder grew the sound until the trail opened into a large clearing and the white water loomed, framing Bran, who stood before it in his long coat. We joined him. It might have been something to look at in the daytime, but now it was just a shroud shape. The sound was like the white noise the aunt put on for me when she noticed I wasn't sleeping those first few nights – only louder, with a hint of music behind it. Or was it humming?

Bran and Anjelica were warm presences on either side of me. I could not make out their faces. "What now?" I shouted over the rush of water.

It was Bran who leaned down, Bran's warm breath in my ear. "All you have to do is ask. Ask the spirit for what you need."

The waterfall was a spirit. I recognized that as soon as he said it. That's why its long pale shape reminded me so of a ghost.

In my other ear, Anjelica said, "We both did it. You see how well it works."

I knew it was true and could guess what they'd asked for: Anjelica had wanted success. That she was considered beautiful was only a part of what she meant by success. Another was her great popularity, another her skill and ease at work. What she'd asked for would take her far. Bran had asked for love. He'd received love from Anjelica and from every other person we knew. From me.

The waterfall hummed. It was clearer and clearer under the rushing, crashing sounds.

I might need success, too, I thought. *I might surely need love.* For a moment I considered asking for everything to go back to how it was before I moved here. I'd not been popular at school, but I'd had many friends and much to do. I could be living in comfort in Grandma's house, with the cousins and friends coming in and out at all hours, with the ready comfort food and the TV always on. What would it smell like if I went back there now?

It would smell of sickness and mold.

No. That was not what I needed.

I needed to move toward my own future, but how? I thought of my drawings, how I loved them and yet how frustrated they made me. Should I ask for skill? Or for admiration, regardless of skill? No. These things were related to what I needed, but they weren't quite right.

"Just try to listen to yourself," Bran said. "You'll know what you need when you think of it." He held my left hand, Anjelica took my right, and this closeness brought to mind a particular drawing I'd done on a rare Sunday when I chose to stroll alone in the park instead of hanging out at Bran's. A fat couple and their little child walking down the path. The parents each held a hand and they pulled her up, swinging her in the air, and said, "Whee!" I'd felt, sketching them, that I was really seeing them. Without judgment or sentimentality. They weren't ugly or beautiful. They didn't make me think of my absent parents,

Bran and Anjelica, or anyone else. There was nothing mediating my experience of them.

And the drawing had been good, so good I'd kept it hidden from others, something to take out and look at over and over. It seemed a threshold had been crossed.

I didn't want to have any more delusions and misconceptions – about myself, about others.

"I need to see clearly," I called before I could consider it. Bran and Anjelica had let go of my hands and moved aside, and the wind whipped spikes of cold water onto my face. I wasn't sure I'd been heard, so I cried, "I need to see things as they are. I need to understand…everything…clearly!"

And that was when I saw the spirit in the waterfall – clearly, fully. An inhuman personality made of watery strands. Like a fall of hair or a beard made conscious and expressive. No eyes, no mouth, but a massive face nonetheless, turning its full attention on me, a speck on the ground.

A chill, a vibration started in my toes and jolted up my spine, coming out in horrible screams.

The nausea followed. It gushed up too fast for anyone to help. It was in my hair, smeared on the blanket. Bran and Anjelica came close again, and I saw their faces.

And that was when I lost my grasp on what people call 'consensual reality'.

★　★　★

Sometimes Grandma used to drink too much, and she would rant and work herself up something terrible about all the ways she'd been mistreated and misunderstood. She would transform into something bitter and spiteful. Those first few hours were like that. I was like that – screaming and ranting – and the world was like that. The world was transformed. I ran and tried to hide from my friends, from the face of the long, fibrous pale water-spirit.

I ran and hid, and wherever I hid would be something more horrific, so I would run out again. Faces in everything, everything swirling with sinister shapes. Chimerical creatures like those I'd so wanted to imagine, but I was not imagining them. They were not images but were all living, all spirits, ingrained into every part of the land here.

It was lucky I kept shrieking, or they never could have found and caught me. Anjelica, so strong and so adept at every little thing, was the one who neatly tackled me, wrapped her legs around me, pulling my arms back. Bran tied them with something, but she kept lying on me, firm but not crushing. She always knew exactly how much force to apply.

People lie down like that on dogs sometimes, to show them they are helpless. I saw that I was helpless. I submitted, just as a dog would.

She stroked my head and shoulder, and that made it all a little less overwhelming. With my eyes closed, with the pressure on my back, I felt I could speak.

"It's like the butterfly with the human face," I said.

Anjelica was panting. "What is?"

"*Everything.*"

"It's only what you asked for," she said.

"I want to take it back," I said, and she gasped. Bran let out a low, defeated moan. I had thought I'd asked to see in order to draw, as a path toward my future. I saw now that was not the reason. I had needed to see for its own sake, and yet it was intolerable. I wanted to go back.

"To deny a gift is a major affront," said Bran. He loomed above me. His face was the moon's. "And you wouldn't go back to the way you were before."

I nodded. I understood, but I couldn't live this way. Bran's face in the darkness swirled and contorted. Anjelica was easing off me, and as she did, she pulled and knotted the blanket around me – I'd lost it somewhere in my terror, and she had found it. She was dressing me, swaddling me.

The scent of acid, of vomit lingered, and yet Bran sat down and took me onto his soft lap. He stroked my sweaty, filthy hair. I became aware of scrapes on my knees and leaves and dirt on my hands, a missing shoe. We spent a long time sitting like that, and then he said, "We'll take her back."

"No," said Anjelica. "Please."

But he stood and lifted the cocoon of me up, over his shoulder. Slowly, we trudged back to the waterfall. They trusted me now, enough to let me stand and let the blanket loosen. They did not untie my hands.

I kept my eyes closed, but the problem wasn't just the sight. It was the understanding. I understood how it was in Grandma's home and understood how deep her denial was – about that, about her own health and happiness and mine, about how she had raised me. I loved her still, maybe more than ever, but I saw her clearly. *I have blocked all of this understanding; I have filtered it out.* I had heard that before, that we filter out so much of what we experience and that dreams are somehow the processing of it. That we couldn't live sanely without this ability.

I opened my eyes and looked, and though the ropey swaying spirit still terrified me, I thought I could face it now. The visions were not less intense; instead, I was starting to develop a thought-shape to deal with them, to think about how I might use them. I was imagining what I might draw, once home.

"Do you have something to say to it?" said Bran. His voice sounded sad and far away. I barely heard the waterfall or the hum. It sounded now like the white noise on my nightstand.

Take it back, I could say, but we couldn't go back to before. There would be heavy interest. I saw myself stripped of all understanding, lying on my bed in front of the window, only now it was a hospital bed. I saw a nurse tending me, sponging me, and Grandma in a bedside chair weeping.

I saw everything falling apart: Bran hated, ignored at school, his family ruined and penniless. He and Anjelica quarreling, breaking up or drifting apart. The saddest thing: Anjelica unconfident, incapable, being bawled out at work and stooping in an oversized hoodie, not ashamed of her body so much as her existence.

"Say what you need to. We won't stop you," said Anjelica. Her hand hovered close, like she wanted to touch me but was afraid. I leaned into her, and she put her heavy arm around my shoulders. I was seeing both of them much less idealized than I had before and yet they were not bad; they were only people. We were all three of us just small shivering animals, after all, and the forces around us huge, monumental.

The spirit was rippling but plainly alive. *To draw its face*, I thought. *That's what I want.*

"I wish I could explain what I see now," I said.

"It deals in needs, not wishes," said Bran.

I nodded. Making full contact with its impossible eyes, I wondered, *Can I keep this gift? Keep it and hold it and act like it's nothing, act like everyone else?*

Or act on my own wishes, act decisively? Can sight and understanding do that for me?

And then it spoke, loud and watery, only to me. "Do you have something to say, child?"

"Yes, I do." The wind threw icy pins in my face once more. The water roared. I was frozen, speechless, but only for a moment.

ONE EYE OPENED IN THAT OTHER PLACE

They were tied up together from the start: Dottie and that other place. That other place, that other eye. Charles didn't like to think of it as a third eye, though that's what it was. It wasn't in his forehead, wasn't in the center of his face at all. Instead, it rested between the right side of his nose and the tear duct. It wasn't actually there, of course, and yet it felt like it was there. It felt like the seat of something.

Call it the seat of daydreams.

What did it see, anyway? Nothing much, only a pleasant dim bedroom (not his own bedroom, not any room he had ever inhabited), the colors burnt sienna with a little rose. Reddish like a bright light glowing through fingers. It felt like eternal afternoon through that eye, the drapes drawn closed with strong sunlight behind them. A blurry, underwater feeling.

Charles had a dominant nose, and maybe that was what focused him on that particular spot in his field of vision. He'd be in a class – or later at work in the Department of Mathematics' main office, making copies, filling out spreadsheets – and the blur of the right side of his nose would distract him and he would focus there, thinking his own thoughts rather than whatever thoughts he was supposed to be thinking. Seeing just the warm ruddy spot of color that was his nose and then, as things progressed, he saw more.

Dottie was tied up with these sights from the first time he saw her. Overfriendly Dottie, always smelling of the cinnamon Altoids she used to cover the desperate parking-lot cigarettes she thought she was keeping secret. Dottie, who seemed to live in her little office across the hall. She was always there when Charles came in at seven-thirty and had never left before him, not once.

Sometimes Charles would sit at his desk thinking of Dottie, his two eyes on his email, fingers moving over keys, and that other eye would open.

The drapes in the bedroom of the other place glowed as red as everything else seen through that particular eye. They were made of tapestry or jacquard, thick but not entirely opaque. He could just make out something of the design and something of the stubbled texture.

The plain office decor around him had often soothed him (Charles hated clutter), but now, set against the warm bedroom, it felt overly cool and stark.

* * *

Dottie initially appeared to be a normal person, but Charles always knew. People like them pick up on one another right away.

She didn't work for Math at all; she worked for the tutoring center located on the next floor, but the tutoring program had overflowed their office space, and because her work was somewhat more independent than that of the other staff, she'd been given that one forgotten office set off by itself across the hall from Math. That space in the hall had become for all that fall term a popular place for people to linger.

Dottie had come to the college from far away and made a good first impression. Cheerful, genuine seeming, she was the kind of person who carried all her weight in the middle and tapered toward all her ends. Tiny ankles and feet, tiny pretty hands, a doll-like face and glossy russet hair. Immaculately put together, too, and in the first months she'd smelled of a subtle department store scent rather than cinnamon and smoke.

Yes, she had been popular during that first term. Young women from the Registrar's office came to take her to lunch off campus, and there were young men lingering in her doorway, too, from time to time. At evening events, such as lectures and film screenings, someone was always calling her over to sit. Charles saw because he attended many of those events, too. He sat alone most times, though if anyone from Math was there, they would wave him over and offer a dry smile.

Dottie didn't stay popular for long. Charles could have guessed she wouldn't even if he hadn't been at that dinner event, though that illustrated the matter quite well. She sat at the table closest to the speaker; Charles at the next table back. She was the freshest-looking person in the room, surrounded by silvery professors and grayed-out staff. Charles watched her speaking; he didn't need to hear. She had some affinity for the subject they were discussing, and she spoke on it with passion, not for a long time but long enough that two of the others at the table shared a look. She really did seem inspired, like she might strike out or cry. She caught herself, blushed vibrantly, fell quiet. Talk at the table went on, and she joined in but only with little bursts of agreement after that.

And Charles caught a 'help me' look from a student one time when Dottie was talking in a group in the hallway. On his way out one evening, he caught another little something. The hall lights were off, and she must have thought that everyone had gone home.

She spoke to someone on the phone (ninety-nine percent chance it was her far-away mother): "I try. I know. I will. It's just…."

Charles watched her even more closely after that. He felt he could work out the story she told herself: she didn't fit in here after all. These dried-up gray people were wearing her down, everyone around her seemed dead inside. She was most happy when she was passionate and loud and they wished her quiet. She'd gone to some trouble to become this vivacious thing, and here they were driving her back into her shell.

Whenever Charles thought of Dottie, his small eye tended to open up to its warm red vision. It wasn't just at the office anymore. He couldn't keep his thoughts on movies or television, let alone games, let alone reading. At times he'd do some dumb thing with his hands – polishing knives, scrubbing pots. He'd look out his kitchenette's window, look out to the parking lot and think of Dottie. Sometimes he dried his hands, sat at his little table and doodled while thinking of her, and when he thought to look down at the pad, he saw surprising things drawn there. A pair of wire-framed glasses lying on a nightstand, an old-fashioned wind-up alarm clock.

The glasses he'd drawn in brick-colored pencil had a regular lens on the left, and on the right was an almost-regular lens with another smaller lens set in near the nosepiece. Glasses for a person with two regular eyes and a third, smaller one near the nose.

In that other place, he sat up slowly and turned to the window. Up close, the drapes smelled acrid, smoky and metallic. Something else, too, but he couldn't catch it. He couldn't stay long, couldn't ever seem to keep that small eye open.

*   *   *

"Hey," Charles said, "do you always have to work so late?"

She stared up at him, her mouth slightly open. She'd just been bent over plugging or unplugging something.

"I'm sorry. I didn't mean to—" He stepped back. He became uncomfortably aware of his own face and set an appealing expression on it. Masculine shyness, soft interest.

"Only killing some time before class," Dottie said. Suddenly she was that old Dottie from a few months before, all open and genuine seeming.

"I didn't know you were a student," he said.

"A night class, just for fun."

"Ah, but that doesn't explain why you're here so late the rest of the week."

They laughed nervously and Charles said he liked her wall-hanging, her peach-gold salt lamp (and didn't her things recall that place? Didn't they seem allusions to it?). The whole exchange was two or three minutes, but it made him feel triumphant all the way downstairs, all the way to his car.

*   *   *

That night, Dottie went to her drawing class as scheduled. The next week, Charles dropped her off late for it – their dinner date had lasted longer than planned. By the week after that, she'd stopped going to class. She hadn't been taking the class for fun; she'd taken it to meet people, and now that she and Charles were dating, there was no need to go.

They didn't kiss until after the winter break when she returned from her mother's. They were chaste for people their age, but eventually they were sharing a bed one or two nights each week. Always her bed, as his poor bare apartment was unfit for any kind of romance.

Her apartment was as red and pink and gold as he'd expected, but it was also surprisingly spacious and plush. Charles appreciated the cleanness and the quality of all that was on display, and yet it was overcrowded for his taste. After an hour or two, the lamps and plants and gewgaws began to feel overwhelming. He would close his eyes, the other eye would open in the other place, and he would shock himself out of it, stand and try to occupy himself or start a conversation, anything to stay in the real world until it was time for dinner or bed or whatever they were doing.

When he was sleeping over, he'd spoon her until she slept and then loosen the hold. He'd let himself slip into that other place.

It was bittersweet now because he knew it wasn't thinking of Dottie that took him there. He was moving away from her to visit that place where she could not follow. It was something about lovemaking, or the way her apartment made him feel, or her scents of smoke and then shower, perfume and then smoke and then cinnamon. She had him smoking sometimes and drinking more than he was accustomed to doing, so maybe that was also part of it. A rise in blood pressure or something. He'd loosen his hold on her, push his face into the pillow, his heart going harder than it should, and the small eye would open right away.

He saw everything now, from the paisley pattern in the curtains to the pale enamel on the old-fashioned alarm clock. He touched the glasses, brought them to his face. They had those deep-curved wire earpieces that hold tight. He saw the brass footboard and beyond its bars a trunk with a striped blanket folded upon it. He saw beyond that to a small fireplace with a wood-framed mirror hanging above it. He wanted very badly to rise and go to that mirror. He always meant to rise and sweep the drapes open, and he very often could rise, but he could take no more than a half-step in either direction before that little eye would slam closed, cutting him entirely out of the scene.

*   *   *

For Charles, work was no more or less satisfying than it had been. He worked in his clean, bare office as before.

Dottie saw things differently. She was back to something of what she had been, on the surface at least. Keeping the secret of their relationship, which she approached as a kind of game, made her vivacious again. New young women came around to take her off campus for lunch. There were always more people to meet.

As the spring semester went on and the days grew longer, it seemed they spent more time talking. Dottie said more than Charles did. She spoke passionately, just as she had on that long-ago day when he noticed her at the dinner. Charles never wanted to escape her. Sometimes when she talked about people they knew, she was surprisingly cruel, and that gave him a little thrill, brought him ever closer to her. She had so many opinions, so many interests, so much derision and even hatred for all the people around them. She unfolded like a flower, revealing layer after layer like an onion.

Charles tried to make his face appealing while she spoke. He stared at the right side of his nose and fell to looking down at the rosy floor in that other place, but when she was awake, she always called him back. She'd ask him a question, and, surprising himself, he'd answer it honestly.

She wanted participation, and so he obliged. He told her how he and she were alike. He didn't have interests or opinions – that wasn't what he meant. It was deeper than that. It was the way they didn't fit in and had always been alone, even in a crowd. He told her stories from his life to illustrate.

With a meaningful look, he finally told her it was all tied up with that other place they both went to sometimes. He referred to the other place casually, as though it were only a metaphor.

Something softened in Charles as they spoke of these things, and when they went to bed they were both gentler and more impassioned than they had been before. He said, "I love you" for the first time and she said it back soft and slow. They didn't try to spoon because the room was overheated. They lay on their backs breathing deeply, all drenched in opioid feelings.

Charles closed his eyes, and he didn't have to try; when his small eye opened in that other place, he put on the special trifocal glasses, rose and glanced at the mirror so quickly he could not comprehend the strange image there. He turned to the drapes—

—and that was it. The small eye slammed shut.

After a while, he slept and woke to a room even hotter than before. Light came from the bathroom, a tinkling sound.

Charles closed his eyes, the small eye opened, he put on the glasses and rose and took a long look in the mirror this time. The face was his own face only thin and old. The small eye blinked out of time with the others. Concentrating more than he'd thought he could, Charles turned to the line where the two drapes met and pushed them back.

The scene before him was red, bright and strange, incomprehensible really. It reminded him of coral, of frilly mushrooms, but it wasn't either. He caught a hint of something (worm-arm?) and the eye slammed shut.

Dottie walked past the bed to the window. "Too hot," she said. She pushed up the old wooden window with some effort. A warm gust came through the room.

Charles was already back in that other bedroom, and this time he was still standing, still walking. He moved around the bed, between the trunk and the fireplace. The paisley drapes had fallen closed. The far side of the room was in dark red shadow.

In the depths of the shadow, he could just make out two doors.

"You want a cool shower?" Dottie said. She'd already thrown off her little nightie.

Charles rose and followed her to the bathroom. He was in both places.

He was not coming in or out but remained in the two places! He'd have liked to say something about it to Dottie, but he was too overcome.

In the other place, Charles opened the door to a bathroom laid out like Dottie's but with a clawfoot tub, no showerhead at all. Maybe showers had never been invented in that other place.

Dottie stood in her tub, waiting for him to get in. He knelt and put the plug in, started the water.

"You want to take a bath?" she said, sitting down. Her voice came clear and close, and in that other place her voice was far away. It seemed far beneath the floor.

He knelt beside the tub while the water poured in.

He saw – in both places, he saw – the water was filling. The strangest thing: in the other place, the bottom of Dottie was there in the tub. Her heels, her calves, her thighs and butt stuck up out of the water, all flattened as though a length of heavy glass pressed down on them. Just an absent pink span of flesh, yet he knew it must be her.

Here in her own dim gold-colored bathroom, Dottie smiled at him, pulled his arm. "Get in," she said. She pushed herself back to make more room, and he moved in, kneeling in the cool deep water between the faucet and her body.

In that other place, he knelt in exactly the same place. Her upside-down feet pushed back toward her upside-down butt. She was coming into that space with him. Like being born breach. He grasped her ankles and tried to pull from that side, but nothing happened; she was stuck and did not move.

He would have to try pushing from this side instead.

He placed his hands on her shoulders and pressed – not too hard, not violently. He pressed from this side, and in that other place her cubelike body came up another inch. It stopped.

"What are you up to? Want to rub my back?" she said.

Charles nodded, and there was an awkward rearrangement, her body going so strange in that other place. Once seated behind her, he pressed again on her back. It had no effect.

"That feels good," she said. "Go lower."

He did. The little eye remained open, seeing the bottom of her, but here on this side, he rubbed her back just like he was a normal person with no motive except to give pleasure. After a while, he poured shower gel on a pouf and washed her back. He washed her front as far as he could and she took the pouf to finish.

She looked back at him so happy, like all her life and energy had come back stronger. "I love you," she said, a euphoric feeling coming off of her. On the other side, she lay before him like a grotesque rose. *I have to push harder*, he thought, *but what if....*

"Can't you come over by yourself?" he said softly.

"Hmm?" she said. She was sleepy again.

"Open your other eye," he said.

She only giggled.

A red-toned image of a violent push came to his mind – splashing, gurgling fear and horror, her nails raking his arms and chest – but he pushed that image away. She pushed back against him and turned on more cool water with her foot.

Something had changed about his vision on Dottie's side. Perhaps his eyes had adjusted to the dim light. Her bathroom was no longer the calming gold color but jarred with blue and yellow-green and a great deal of staticky gray. He closed these eyes and opened the others wider.

In that other place, all was still red. He looked away from the terrible thing she was. The window called to him. Somewhere there was a door to the outside. He just had to find it.

"You'll follow when you can," he said. On the one side, his body stayed behind her, just a flesh-chair for her to lean back against, but on the other side, he eased away from her and carefully stepped out of the tub. He knelt and pressed, gently, until all of her was gone, until nothing but clear water remained in the red-lit bathtub.

"Are you asleep?" she said, but it was far away. He did not feel her turn and put a hand to his face.

He stood and found he did not need to dry himself. All was red, pleasingly warm but not hot. His element. He left the bathroom, hovering toward the enticing window.

He heard her screaming for a moment, but it was very, very far away.

THE PORTRAIT OF BASIL HALLWARD

I came awake when I was little more than an outline. With no sense organs, still I could sense Basil near me, the pressure from his breath and his brush, the lightest touch of his smallest finger. I loved him even then, I think.

I came to myself slowly, in layers. *Fat over lean*, I heard Basil thinking, reminding himself of some long-ago edict. *Fat over lean*, the thin dark washes of sienna and cobalt built up to thicker, paler dabs of gold and rose. Basil's broad violent gestures gave way to careful, controlled motions.

My eyes, when he made them, caught first on his beautiful roving eyes. They were hazel, pure green at the center bleeding into tawny speckled brown, the skin around them lined and bruised with lack of sleep.

My nose's first taste was of linseed and turpentine and then his warm, sweet breath. I loved him; I was sure by then.

My mouth he created in loving strokes. He called it in his mind *rosy, bright* and *young, pink, delicious*. He remembered the taste of salt, cream, and honey on his tongue – and I anticipated the same flavors on mine. Yes, my tongue! I felt it growing there behind the painted-shut lips: a tongue ready to do so much but still caged. For now its very being was enough – a miracle, in fact.

I began to taste slick teeth and the bony ridge of a palate.

Soft, he thought, *sweet*. His own mouth came an inch from mine as he worked on something above my face. My hair. He thought it, *thick* and *crisp gold*. It was almost a taste. He touched me again with his breath. My beloved's breath was sweet with all its animal warmth and its accents of oregano, mint, pepper. Basil. My mouth strained toward his, but I could not complete the link.

That hateful space held between us. I could not fathom how we never touched.

★ ★ ★

We never touch, even now. He stands before me with love written in his face. His touches are only brief and tentative caresses now. More and more, he stands back, gazing. This is good, too. He gazes, and I gaze back. The admiration is mutual. He admires how real I am, which is a mark of how skilled he is. In truth, he worships himself, and I worship him as well, and do not think of myself, though I feel at times new organs forming behind or beneath the slowly drying final layers of oil.

Over time, my vision broadens. I am stunned to learn there is more in the world than my Basil.

★ ★ ★

The terrible boy Dorian cries out that he hates me, or something along those lines. He resents me. He does not see why I should have something and he should have less. Is he speaking of Basil? I have Basil and he does not? Oh, if that is the case, I am glad. My tongue pushes against the barrier of my lips once more, but it is still too weak.

I must listen, try to make sense of this.

Three of them speak. They are saying the boy is like me in some way. There is a comparison to be made between us.

The third man wants me.

Basil wants the boy, and the other man wants the boy. The boy wants me. Basil assures him that, yes, he can have me.

"No, I won't go," I want to cry. But I will go, if Basil wishes it.

"That thing can have my soul," the boy says, or something very like that.

Yes, yes, I want it, I think with all my power, and their eyes refocus on me, or Basil's and the boy's do. The other man is looking at his fingernails. He says it's time to go. The two keep scanning my face, Basil thinking, *There's something there. What is it?*

The boy's thoughts are more opaque, but I read his face: he's unsettled. The other man says again that it's time to go, and though Basil asks, or rather he begs the boy not to leave, the boy leaves.

Basil's body slumps when they're gone. The image of me runs over and over in his mind, my hair and mouth and hands. All he needs is to look up at me, but he doesn't look. I feel new dimensions to my hands now and sensitive inner parts growing behind my painted costume. My new fingertips feel him feeling my hair and running his hands down my neck to my naked shoulders, but it is all only in his mind. His shoulders shudder, and I know he is weeping though he will not show me his face.

*   *   *

I belong to the boy. He keeps me under cover, and there I wait, thinking of all the colors in Basil's eyes. I think of the dark hair on his head and face. My fingertips still feel him feeling my hair and skin, but the smell of him is gone.

I ruminate on the injustice of it all, which builds anger, and maybe it is the anger that builds strength. All the inner parts of me keep growing behind the paint surface. Behind the cover where no one can see, I am moving now, slowly opening up a space.

The cover comes off in a sweep. The boy gasps and swoons. I do not know what he sees.

Another man comes. The two of them talk about moving me, and then I know they are doing so because of the rocking motion.

All alone in the dusty room for years, I keep Basil sharp in my mind. I rock back and forth, opening up more space. One day I strain out with all my might and touch my nose to the rough stinking fabric of the cover. After that exertion, I realize I am breathing deeply – I am breathing into lungs for the first time! Air rushes in and out through the nose, since the mouth still will not open. The space between me and the cover grows humid.

I rest. I strain again. I rest.

★ ★ ★

The cover comes off in a sweep, and there he is standing beside the horrible boy.

Basil! I knew you would come! I strain forward, thinking this time I will come free and embrace him, but of course that cannot be, not yet. I move perhaps a fraction of an inch beyond the surface, and he shudders back.

He looks away. He's saying terrible things – thinking even worse. He hates me now. Inexplicably, he is disgusted by me, disgusted by the boy, in fear for the boy's...soul?

But I have the soul. I have it, Basil. Don't you remember?

He is on his knees praying, begging the boy to pray.

The boy. Oh, and here is why I have always hated this boy. It's because I knew, beneath the surface of thought, that it would come to this.

He moves away, and here he comes, knife in hand. Basil does not hear me scream, *Turn, Basil, now! Rise, run!*

No. Oh, no. I cannot turn away.

The boy leaves my cover down all the time he does his evil and then replaces it to keep me from gazing on my murdered love.

★ ★ ★

Basil was in this room with me for many days. His body bled and stopped, and I felt his spirit rush around unaware of me. It was like having a large, frightened bird loose in the room. I reached for him over and over with my mind, but I could not catch him. I think he could not hear me. I do not know if it was the cover that kept him from me or the prison of the paint itself. I kept on straining, resting, straining. I kept on hoping and calling for Basil, but nothing helped.

A man came and took away the body, and all has been quiet since. I suppose his spirit went along with his body. I do not know.

I keep working. Months or years have passed, and by now my lips can part. My hands can turn. All at once, I feel the fabric on my fingertips. I push against it, brush against it. My touches are too light.

★   ★   ★

More months, more years? I push the thumb and index fingers out so far that they not only brush the fabric but are able to grasp it, pinch it tight, tug it down. Two strong tugs, and it is finally happening.

The curtain falls to the floor in a heap, and I am naked.

Naked, too, drawn on shadows at the far end of the room, is Basil. Nothing more than a charcoal sketch against the blighted wall, he shivers and weeps soundlessly, arms crossed, and long, beautiful hands caressing his own shoulders. His head is bowed.

"I did not know you were still here," I say, and he hears me for the first time. His head rises, colorless eyes turn toward me.

He touches his mouth, shakes his head. He cannot speak. It seems he cannot send his thoughts to me as he always did before. He is too weak.

"Come to me," I say, but he cannot.

He can hear, so I tell him all I have to tell him, most of all how glad I am to gaze on him again. If I never have anything else in the world, this is enough. I speak to him, and though he cannot answer, the shivering does lessen over time. The arms relax. Something of the old expression comes upon his face, and I am glad.

I tell him that though he cannot come to me, one day I will be strong enough to come to him. I am stronger every day.

The boy will rush into this room again sometime and look on me in horror. He will reach for the blade he used on Basil. He will try to use it on me, but he will not succeed.

"My hands, you see now, Basil? My hands are free. I will take the blade from him, turn it on him. You do not think I can do it?"

Basil smiles, shakes his head.

"I can do it. And do you want to know what will happen then?"

I want to say that I will come to him then. I will have the strength to break out of the layers of hard-aged oil and stride across the room, and then what will happen? Will I carry Basil out of this terrible house? How can I separate him from the shadow that holds him?

My fantasy makes no sense, but he watches, eyes wide, hoping for something, longing to hear that we are not doomed, even now when everything seems so bad.

And then suddenly an inspiration comes, and I think that it is true. I think this is what will happen:

"I will come free. Once vengeance is done, I will step free. It will be a miracle, but it will happen. I will kneel on the floor beside your murderer and lay these hands into his blood. There on the floor beside him, I will paint your portrait. You are doubtful? Only because you do not know how much I learned from you. I will paint you right here – I know how to do it – and you will wish and I will wish. Very hard we'll have to wish, harder than we've ever wished for anything before, that the painting of you can have your soul. And then you will strain like I have strained, only faster, harder. It will have to go fast. You'll strain yourself up off the floor, and you will still be weak, though not so weak as you are now. I will take you in my arms, and I will carry you out of here. I promise. Do you hear me? I promise."

I stare at my love as I always do. I try to read his face. Perhaps he should not dare to, but I think he does – I think he believes.

My eyes have blinked before, though not so strongly as they blink right now. Tears flow from them for the first time, and I think that I have never felt so clean.

THREADS LIKE WIRE, LIKE VINE

I'm in the thrift store with my friend Tina when I see it, just a flash of rainbow color hanging between two black swimsuits. Already feeling protective of the thing, I tuck it between the jeans I'm getting, but Tina sees.

"What's that?" she says, and I pull the jeans against my chest too late. She pulls out the thing.

"Oh, this is nasty," she says, unfolding it and working out how to hold it up the right way. It's not a swimsuit, or probably not, more like a see-through teddy crocheted out of what looks like multicolored embroidery floss, but it's super stretchy. She's stretching it now. Oh God, the crotch is all bunched up.

"I don't think this has been washed," Tina says, and it does look a little yellowed and grimy, on the back at least. Still, I'm getting it. I could pretend to put it aside and come back for it when she's not looking, but I'm not going to do that. I'm just placing it on top of my stack, going through the checkout, getting into Tina's truck.

The ride is awkward. She doesn't try to talk. I'm thinking of how, once we're back at my apartment, I'll soak the thing in Woolite, rinse it, press it flat between two towels. I'll hang it, let it dry thoroughly so I don't damage it when I put it on. That might take a full day. I tell myself I'll have this patience, but when the time comes, I don't have any patience. I can wait for Tina to stop the truck and say goodbye, but that's all the time I can wait. I rush across the lawn and up the stairs, unlock my door, drop my bags. I'm already unbuckling my jeans when I close the door, ready to pull off my T-shirt. I leave my panties on and slither into the thing.

It feels loose around me that first second, but as I'm walking back to the bedroom, it pulls tight so that, by the time I look in the floor-length mirror, it's a second skin. It's tighter than second skin and pulsing now.

I sit on the edge of the bed and watch it move. There are layers of it, three or four, moving subtly in different directions, massaging me. The layers are all crocheted out of that rainbow thread – the kind that shifts through all the colors from blue to red to yellow – only no, they aren't. I pull at the threads and see that the inner layer is all the shades of purple and blue, the middle one green and aqua, the next layer yellow to orange to red, and only the top layer is all the colors. All the layers are moving, east to west and west to east and so on.

Nothing like this has ever happened to me, but it doesn't feel wrong. It feels like I've gotten something back that I ought to have had all along.

I wish the thing covered more of me. It's high in the front but low cut in the back, and there isn't anything much on the sides. I keep thinking of going to the kitchen and using the shears to cut off the sides of my underwear, slipping them off, but I can't quite bring myself to get up. There's a warm feeling here on the bed.

I keep pulling the threads away from my belly to study the layers. They're knotted into complex patterns like flowers, like sunrays or mandalas, becoming smaller and larger as the threads shift. I try to work out the patterns, but it's too confusing. It makes me think of the terrible concentration it took for me just to make knot after knot for the stripes on a stupid friendship bracelet back when I was a kid.

I lie back and find myself thinking of another thrift store that Tina and I go to sometimes, the one that's closest to my apartment. The smell of leather and sweat, the tiny slutty clothes they have there. I think of myself picking up a pair of blue cowboy boots, checking the price again. They haven't been marked down. I hear the music but can't place it, can't name it.

When I roll over onto my belly, the butt of the thing pulls down as far as it can. It wants to cover more of me, too. We want the same thing.

My eyes focus on the blue boots and then refocus on something beyond them, there in the back of the thrift store, under a stack of black and white leggings: a flash of rainbow.

I'm standing in the thrift store in the jeans and T-shirt I had on earlier, but I have the bodysuit on under everything, and it's moving deeper now, feels like it's cutting its lines and whorls into me. Slowly, as I lift up the stack of leggings, as I retrieve the rainbow-colored thing and take it to the cash register and pay, the bodysuit loosens.

Just a strange daydream, after all. I am still lying on the bed, but it's later. It's dark out. Only the pink and yellow salt lamps light the room. I can't see all the colors of the bodysuit now, just shades of gold and rose.

But as I relax, the daydream rolls on. I'm walking home with the new thing in the bag. I haven't unfolded it. I'm hoping to make it home, but I can't wait that long. I move into a coffee shop, order and head for the restroom. I unfold the item finally, and it is what I hoped for, a pair of high-waisted cigarette pants made of the same layers of crocheted thread. I kick my jeans to the back of the stall and slip into them. I lay my cheek against the cool stainless-steel door. The new pants sag at first, but the threads come awake. They crawl and pull.

This is the first time my legs have had this sensation and now, from my bikini line all the way up to my ribs, I'm compressed in the four layers of the bodysuit as well as the four new layers of the pants. All eight layers move in eight different directions, pressing in. I sigh.

I come back to myself, on the bed. It's still dark, but there are sounds outside like morning. The thing I'm wearing is soaked with oily sweat. The whole room smells like sweat, mine and someone else's.

Or other people's?

The phone lights up green and there is a text about work, a notice about missed calls. I turn the phone on its face.

I take a deep breath, soaking in the smell before it fades, before I become too accustomed to it to notice.

I take that deep breath, and I am in another shop, one I don't recognize. I have on the bodysuit and the pants and nothing else but spike-heeled shoes. I catch my reflection in a mirror, and I look different. Dangerous, older, with wild unwashed hair. This store is small and upscale, stuffy, nowhere I would normally go, and the cashier is eyeing me hard. I search the shirts and sweaters, pacing nervously. I search the coats, and then I see it, a blaze of color close by in the formal wear section. A cropped blazer with angular shoulders. This time I don't wait at all. I slide into it, button the strange little pearl buttons.

I make a sound of pleasure right there in the middle of the store. My arms are feeling the layers for the first time. My core is alive under twelve layers of the threads, head all dizzy in a haze of sweat.

I slip my hands into the high pockets. My hands are tingling, feeling the threads finally surrounding them, and in the right pocket is something cool and sharp.

I can't wait. There's a nasty look on the cashier's face as I check out.

I am lying on my bed, drenched and spent, alone in the building dread. It's dark, but it has been light, and someone is pounding at my apartment door. Tina. I'm on the inside of the door now, saying something to make her go away, promising something. I'm crouched down on my side of the door, begging her to please go now.

Out on the shade-dappled street, I draw stares. I feel taller, more upright. The layers are bracing me, the legs of the pants moving me down a side street. I feel the breeze hit my sweaty back where there are only the four layers of jacket and nothing else.

I'm walking with my own legs most of the time, but when it wants me to turn, it turns me by pushing into the opposite hip. This is how you turn a horse.

We snake our way along city streets to a section a lot like where I live, the apartments cut up from battered Victorian houses. We slow, passing a blue apartment house and a maroon one. At the base of a green one, we slow again. It isn't the green one; it's the one behind that. The white house isn't noticeable from the street, but I'm taking a shortcut, I guess, through a dry stretch of lawn bordered by lilac bushes. The blossoms are all still in tight little pearls, but their scent is overpowering full-blown lilac. I stop to wonder at this, but the backs of the pants press me forward.

We move over a greener lawn and around a corner. This feels too real in some ways and unreal in others. I catch a glimpse of white-capped mountain and white sky between two houses, and there are rose petals and cigarette butts and broken glass on the ground. There are fall leaves on the ground, summer insects in the air. My shoes cut into my heels.

I feel afraid now, and I try to wake myself back into my bedroom, but I can't. I'm climbing a rust-colored staircase, moving in a winding hallway that smells of mold and mice. I am before an unclean, white-painted door, and the shushing sound rushes in my ears. I hold the key before the lock.

I come back to my bedroom with the phone in my hands. I'm crying, trying to call Tina, but I can't see the screen. It's blurred. The smell of sweat and scalp and lilac floods my bedroom. There is a green circle on the screen, and I am trying to press it, but I am pulled back, pulled back into the doorway. The key is in the lock, and I'm turning it.

I'm on my bedroom floor on my knees trying to pull the bodysuit off. It is bound to me, grown into me like ivy vines into the side of a house. I rip at it, see for a second the channels cut into the soft skin at my hip. I tear a hole, and the severed tendrils weave back into place. I pull, and the whole of it presses back hard, and I swoon.

I am in a front room, all gray. The windows have thick gold drapes. The stained-glass lamps are off, but they glint in the semi-dark. I smell cat.

I am in the bright cold bedroom, which has nothing over its slim window. In an oval stand mirror like my own, I see myself for the first time fully dressed, and I am beautiful. Older yet, harder, hardened. We are beautiful, the threads and I, but I am not quite fully dressed after all. There are many places that have just four or eight layers. Skin shows through. And the feet, hands, throat, face – all of them are entirely bare.

I turn. Behind the bed, a wrought-iron staircase spirals up to a strange little loft, and I climb.

In my bed, I lie still. I feel the smooth rough cold of the painted iron on my palm.

In the loft, a chair and a knitting bag, crotchet needles, a red and yellow eyebrow window. A ghost-woman sits in the chair for a quarter-second, no more, and then the chair looks inviting. Seated, I take up the needles, one in each fist. I have never used these before, but it doesn't matter. I lean to look in the bag, and it is sitting there, a hefty spool of thread, its end already rising up to meet my needles.

AN EDUCATION

1.

"Seeing *can* be taught. Close your eyes," the new tutor said in response to my tales of past failures. She pushed away my file, leaned over her desk. She was all long spirals of salt-and-pepper hair, flaking lips, tiny eyes behind thick glasses.

Accustomed to being interrupted, I often make a glottal sound without anything planned to say, just to take up my part of a conversation. I made that sound now.

"Your eyes, girl," she cut in, "or I'll close them for you. Sit up and cross your ankles."

Her voice became soothing, as soon as I did what she asked.

"*Very* good," she said.

The blackness soon came alive with dim little sparks, same as always. Time passed.

"I can see a few points, but I can't go further," I said. And yet there was a cluster of sparks in the back corner that were brighter, firmer than the others.

She didn't answer. I heard the whistling of her nose-breathing, the wet grind of her teeth, and from that back corner, I heard a basket tip, its stack of wooden dowels clacking onto the floor. I knew just what they were.

One, two, three, four, I thought.

"*See* them," she seethed. "How many?"

They grouped themselves like this: IIII IIIII II II.

"I see, I do," I said. "Thirteen."

And the dowels formed themselves into a chair, with the IIII being the back, IIIII the seat, II the back legs, II the front legs.

Made of swarms of greenish sparks but clear enough, it rose above the desk. It spun and tipped slowly like a dancer.

It spun so that I could see every angle? No, it spun to show her power.

If I'd opened my eyes, I'd have seen it no more clearly, only differently. There were things clearer and some less clear in this space. Color, for example....

But no. The color *was* clear. Red, though I sensed red in a different way, through a different organ. More like taste than sight. It was sweet....

I was telling her I could see everything – the red paint, the dowels' texture, their interior structure. I saw how one splintered on the end. I laughed as I told her. Triumphant, relieved.

She touched my arm. "Of course, beginner's toys," she said, "but you will get there."

"Beginners?" I said.

"A special wood, easy to see. But you see them. Can you move the chair? Move it a little and then you can go. Or, loosen one of the places where it's bound. That would be enough. These bindings are weak," she said, and she went on trying to tell me how.

But I couldn't.

2.

My tutor and I sat in chairs across from each other, eyes closed, end of session. No desk stood between us.

I tipped the pouch and spilled sand onto the floor. With a firm grasp on each grain, modeling as I went, I pulled the figurine up and set her on her axis. A dense little ballerina sparking with thousands of glassy points. She spun and tipped, spilled down.

By this time, I could see the tutor more clearly with my eyes closed than with them open. She crossed her legs like a man and looked into my folder, frowning. Her lunch bubbled in her gut, some mix of chickpeas and greens in a bitter spiced sauce. A back tooth festered.

She frowned at the folder, drew an X beside the date for today.

"Fine if I go now? I'm so busy," I said.

She looked up at me, rubbed a thumb tip over her chapped lips. "Practicing anything else lately?" she said.

What else could I do? I raised the big sandcastle for her, just a three-dimensional drawing but rich in detail, interiors drawn out, doors and furniture and such, just a shaky line to it here and there, then a general shudder and a shimmery sound. I could maintain it for ten seconds before it fell. Grains bounced up on my sweaty leg.

I flinched, sure she'd say something demeaning.

Instead she said, "Ambitious. I'm proud."

3.

We were on the subject of 'What comes next?' Where would I go? Would I tutor, begin touring and try to make a name for myself?

I've outgrown her, I thought. Silly me.

She asked if I'd like to take a practice together, for old times' sake.

I humored her. Back in our spot, when my eyes were closed, she asked if I could see her well.

"Of course," I said.

She began to double. Slowly, slowly, another tutor came to sit before the first. The new one stretched and stood, approached the door, creaked it open.

"Try to follow," she said.

I stood.

"Not that way. The way I did."

Shocked to find that I could, I slid over and out, stood again in that *different* way. I didn't need to turn in order to see, behind me, my body sitting at rest. It was comfortable, vaguely smiling. I followed my tutor out into the vestibule and saw nothing but the familiar glossy red doors, one in front, one left, the stairs on the right leading down to the alley – only there was no alley but, I thought, more doors down there.

I didn't have time to ask or wonder because she opened the left-hand door into an identical vestibule, only with the stairs in front. She went quickly through another left-hand door. The stairs were on the left now. She kept opening doors. Too rushed to examine my confusion, I followed.

Too trusting (too arrogant) to question her, I followed.

Sometimes the stairs led up, sometimes down. I followed her to the bottom of one staircase, where there was another vestibule just the same. I followed her up twice or three times, and then down again, and then up again twice in a row.

The doors began to look older, peeling paint, dirt, dark shoe scuffs. I smelled piss, garbage.

She stopped, and the doors...sped up. Like cards flipping, a film missing frames? Only her figure was still smooth.

She turned toward me.

She brought her face close.

"If you get back to where you want to be, you're as smart as you think you are."

(My body)

"Oh, no," I said, the words all husky in my throat.

"Open your eyes," she said.

I tasted my mouth, not my mouth. I took a flake of skin between my teeth.

"Open your eyes."

And saw my own mouth open into laughter.

THE MAIDEN IN ROBES

Grandma always had a lot of what Bill called cooter-plants growing in the greenhouse back behind the ponds, but we paid them no mind. When we kids first came to live with her, she told us we were not to touch anything back there or else. Other kids might have taken that as a challenge to enter the greenhouse and touch all the things, but not us. Our grandma was mean as could be, and we did not cross her. I never even knew the word or why the plants were called cooters. We only ever saw them through the dappled greenhouse glass, so they just looked a little like flame shapes.

There were a lot of other things in the greenhouse that we never saw up close because we were obedient children. I suppose our friends always thought it strange how we grew up without any piss and vinegar. Never a spanking, never the need. We *were* docile, maybe a little fearful, but not maimed in the mind or anything like that. Grandma was fair; she set her limits and we obeyed.

How do you keep children from wandering into the road or jumping into the river? You tell them not to and show them how serious you are, and they by and large don't do the terrible things you fear they'll do. Well, Grandma was the same way; there were just more things she was serious about. Never lie, cheat, steal, and so on, but also:

Never go into the greenhouse.

Never bring anyone home without permission.

Never go up the stairs. Those are *Grandma's* rooms.

Never cross Grandma – with your words, with your mind. Don't get in her way. If she's headed past you, step aside.

Respect and boundaries were what it came down to. It was easy enough to be good with rules so clear, and the four of us grew up strong and good and kind. My cousin Bailey married young. She made a fine mother. Cousin Bill went into fixing people's houses. He isn't married yet, but we hear his work praised all around town. My brother, Henry, was supposed to work with plants, like Grandma, but he became an apprentice to the baker and has a little sweetheart named Emily. Grandma would like them to live here when they marry, but they'll want a place in town, I'm sure.

I'm the baby, but now I'm old enough to have a sweetheart too. Absolom Eugene Underwood the Third, possibly the most eligible bachelor in the county, the light of my life! His people are not happy about this match, but his money is his own. I wonder what he sees in me except I'm sweet. I hope that will be enough.

We have permission to sit on the front porch, so that's what we do. I gaze into his piercing eyes and hear of his education, his travels and adventures, all his wants. I'd say he's censored things for the benefit of one so innocent, but one day *we* will travel, we will adventure, and everything long concealed will open up for me!

★   ★   ★

"We'd like to walk around sometimes," I tell Grandma. Eugie's so full of life he gets restless sitting all the time.

"Walk where?" she snaps. She washes dishes so tensely I'm afraid she'll break a glass. I watch the water for blood.

Nervous, I clasp my hands. He hasn't told me just what to ask for, so I say, "We might like to walk around the pond."

"Your idea or his?" she says.

"Mine," I say quickly. I hope she won't see how I flush with the lie.

She rocks back from the sink, dries her hands. She looks me up and down. "You sure? I think that boy tells you what to do sometimes, no?"

"No," I say, going redder with the lie and with indignation. If she didn't want me obedient, then why on earth did she make me this way?

Maybe she is the only one I'm ever meant to obey? No, it isn't that. She wants me happy like all the rest of them are. Eugie will make me happy. He's the only thing that will.

★　★　★

The ponds are unlovely, but it feels good to walk. The damp between our clasped hands unnerves me so much I can barely focus.

Eugie points and asks, "What are those?"

I say, "Grandma's cooters."

He's stunned for a second and then he laughs deeply. He drops my hand to shield his eyes for a better look past the greenhouse glass.

"Just some old cooter plants," I say.

"Why, that they are," he says. His mouth twists as it often does, like he'd like to laugh some more right away but shouldn't. He takes my hand again, and on we go.

I'm glad. I never have liked the greenhouse. I have a memory from long ago — maybe when Mom and Dad and my aunt and uncle were all still alive — the greenhouse filled with smoke or mist. Glowing, anyway, gray-white against the starry night.

★　★　★

Family dinners are rarer now. Usually it's just Grandma and me, but tonight my sweetheart shares our meal.

"What are those flowers called, those pink and brown ones in the greenhouse?" Eugie asks. I do not mention that I've already named them to him.

Grandma pauses, wiping her lip with the napkin, then says slow and clear as if every word is its own pearl on a strand: "The Maiden in Robes."

I do not cross her by correcting, or asking, or anything. I hope that the conversation will veer elsewhere, and it does. We speak of Bill's construction projects, Bailey's children, Henry's early hours and the magnificent loaf of bread he left for supper.

I wonder when I'll have anything of my own, but I do have something. I do.

Eugie squeezes my knee under the table when Grandma's absorbed in her pie. I nearly choke, fearing she'll see, fearing and relishing the strange action of my nerves whenever I'm touched by him.

* * *

"No, we can't," I say.

"How will she know?" he says.

"It doesn't matter whether she knows. What matters is that it's forbidden."

He looks at me as though I've raised in value. That's all well and good, but he *will* ask again next time. It's all he seems to think of now.

Respect and boundaries. When we marry, he'll be the one I obey and vice versa. For now, it's still Grandma's house and Grandma's rules.

* * *

"You have permission," I say when he arrives on the step. I didn't expect to feel sad saying it.

Eugie pauses, looking stunned. Maybe he wonders what I might be granting permission for. I'm suddenly aware of sweat between my crossed knees.

"I asked, and she says you can," I say. I nod gravely toward the ponds and greenhouse.

"Well, come on, then," he says, reaching for a hand. I don't reach back but fish in my apron pocket for the key and pass it over to him.

"*You* have permission. I have to stay here."

He will stay here, then, if I can't go. We will make distracted talk on the porch with his eyes all out of focus until I say, "Please. Really, just please, just go." He will go and come back more quickly than I expected, but he will be flushed and will hurry off toward his car too soon. I will have to call him back so he can give me Grandma's key.

I'll think he's going to be back soon and pester me for it again, but he doesn't come back.

* * *

The Maiden in Robes is not a pretty flower. At its best, it's just a flat flame, like a single spike of bromeliad, and yet those who encountered it in the field spoke of its great beauty. I read a few of these descriptions much later, in a library in the country where this plant once grew wild. I was completing research for a book, something I'd have never imagined doing when I was young. But that was half a lifetime later, or so it seemed.

Only one firsthand account remains, but the secondhand tellings confirm that the flower looks like a lovely woman shrouded in heavy robes or blankets with only perhaps the curve of her head sticking out near the top.

She moves under the burden of the coverings. She struggles to open them, and you strain and struggle to see.

Your eyes are so heavy looking at her.

She says if she has one night with you, she'll be real. Though swooning, you're ready for it – about to burst your skin.

The longer you look, the more of her you see – and the farther away she appears. She had seemed a Thumbelina right up by your nose, and now she's a full-sized woman far in the distance. Nearly free of her blankets now....

★　★　★

We haven't left the house in ages. I'm restless from sitting and from the lack of sleep.

"He's never coming back," I say. I can't hold in my tears anymore, so I turn away from Grandma.

"He is," she says.

"He isn't," I say, and I get a strange chill. *Never cross Grandma.*

But she is not angry when I turn back. Her face is soft and sweeter than it ever was before...and frightened. Someone who's chastened herself realizing she's gone too far. She says, "He never left, not really."

My eyes focus past her to the starry night beyond the windows. I turn and, weeping, climb the stairs. *Never go upstairs. Those are Grandma's rooms.*

I am searching for the key. Digging in pockets and crashing things to the floor. These rooms are nothing special, nothing different from what's downstairs.

She is speaking. I don't catch it all.

Your house now, soon enough. Your rooms, your rules.

Take the key.

I can't find it.

Take it all.

Hate me if you will…only stay.

★   ★   ★

If a single flower can bring a man to ruin, what could a few dozen do – and in a closed-up space, besides?

I anticipate the white-gray glow before I come upon the greenhouse. What happened here long ago? My parents and Bill and Bailey's mother – this must have been not so long before they passed. And then why can't I remember why they passed? All three of them ill or injured for a time, it seemed. They were somewhere else. We weren't allowed to visit.

I wish I could bring it all up, but once I'm at the door it's all I can do to throw the rock and find the inside handle. In the gust, I see the maidens. They look just like me. They do look far away and lovely. They're calling to me, but there's something else too. Mist, I thought, and there is something more. A web? Not fine as spidersilk but more like a lacy sponge.

"The Bridal Veil," an awe-filled voice says right behind me.

The veil's tendrils catch on me before I swoon. I fall, and Grandma catches me.

★   ★   ★

Boundaries. Respect. They're mine now. I say what happens.

She sleeps downstairs. Eugie and I sleep in the same room but separate beds. No one would see if I climbed into his, but it wouldn't be right.

We'll wait for Grandma to bring the preacher. He'll probably have to come upstairs, as we're too weak just yet to go anyplace.

We'll rest up and feel better soon, or I will. Eugie already feels quite well. Though he can't yet walk or speak, his face rests in perfect bliss. When I come back from the bathroom in Grandma's robe, his eyes track me. His lip trembles. That is all.

I've been picking the bits of veil-root out of him a little at a time. "An hour or two a day," I say, "and we'll have it all done by the wedding."

Today it's the leg all bumped up like chicken skin. It's a beautiful leg. He's a beautiful man, still. He manages to look like he has his wits about him, and I think the illusion will hold up even when he speaks. I don't know how bright he was, really, before.

"We can still travel. We can still have adventures," I say. His money is still his own. No one will cross us.

I'm tweezing out a spike large as a cat's fingernail when he flinches, making me leave a little tear in his pretty skin.

"Don't do that," I say. "Don't move."

And he doesn't. The rest of the night, he does not move.

SMALLER STILL THAN ME

I thought my smallness might be valued here, but it turns out these people are proud of their height and heft. Despite the prestige of my residency, despite the pity they might feel for me, I've gotten not one come-on.

I go to the readings and receptions, more of them than I'm obliged to attend. I stay later than I'm obliged to stay, and still all anyone asks about is sculpture. Full of hors d'oeuvres, I stammer and sweat, mispronounce words from a long-ago artist statement.

It's the loneliness as much as the insecurity that makes me blunt. I sit in on a critique, say, "Your problem is you don't understand how to work in the round. Everything you do is frontal. It might as well be a drawing."

"Oh, thank you," the student says with a nervous bow and comes back next week with another piece just the same.

I'll remember him, but the other artists and dabblers I'm called upon to influence are equally blithe, unreachable.

I do have every afternoon for work. I tell everyone I'm obsessed with fiber and, in fact, there is much planning I need to do for a hangar-sized string thing to be installed this coming winter, but when I request modeling clay and wire and wood, no one asks questions. The materials arrive on my doorstep the next morning.

It takes two weeks of idle fussing with the frame before I realize I'm making a self-portrait. After that, the work goes quickly.

I love the smallness of it, the way the thighs swell to the sides. It is just slightly smaller than me. Smaller than I? I never know how to speak. Maybe that's part of why people don't take to me or respect me or love me or whatever it is they don't do. I think this way as I linger over the dimples at the hipbones, the weird creases in the lower belly, the well-earned folds in the neck: I'll love this body if no one else will.

During weight loss, applying lotion is important, not only to improve the skin's appearance but also to help one's mind map onto the new contours of the body. It's been years since my loss, but I still use lotion every night. This is like that. Once the masses are built up, smoothing and burnishing the costly green-gray modeling clay feels like rubbing myself from behind myself.

★   ★   ★

You haunt me for weeks. When I'm lying awake in bed, you knock over accent tables and squeak the floorboards. When I shower, you finger my things and then freeze in position, leaving me to wonder at a suit that's moved from the bed to the chair.

With a pounding heart, I hold up a wire earring and squint to be sure I'm seeing the gray-green substance stuck in its coils.

I am miserable.

I begin seeing your smudges on all of my clothes, my notebooks, my bags. I arrive at tutorials disheveled and without my cruel remarks. I neglect wine parties, then miss a morning panel because I've stayed up late pacing the cottage.

What's odd? This only seems to boost my reputation. I am more in demand. I see my first smoldering look from across a banquet room.

I suspect another person is breaking into the cottage or stowing away in the day to rise at night. I search closets before locking up, look under furniture.

I know I'm fooling myself.

When you slide into my narrow bed, so smooth and so cool, I stiffen and feel I might cry out, yet I'm not exactly surprised. You play dead until I relax.

It's a nightly thing after that and each day something more. You walk behind me to the shower, mime the motions of tooth-brushing and dressing, undressing. You begin to speak.

I think of putting something on you, but I like the sight of your body. You stay naked and do not seem to mind.

But you're minding other things.

"Who are you with when you leave here? Why do you stay so long now?" you say.

"Do I stay long? How would you know?" You've implied that when I go, you lock in place and are lost to all sensation. Is this not so?

You don't answer. I think you forget you can speak. You mirror my movements as I tidy the cottage until I stop to guide you forward. Now that it's your hands on the broom, you freeze.

"You know the movements," I say. I sway behind you as you've swayed behind me, and you sweep the floor for the first time.

And so we've gotten along these last weeks. I warm you on the nights I'm home, and you do the chores.

I've made an admirer, one of the big locals who wants some of my evenings, and I've been more conscientious about the days – to leave everyone with a good impression.

The time we've had has been lovely. I think you were something I really needed. The whole experience – everyone here and the place. I needed this.

Here is where you cry and slam the doors, just as I would in your position.

"You can't. I'll have no one," you say. It doesn't matter that I made you. That doesn't give me the right.

So I stand behind you, teaching you how to work with wood and wire and then the clay, which sticks to your hands. It takes parts of you with it.

My hands guide your wrists, but it has to be you who makes the thing, and you are weak and impatient. It shows in your work, which is over-small and frontal, a stick drawing with cartoonish masses at the hips and a neck wattled like a goat's. Your pride and your love for it overwhelm me, but they aren't enough.

You want privacy and lead the thing stumbling out to the garden sooner than I would have expected. As I watch, I'm aware of clay inside my shirt, inside my underwear, and I know you have been trying on my things again. The night is dark green and you two glow against it like marble.

THE GLASS OWL

Grandpa's gone. He wasn't in his tent or down by the river this morning. Time has come to pull up camp, and he still isn't back.

We're just a half-day away from our city – not far enough. We have to keep moving. If everyone could run, we'd do that. We can't all run, and so we walk. We're in flight from something and know not what.

Virginia comes from her washing-up at the river to hear the news. Everyone's comparing notes and saying it couldn't have happened. Grandpa can't be gone.

"He wouldn't," we say and, "You don't think he'd go back?" and so on.

She doesn't hear.

She's already crashing through brush, running so fast the sun strobes through the canopy, thinking, *This is a disaster.* Something terrible rushes toward their city, and now here she is running back toward it.

Birds fly over, heading away from what she's running toward. She catches little flashes of wild things on the ground, all of them headed the opposite way.

Trees are sparser now, her breath already rhythmic, body light and reactive. She's glad to run so well, but she hurts inside.

Her thinking comes in short, repetitive bursts to match the rhythm of her body: the other people won't wait at the camp. They'll be gone when she gets back. She'll be alone. She has to find him. She can't find him. It's too late. The people won't wait. She'll be all alone with nothing, no one.

She has to find him.

Has he gone all the way back to the city?

She'd half expected that to come during the days of packing – that he would refuse, say, "Let me stay, let me be," as she'd heard the old ones sometimes did – but he had not wavered. He had felt the need to go as urgently as anyone. Just like you feel a storm coming.

Just like you feel the fire.

And he'd packed and helped others pack, rested up for the trip, kept himself limber.

The change in him, it came last night at the fire, didn't it?

That little Cindy begging for stories – that's what set Grandpa thinking wrong. He told of the glass owl, the only living thing that rose from his boyhood village decades ago. He spoke of how that owl passed over those fleeing villagers with its shimmering sound, glass feathers on glass feathers on wind.

"Could you see through it?" Cindy had asked last night. She was warm in blankets, ready for bed, a cup of peppermint tea in her mittened hands. Her eyes, they were so large just then.

"No, it was just...white," Grandpa said. He squinted into the fire as though he saw the owl there, all brittle and shiny like crusted snow, hard and sharp as the crinkled, glassy hairs on his own head and face. He had not just seen the glass owl; he had touched it, though he did not say this to Cindy.

Our eyes moved to his right hand, burned all those years ago. He was lucky he pulled back so quickly. If he had not....

But there at the campfire he said, still amazed after all these years, "That owl and who knows how many other creatures, they *stayed* when the bad thing happened! They *didn't* run. That time it was fire, a fire so sudden and hot it melted the village to glass."

"What is it this time?" asked Cindy.

★   ★   ★

We don't know. Something terrible.

We're anxious now.

★   ★   ★

"Lunch, we'll have it here, then?" we say, as a way of waiting for Virginia without waiting.

"Lunch," our leader says, "and then we'll tarry no longer."

This restlessness in us, it's what told us to leave our city,
the city my grandfather founded
where I was born
where I bore my
buried my
Leave my only home?

It wasn't a question. Along with shared nostalgia, we all felt the same urgency in our minds, in our muscles. We thought some might...but no. *None* wavered, not in our neighborhood anyway. Three days of packing and readying. We couldn't wait longer.

We *can't* wait longer. Those who aren't busy with lunch preparations begin taking down tents and getting them back into the mules' packs so we'll be ready after lunch.

"This one?" calls a teenage boy.

Tears come to our eyes, that quickly. The boy stands beside Virginia's yellow tent. Grandpa's blue tent is just behind it.

Our leader calls back without hesitation: "No. Leave both of those. They might return."

They won't return.

★   ★   ★

Virginia can't stop. Her only rest is a brisk walk, a pause to sip water. She missed breakfast; now the sun's at noon. Her limbs still feel light, electrified, but her belly is another matter, and her head weighs down her body like a heavy stone.

She keeps to the river because it leads to the city, and as she walks, she comes closer to the edge and finds herself watching the water.

What does she think, that it will run red, that ashes will rush down? Or that pieces of the city will bob along in its current any moment?

She looks away.

The running hurts now. Good. When something like this happens, it should hurt.

★   ★   ★

The food is spread on clean blankets, plenty of food.

We do not know where we go. We are just a half-day from the doomed city, and yet we sit down to take our second lavish meal since leaving. How long will our food hold out? How far do we need to go to be safe from whatever it is that's coming? Where will we live now, and will we stay together? These things we don't mention. Instead, it's, "Oh, that looks wonderful." It's, "Could you please pass the salt?"

One says, "Little Cindy reminds you of Virginia, doesn't she?"

Another, "All rapt over Grandpa's stories, with those big eyes of hers. Yes."

"She'll be devastated if they don't come back."

"It's not 'if', though, is it? I mean…."

"You're right."

"We shouldn't have let Virginia go."

"Some always waver. That's what all the old-timers say."

"We thought everyone was strong this time."

"There could still be others who fall back. There's no way to tell."

"That's why we have to get moving. I don't want to wait anymore."

"I can't wait."

"We can't. We all feel the same."

"Let's just enjoy our meal."

We are quiet for a time, and someone says, "Did you know Grandpa went back to his childhood city, after the fire?"

Another says, "Even Cindy's heard that one a dozen times by now."

"Years later, as a young man he walked there, had to see it. All the ground was glass, parts of the buildings turned to glass."

"He thought there might be more glass animals."

"When he saw the owl – when he touched the owl – he thought there might be others."

"Or people risen in glass. The ones who fell back."

"The ones who refused."

"That's just a story."

"I know."

It suddenly occurs to us that now, without Grandpa, we can move more quickly. The mules can run; everyone here can run or be carried by a running parent.

That's good. That's something.

★　★　★

Virginia does; she runs. The river rushes to her left. She begins to feel faint and walks briskly and then walks slowly.

She should have overtaken him by now, even if he left just as they were bedding down. He might not have kept to the river, though, if he was thinking to lose a pursuer.

Something terrible rushes toward the city, even now. Fire, or murderous people, plague, flood – but it can't be a flood, not here.

Something.

Some are drawn toward the destruction every time, just like that owl was. Virginia herself is being drawn back, though it doesn't feel like she's wavered. It feels like she still wants to bolt back to her people, resume the flight away from the city and toward whatever is in their future. Other cities or villages, presumably. It feels like she's walking this way for a noble purpose, sacrificing her time and risking herself for a greater purpose.

It always feels that way to the ones who waver.

And there Grandpa is, unmistakable and sudden, a sunbeam hitting his white shirt up past a loose group of evergreens.

She jogs toward him slowly and painfully. She sees how he limps now. He's hurt his foot. He's quivering, turning, confused.

Oh, you impossible man. Will there be a fight, then? He's still strong. She can't drag him away.

"The glass owl," he says when the snapping under her feet turns him toward her. His eyes are as large as Cindy's were last night. "It was just here."

"What were you thinking?" Virginia says, embracing him. He leans into her, he's so exhausted. The air is different. Are they too close to the city, too late to flee?

Drawing back, Grandpa looks pained. He says, "I heard the owl just outside my tent. I told you all about it in the note I left. Oh, *why*'d you come?"

"What note? You didn't leave a note." The note shows clearly in his front pocket.

"Go back, Virginia. Are they waiting for you?" He looks to the sky, for the time or for the owl, she can't tell. Is the sky different now, more muddied?

She pulls the note out before Grandpa's eyes, but he doesn't focus there. He's scanning all the trees.

"I saw it. Last night and then just now, *just* now," he says.

His body turns as he catches the owl again. Virginia follows his gaze, and it *is* there, or something is. She catches a flash of hard white shuddering near the water. Is it drinking, bathing?

Grandpa puts a fire-marked finger to his lips. *Shhh*, like the sound its glass feathers make. Virginia doesn't hear the bird over the river noise, but her arms and scalp prickle. She's going to hear it.

Is she going to touch it?

They approach very quietly, holding hands. She's going to get to see it, finally. She'll hear close-up its shivering glassy sound.

Will this owl lead them back to their city and certain doom? What else could happen? It doesn't feel like it matters, so proud she is to have come back here to be with Grandpa inside this old, old tale.

A CHRONICLE OF THE MOLE-YEAR

Mom and Dad spent November deep-cleaning the house and stocking up on every little thing we might want to eat. Glass canisters stood full of pasta, rice, beans, and nuts. Every kind of jarred and canned good crowded the pantry shelves. On the counter, outrageous displays of fruits, vegetables, bread, cakes (a white, a chocolate, and the pineapple that was my favorite), fruit pies and pudding pies, boxes of candies and plates of cookies. The fridge and freezer held tofu and imitation sausage as well as real sausage, bacon, several varieties of beef and chicken, and an extensive collection of milks, creams, sauces, and condiments.

So overwhelmed with choices, our Mole-Year's Eve dinner was a simple baguette sandwich cut in five, accompanied by a pitcher of lemonade. We had to eat quickly and get to the meeting.

"This will be our year," said Mom, as she always did.

My little sister, Lucy, said, "It doesn't ever happen. None of us have seen it."

"That's not true! You know your brother had a mole-year," said Dad.

"Only I was a baby and can't remember," said William, blushing fiercely. He was sixteen and unpopular, thinking surely of something vile and debauched he planned to do if, this once, our prayers converged and the time was granted.

Unlike my sister, I believed. The new gray kitten sat tense on my lap, getting bits of cheese from my sandwich, and all I could think was that if we woke to a mole-year, she would be gone. She didn't even have a name yet, and if everyone here had their way it would be a year before she had her name, or grew, or anything. And I would have to live a year apart from her.

"Why don't animals get to, though? I don't understand," I said, stroking her soft head.

"They can't vote," Lucy snapped.

Mom said, "They can't pray for it, dear. They can't wish."

Dad scooted his chair closer and said, "What will *you* do, Perrie?"

The kitten had dropped off my lap, and I hardly thought of her now, absorbed instead with 'the plan'. I said, "I'll live in the forest with Rosie. Can we?"

"Good idea," Dad said.

"In the green cottage that's empty now. Can we live all alone if we like?" I added.

"Of course," he said, "if Rosie wants the same, that is."

"We always want the mole-year to come, don't we?" I said.

"Well, you and William will vote as you like," said Dad.

Mom held the kitten belly-up in her arms like a baby. With a worried brow, she said, "Dad and I always pray, and wish, and vote in favor. Who wouldn't want more life?"

"But people do vote no," I said, and we were quiet, each perhaps imagining what might bring someone to vote no.

In a moment Mom had put on her coat and was holding out Lucy's.

"What will I do?" said Lucy.

"You're too little. Can't vote, can't choose," said William.

Lucy stood and backed into her coat, scowling. "It isn't real anyways."

★   ★   ★

The meeting at Town Hall was quite short: once we'd filled the folding chairs, the mayor went over voting instructions. We voted on slips of paper and passed them to the end of each row, where children my age collected them in baskets. A group of four women got up to sing about winter and endless time. Lucy sprawled on the floor by our feet with coloring books, oblivious to it all, and I thought wistfully how a year ago, I had lain right beside her sharing crayons.

The mayor came up and said the discussion was open. People lined up in the aisles.

"What are they doing?" I whispered to William.

He only rolled his eyes. He was playing a game on his phone.

A large woman took the stage and started talking about how, now that she was widowed, her dogs and horses were all she had. She broke down in tears and hurried back to her seat.

Another woman helped a sick-looking old man to the stage. He spoke about how painful his illness was, and she chimed in, saying he was not expected to live one more month, but the family was all resigned and prepared.

"Why are they speaking?" I whispered to Dad.

He only petted my head and gave a thoughtful look. At that moment I spotted Rosie with her parents. We waved.

Two hollow-eyed young people with a bundled-up baby came up and said how hard it was to miss so much sleep. The baby squalled, and they sighed.

"We've already voted, but we can still change our wish," I whispered.

Dad said, "Yes, that's what they hope," and then, frustrated, he stood and said how he'd spent a mole-year with an infant, and it had bonded him to his son William, like nothing else. Hearing his name, William looked up and nodded.

Next was a small group of people who were concerned about gaming. I didn't quite understand. The meeting fell apart then, with people in the audience following Dad's lead and speaking out of turn.

We left when it became clear that no one would put an end to the disorder. When we sighted snowflakes on the drive home, Mom wept about how beautiful a good snow is on Mole-Year's Eve.

I don't know about the others, but I was a long time getting to sleep that night. I stroked the sleeping kitten curled beside me. I had voted yes, and I wished it too, not without a pang for the sick man and for all the pets we would all lose from our lives for a year.

I woke too early and had to wait to be sure. It was dark outside at seven, dark still at eight, and that's how I knew we had made it into the first mole-year of my young life.

I looked for the poor kitten, though I knew I wouldn't find her. Mom didn't emerge from the bedroom, and Lucy was so angry to be wrong she was playing sick, so it was only the three of us going back to Town Hall for the second meeting. It was foggy outside – nighttime but with bright moonlight falling on all the white. Indeed, the snow had made everything beautiful, and plows had come by in the night so we did not have to fret about the roads. I thought the air felt warmer than it ought to, with a strange blur in it giving everything a rainbow aura as though glimpsed through pearly glass. Sounds were muffled.

"Strange," said William. "Everything seems a little strange."

Dad passed him the car keys, and I noticed how happy both were.

★   ★   ★

The four women came up again to sing about winter and endless time. William wasn't playing on his phone now because the internet no longer worked, but everything else was as it had been twelve hours ago. We sat in the same seats, most of us, and yet it felt a long time had passed and that we had entered a different world.

The mayor tried to read off facts and rules about the mole-year, but soon the chattering drowned him out. Dad hopped up and went to the aisle, where Rosie's dad joined him. They talked seriously for just a moment and then laughed together. Dad then went to a group of older ladies.

When he returned, Dad passed me a key on a rabbit's-foot chain. "Your cottage, my dear," he said. "Ralph can take you tomorrow."

Rosie waved excitedly, and I waved back. I felt hopeful and a little disturbed.

"You're the best age you can be for your first mole-year, Perrie," Dad said.

I looked toward William, but he was not in his chair.

"Older and you'd have more to worry about. Younger and you'd have to stay home like Lucy."

"Where's William?" I said.

"Oh, they took the teenagers to learn about birds and bees. They'll be done soon."

They were done soon – William looking pale and cowed – and we hopped back in the car. William drove again. We were quiet most of the drive, Dad gazing across at William and then back at me.

There was something on his mind.

"You were a baby last time," Dad said, "so that was fifteen years, but there were only five years between that and the previous mole-year. Your mom and I were newlyweds that time."

"We've heard," said William. I didn't see his face but watched his neck blush.

"Can you imagine?" Dad said. "We'd just gotten the house – we were working hard to afford it, and then we were gifted a year with no work, a whole year to just enjoy each other."

William said, "Some of the kids were hoping to set up in the high school this year."

"We'll talk about it later," Dad said curtly.

He turned back to me. We were pulling up in the driveway.

"Are you trying to tell us something?" I said.

He sighed and said, "When a person goes into the year pregnant, they stay that way the whole year. When they come out, the pregnancy finishes. They have the baby."

"But if they get pregnant during the mole-year—" said William.

"—or, rather, if it's early enough that the baby's born before the end of it, then, well, the baby stays...suspended in time. You only see him during mole-years," said Dad.

We were at the door. I felt uneasy.

"I mean to say," said Dad with his hand on the doorknob, "you are just about to meet your brother Jeffrey."

In that instant I imagined a boy older than William – a man – who had raised himself in this strange dark mole-time. I shivered to think of what a brute he must be, but when Dad opened the door, we saw Mom and a transformed Lucy cuddled in blankets before the fire, a happy baby between them.

We went and knelt and met our brother.

"He was still sleeping right where I left him fifteen years ago," Mom said.

"Do you remember him, William? You played together when you were both babies." But this baby couldn't play anything much. This baby would forever be about three months old. For the first time it occurred to me that William had spent a whole year being one, and I wondered how that had changed him.

The baby slapped at William's hand. My brother only shook his head slowly. He didn't remember at all.

"How did he get to be as big as he is?" I asked.

But Dad, Mom, and William were all absorbed with the baby, pretending not to hear.

Lucy said, "Yeah, if you're saying he never gets older—"

Dad said, "We think his body didn't know, at first. There's a certain …momentum in the body."

Mom said, "He grew for a while and then he couldn't grow any more. It's a blessing, don't you think?"

We let it be.

★   ★   ★

Late morning, we ate whatever we wanted. I had pineapple cake and a slab of ham. In the evening we all had chocolate pie and cherry pie with ice cream, and Dad made fried chicken and a tofu stir-fry to go with it. We'd suffer no bellyaches, couldn't gain or lose any weight. Most importantly, we wouldn't run out of anything.

In between the meals we played board games and napped. Some of us set up with books. It didn't snow or melt. The fire kept burning all day with no one adding a log to it. It would burn all year if no one choked it or threw water on it.

"Do you miss the kitty?" Dad said.

I nodded, and he laid the little baby in my lap to play with.

Mom was packing some of the food into brown grocery sacks.

"Are we going somewhere?" I called.

"You are," said Dad.

Oh, yes. Off to the forest with Rosie.

"I'm just so happy to have everyone together," Mom said, "even if it's only one night."

*   *   *

Rosie's dad, Ralph, had her bike latched to the back of his car and made a big production of latching mine on there too. In the cargo space were my bags of food and Rosie's, as well as a big backpack of clothes and books and things for each of us.

My family gathered by the front door to wave one last time. I noticed all our footsteps from the day before were gone – everyone's were. The snow would be fresh each morning all year, just as the pineapple cake at the bottom of my grocery sack would be whole, fresh, and uncut each time I thought to have a slice.

Rosie and I got in the back seat and started talking about what all we'd do. It felt like we both were trying too hard to be excited, but it worked. We faked enthusiasm until it became real.

"You'll be safe," her dad said. "Don't worry, and if you're afraid, or if you're lonely, or if you want anything—"

"Yes, we know," said Rosie.

"You can call on the landline and I'll come, or you can get on your bikes. The roads will stay plowed."

There wasn't so much snow in the yard at all, so thick were the trees here. This little green cottage had been Rosie's great-aunt's. No one had the heart to disturb it yet, so when we walked in, it was as it always had been, everything sweet and small and girly.

Rosie's dad set about building a fire for us while we put away our food.

As he was leaving, he said, "Listen, girls. I don't know if anyone's said...." He fiddled with his keys so that I didn't want to hear what he was going to say.

"Sometimes there's magic?" said Rosie.

He smiled. "Yes, that's all I wanted to say. Sometimes you see magical things during the mole-year, and sometimes animals – not the normal ones, but you'll see. You'll be safe. The fire will warm you, but it can never burn you, and that's true for anything you see that's strange. I think this is a good place for you girls. I think you will be happy here. But if you see something, don't be afraid, and if you're afraid—"

"Call," we both said.

"Or get on our bikes and come home," said Rosie.

We hugged him, and then he was gone, and we were all alone in the forest.

★   ★   ★

We managed quite well, I think. Though no one was there to tell us to, we checked off a day on the calendar each time we woke up. We bathed and brushed our teeth, got exercise and, after the first few meals, ate quite reasonably. We spent a great deal of time exploring the forest, which was lovely with a great many evergreen plants and strange rocks and barely any snow at all. We grew accustomed to the dim misty light that lay over everything, and the rainbow edges, and the silence.

Inside, we sampled each other's books, and though we were too old for it, we played dress-up in the old lady's clothes and jewelry, rubbed her strange-smelling cosmetics into our faces. We explored the little cottage from attic to cellar and tried sleeping in the guestroom beds until we settled together in the great-aunt's queen-size bed, which was heavenly soft and smelled of lavender.

Mostly, we lazed around the living room talking, playing board games and card games, and making each other laugh.

It was everything we'd hoped for.

We both kept one eye out for signs of the magic Rosie's dad had spoken of. A rock with a greenish glow to it, was that magic? Was the sparking sound we sometimes heard in the forest magic?

But no, when we saw magic, we were sure. Our first sighting was a ghost, the little great-aunt. She strode through the kitchen while we made tea, sending a chill down my spine. We searched the cottage but saw no more of her until several days later when, returning from the forest, we caught her squatted down pulling weeds in her vegetable garden.

"She never was able to get much going. Not enough light," Rosie said.

The great-aunt was not see-through, but she had that foggy, rainbow-edged feel to her that let us know she was a ghost and not a real old lady come to challenge us for the cottage. We let her be that day, but after that she appeared more often, always bringing a chill and a jolt.

One night she sat up in the bed between us, shrieking, "I know someone's here."

"Are we afraid?" said Rosie, after.

"Not precisely," I said.

*   *   *

It was as though time had a geography we were learning our way around. We were no longer sleeping exclusively in what we thought was night, and yet the time did have shape. There was a recognizable length for what we still referred to as days.

Certain things had no fixed time: the regrowth happened nonstop, for example. Often we'd watched our footsteps filling up with snow and the pineapple cake slowly weaving in around its missing slice. We wrote or drew and then watched the page erase itself from the bottom, the pencil slowly sharpening. A smear of icing left on a sweater would evaporate like water within an hour.

Other things had a cycle: fog at a certain time and then breeze and a light dusting. The snow and fog would clear and the stars come out bright as we'd ever seen them, and that would last a few hours before the fog rolled in again. We knew a spot in the forest filled with large rocks that had, above it, a clear view of the stars. We'd take pillows and blankets out to watch them. After we'd done it a few times, we spoke and found we both felt better there than in the house.

It should have been cold, but it wasn't. We felt braver out-of-doors.

When we had planned this year in the woods, we had expected to have visitors, even parties. We expected our parents to call and check on us all the time, but they had not, and after Rosie's dad's reminders I suppose we thought we should call only when we were afraid and wanted to be brought home.

We had stopped marking days on the calendar, had stopped laughing quite as much. Our time inside was beginning to feel like a chore.

"Where are all the moles?" said Rosie.

"I think we're the moles. I think it's called that because we burrow down," I said.

Rosie sighed. "Would you like to go back home?" she said.

I thought of the great variety of food in the kitchen, the little baby Jeffrey, my loving parents, and yes, even Lucy. "Sometime I'd like to. Not yet."

"How would you feel about an adventure?" she said.

★   ★   ★

We loaded my backpack with a thin blanket, bread, cheese, jars of lemonade and water, cocoa packets, oranges, and a few nuts and candies. Rosie's backpack held two pairs of sweats, extra socks, a box of matches, a large shawl of the old woman's that we thought we might make a tent of, and all the bills from the old woman's jar of mad money. The poor pineapple cake was abandoned along with most of what we'd brought. We thought about books but didn't want the extra weight.

Besides, we were done living in books for the moment. We were going to have an adventure.

Perched on our bikes contemplating the foggy road ahead, we turned to each other with nervous smiles.

"Are we afraid of anything out there?" she said.

"We haven't seen any animals."

"People?"

I didn't know. My feeling was that everyone had all they needed, that everyone stayed home happy with their families, but I knew that was not true. I had been to Town Hall and seen those bitter, anguished people crying for us to change our wish. I knew that most years – the last fifteen in a row, in fact – there were more of them, or anyway they wanted what they wanted more than we wanted time. Not to mention that I was certainly old enough to know that people sometimes hurt children.

Only I was not afraid.

I said, "I think our parents would not leave us out here if there was anything, really, to fear."

She nodded. "I had the same thought."

"So what does that mean?" I said.

"If we die in the mole-year, we aren't really dead."

"If we're hurt, we're not really hurt."

"We'll *hurt*, for sure—"

"—but we won't be damaged."

That was that, then. We set off down the dirt drive toward town. It would not be a forest adventure, not with the bikes. Besides, I had an urge to see people.

What we saw first, though, was our next bit of magic. Ever since Rosie's dad had told us we would see an animal, we'd been looking everywhere for them. It took only ten or twenty minutes on bikes to see our first, at the side of the road. We slowed and circled back to catch a second's worth of pewter-colored salamander slithering into the snow. I thought I saw folded wings.

"Too cold for something like that," said Rosie.

"It isn't cold at all," I said.

"But the snow." .

It was strange. We had both touched the snow before, but she kept forgetting.

"It isn't cold," I said, bending down to press a palm into it. Cool but not cold.

Rosie smiled anxiously. We circled back onto our route.

Rosie didn't like to watch our footprints fill with snow. She didn't like to talk about anything strange but rather, she liked to pretend that life was as it had always been.

I realized then that she probably wanted to go home – that's all this adventure would add up to for her.

We did manage to have an adventure, though. Picnicking in a pasture, we saw creatures far off walking against a fence line. Three adults and a long line of their young moved like great apes, though they came up just above the grasses. When the breeze arrived with its dust of snow, we stopped again to sit on a fallen log with the shawl over us and saw something like a rainbow forming in the sky above a cluster of houses.

"I've never seen one at night before," Rosie said.

"I think there's more magic than we suspect out here," I said, and just then we saw our third type of animal, which was something like a slender white deer. It came close, showing its pearly coat, delicate goat-like mouth, and oversized eyes. We sat rigid, barely breathing, and when it was gone, we felt satisfied.

The stars came out, and the going was easy. Clusters of houses became blocks of houses, and then we entered the small downtown. We passed the mayor sitting on the Town Hall steps. I kept Rosie company all the way to her tall yellow house in the blocks past downtown. The smoke billowed happily out of its chimney. Her parents came out on the stoop.

"I'll be in, just a minute," she called, and they went inside.

"Thank you," I said. "It was wonderful."

She drooped in relief, got off her bike, and hugged me. I stayed on my bike, and when she backed away, I kept my hand on her backpack strap.

"Of course," she said. She scrunched her backpack down into my bike-basket.

"Thank you for spending all this time with me," she said, the tears starting in her eyes.

"I'll never forget it," I said. I was crying too, and so I turned and pedaled away before I changed my mind.

I pedaled right back to the mayor. I had questions for him.

★   ★   ★

My adventures alone brought me almost to panic sometimes. Alone, I saw ghosts walking the roads and heard unsettling sounds. The first night I planned to sleep in an empty barn that still smelled of horses, just off the road that would lead me, with any luck, to the farm of Margorie, the large woman who had lamented the loss of dogs and horses. The mayor had given me her address and others', after I explained what I wanted to do.

I had never slept alone and couldn't seem to do it, so alert I was to the sounds around me. I tried to tell myself the worst I could do was die, and then I'd wake up whole and new on Mole-Year's Day. No harm in dying or anything else. I wrapped myself tight in the blanket and the shawl, thinking that might help, but the best I could do was lie alone and alert with no book and no light. I tried to rest my body for the day ahead.

I set off early in the fog, sure that I had learned something: there need not be more than one night like that in a life. If, at any point soon, I had the chance to sleep, I would sleep long and well and would not be afraid. I would sleep when I should, and when I could, for the rest of my life.

I came to the farm, thinking to help Margorie. I wanted to tell her about all the animals living in the mole-year, but long before I reached the door, I realized she already knew. The closer I came, the more I saw – the deer and the apelike creatures, and so many metallic-looking winter birds. She'd strung the trees with feeders and left pans of water and food out in the snowy pastures with salt and mineral licks beside them.

She answered the door in drapey velvet pajamas with a glass of wine in hand, a pair of binoculars around her neck and a soft, curious expression. "Yes?" she said, looking beyond me for a car, for someone she knew.

Soft music played in the house. I glimpsed an easy chair pointed toward tall back windows framing a view of pastures and hills. She'd been sitting there watching for animals.

I hadn't decided what I'd say, and so I went with the truth. "Ma'am," I said, "I know this is odd, but I was touched when you spoke during the Mole-Year's Eve meeting. I came out here to make sure you were all right."

"Oh honey," she said, stepping back with a welcoming gesture so broad, I knew she was tipsy. "I'm good. I'm good, but come in. Did you walk here? What are you doing for mole-year?" We walked past photos on the wall – Margorie on horseback, Margorie and her long-gone husband in fancy rodeo clothes, two golden retrievers playing in a stream.

She fed me well. As we watched out the window, she told me what she knew of all the animals I'd seen and of other, rarer ones she'd glimpsed. One of the deerlike animals had taken oats from her hand that morning. While she spoke, her husband passed behind her chair on his way to the kitchen. He was all rainbow-edged and dim, but I thought it must be nice having him around again, even if he couldn't do much.

Margorie's eyes got tired and she reclined in the chair, but we kept talking about how I was doing, what all I'd learned during the mole-year so far, and what my plans were for the rest.

"Sleep here, honey – in my bed, or the guest room, or where you will. I can't drive you now, but in the morning I'll take you wherever you like."

"I can't," I said. I was about to say that my dad was picking me up. It's the kind of meaningless lie that comes to mind. Instead I said, "I chickened out on sleeping alone, and I want to try it again. I think I'm tired enough now to do it, and if I do it, I might not be afraid to do it again for the rest of my life."

"Good idea," she said. She was almost out.

"Can I ask just one thing, before I go?"

"Oh sweetie, sure. Ask away," she said, perking up a little. She still didn't open her eyes.

"You're old enough to have lived through the last mole-year and the one before."

"And others besides."

"Then why were you upset at the meeting? Didn't you know it would be all right with the animals to watch and your cozy house and all?" With the wine and the music and the friendly, harmless ghost.

Margorie laughed lightly, opened her eyes. "I forgot how it was," she said. "It's been so long. Maybe you'll forget too. Some do."

She asked me to wait until she was sleeping to leave. She was unafraid of sleeping alone, and yet it was nice to have someone beside her this once. It was a treat.

On the way out to my barn, I thought long on what she'd said. She had forgotten, William had forgotten because he was too little. My parents had never forgotten, and Jeffrey had to be the reason for that. They couldn't forget him.

Rosie would forget much of our time together, I felt certain. She would remember only that our days were pleasant and that we were closer now, like sisters. We would be best friends for the rest of our lives.

I felt I would not forget the details of this time, but how could I be sure?

The barn appeared on the horizon. I pedaled toward it, certain that when I reached it and wrapped myself in the blanket, I would sleep instantly, well, and long. That's just how it turned out.

When I woke, I was hungry but not for cold bread and cheese again. I made a fire and treated myself to a toasted sandwich, all the time congratulating myself about how grown up I was and assuring myself that I would never forget this moment or any of the other vivid moments that made up this most extraordinary year.

★　　★　　★

The next stop was right at the edge of town, a neat white mobile home in a park of such homes. The hollow-eyed husband, Troy, opened its door and welcomed me in without question. Their place was very pretty, everything new and pastel-colored. Lots of houseplants all around. Billie was at the table feeding mashed carrots to their baby, Lillian.

"Come on in, sit down," she called.

We introduced ourselves, and I sat. Billie looked very tired still – but happier than she'd been at the meeting.

"I should say why I've come," I said.

"Oh? Didn't you come to babysit?" she said.

"No— I mean, I can if you need me."

"There are so many kids around here we lose track," Troy said, "and they're all bored. They're over here all the time. But not you. I know you."

"I do too," said Billie, pointing at me like my name was on the tip of her tongue.

"You're old enough to vote. You were at the meeting," Troy said, and both of them laughed.

"It was my dad who got up and talked."

"Ha! We thought he was such an asshole."

"But was he right?" I said.

They looked at each other, smiling but not sure. "Yeah?" said Troy.

Billie said, "It's complicated. But hey, if you don't mind, watch her while I get a shower and a nap?"

Troy had moved to a stool beside the door and was putting on snow boots and a coat. He noticed me watching and said, "Not everybody has the mole-year off."

A knock at the door, and a boy my age came in with a shy little girl about Lucy's age.

"The real babysitters have arrived," Troy said. "Hey, Perrie? Want to come with?"

We went out behind the trailer to his pickup, the back of which was loaded with plastic sleds.

As we drove, he said, "Yeah, most jobs just pause. No teaching, no selling groceries or selling anything much, no cleaning, and the electric and such takes care of itself just like magic – but some folks still have to work. I work for the Parks Department, which means I'm in charge of winter recreation. Surprised I haven't seen you at our events."

"I haven't been in town," I said.

"No? That's the best part of mole-year, all the events. No school and all the kids playing all day. I was seven years old for the last one, had a blast. Hadn't thought of it before, but that might just be what got me working in this field."

"Do they pay you?" I asked.

He laughed. "It's more like a bonus. Not a year's pay, that's for sure."

It was the breezy part of the day, just before the little skiff of snow.

Soon, we'd arrived, not at a park but at a steep hill ending in pasture. Many cars were parked along the side of the road, many families waiting in coats and scarves passing around boxes of donuts and thermoses of hot cocoa. The snow wet their shoulders and caps. They cheered for us when we exited the truck. They lined up for sleds.

One little girl came running right into my arms.

"Lucy!" I cried. I hugged her, set her down, and looked around for our parents.

"I came with a bunch of kids," she said.

"She comes every day," said Troy. He passed us a large sled, and it was strange: for a while, with Lucy, I was a kid again. We slid down the hill together three times in a row, shrieking and laughing, and then we had cocoa with her friends.

"Everything's fine at home?" I said.

Lucy touched my arm. "They finally let William go off to live with the other kids, so it's been lovely. You're coming back?"

"In a while," I said. My adventure wasn't over just yet.

I found Troy leaning against his truck. "Thank you for bringing me," I said.

He nodded.

I turned away and then back and said, "If you don't mind my asking, are you glad the mole-year came? Would you vote the same way if you had it to do over?"

He looked down at the ground and back up, grinning. "Well, Perrie, I just don't know. I suppose we were afraid of things going on like they had been for another year. Lillian was nice today, but she's fussy, doesn't sleep well. The neighbor kids didn't used to come by to help. Not to mention one big thing we were thinking about, which was a whole extra year of diapers."

My nose scrunched up. "I hadn't thought of that," I said.

"The diapers aren't a problem, as I'm sure you realize."

I hadn't expressed it to myself before he said it, but I did know what he meant. In the mole-year, we still went to the bathroom. We felt the same sensations, maybe smelled a little something. Though I didn't know about others, I still wiped and flushed. But there was never anything there. Whatever was in our bellies must have transported back to where it had been before we took it in.

"The diapers aren't a problem, and you have help, so it's been good?"

"It has. I still don't know if I'd do it over," he said. He frowned. "I can't wait for her to start growing again. We were so excited about every new thing that she did and now she's just…arrested. It's creepy."

It was, if you thought about it that way. It was a little creepy that William had such a year as a baby, and that I was spending an extra year at this age. While I did not question that I'd become much more adult over this time, my body hadn't, and how could my mind mature if the matter supporting it did not?

And what of Jeffrey? If he always stayed three months old, he would still be a baby when Mom and Dad were (I shuddered to think it) gone. Would he be mine – or William's, or Lucy's – to care for then, and what about when *we* were gone?

★　　★　　★

I procrastinated the last stop, wasn't sure I wanted to make it at all. The sick old man who'd had his dying extended lived close to our house, so I knew that once it was over, I would be going home for good.

I slept in the furniture store during the starry part of the day. I was walking and happened to test the knob and found it open, the store free of people and a half-dozen beds to choose from. I chose the best one, which was wide and soft with thick pillars at each corner and a lacy canopy. I slept so well I wished I could have it for my room. I stayed at the store more days than I meant to, then I rallied.

The old man didn't live in a house but rather a basement apartment in an old Victorian that had been converted to rentals. Huge place, pretty but not well kept up. For the first time I realized that just as all the things that were perfect remained perfect over the mole-year, the things that were not perfect could not be improved. The peeling paint would stay that way until Mole-Year's Day at the earliest. If I brought a scraper and a pail of paint, I might change it, but the paint would reappear back in the can. The chips would disappear from the trash and rebuild themselves here on the old man's door. Finding this quite sad, I couldn't bring myself to knock, but I didn't have to.

A woman – the daughter, Henny – opened it for me. She looked older than she had at the Town Hall. "He's sleeping," she said, "but please come in."

We introduced ourselves and sat on comfortable couches. The room was plain, clean, and larger than I'd expected.

She said, "I don't know if he'll wake while you're here. He sleeps more and more, which is good."

"I was only coming to see how he's doing and see if I can help in any way," I said.

"There's nothing anyone can do," she said.

I wanted her to say he was doing fine, but I did not want her to say that if it wasn't true. It wasn't true – everything about her told me that. I was uncomfortable, about to excuse myself, and then I said, "I can sit here. I can do that much."

She said, "No, I couldn't—"

"Yes, please, go and do something nice, and I'll stay here."

"He wants to die," she said.

"I won't let him," I said, though I had no plan or conviction to keep him from it. If he died, he would be reborn on Mole-Year's Day with the rest of us and live his month and die again, I guessed.

"There were others here with me at the start," she said. "We prayed and wished all that night, and we were so sure this would not come, and then when it did, they went away to live their lives. I don't have a life."

I didn't have an answer.

"But I will go out, since you're so kind. I'll go out for a while."

"Please do."

"I'll be back in…two hours?"

"Oh no, please, be at least—" But I didn't know what to ask for. "Three days? You can stay in the furniture store if you have nowhere else."

"I have somewhere," she said.

The old man was no trouble at all. He slept most of the time, waking during the breezy hours to watch television in bed and then take a painful-looking stroll around the living area. He had pain medications and other pills arranged on the kitchen counter with instructions all spelled out, and he made sure I looked over everything carefully before he took it. The fridge held homemade casseroles, soups, and many flavors of protein drink, but he didn't want anything. He said it was chore enough to do it during what he called 'waking life'. He'd eat when he had to stave off hunger pangs. He didn't need to eat or go to the bathroom during the mole-year, and so he wasn't going to.

His name was Ralph like Rosie's dad, but he pronounced it 'Rafe'. He didn't want to do anything but what he had been doing. He was concerned about taking the right pills. He'd lived through nine mole-years, thoroughly enjoyed every one except this one, and claimed to remember them, as well as his other years, in vivid detail. He didn't like to answer questions, and so that's about all I ever learned about him.

It was boring in the apartment. I sampled all the sick-food and fantasized about what would happen when Henny returned. I resolved that she would be cheerful, we would talk and play games and make the old man cheerful, get him in a wheelchair, take him to watch the children play. I would go home and clear out the back room for them. They would stay with us for the rest of the mole-year, which couldn't be all that much.

Only when she arrived, she thanked me profusely, gave me a huge bouquet of flowers, and said to give them to my mom. Suddenly I was on the step and she was in the entry.

"Tell her I said she's a great mom and that you're a good girl," she said, closing the door on me.

My backpacks were still inside, all my food laid out on the counter, but I didn't knock. I hurried home.

★   ★   ★

For the first time since the mole-year started, I missed my little kitten. Being back in the house reminded me.

Dad and Mom both cried. "I'm just so happy to have everyone together," Dad said, "even if it's only six more months."

"Six more *months!*" I said. I'd had no idea. They were smothering me with hugs and kisses. "Everyone's home? I thought William went to the high school."

"It was too much for him," Mom whispered.

"But he has a little girlfriend now. So cute," said Dad.

"Did you have an adventure? What animals did you see? What have you learned?" they asked, and other questions. I couldn't get a breath.

Lucy came downstairs holding Jeffrey. I wondered if she'd been carrying him around all this time. When Mom and Dad had settled down and the flowers stood in a vase, she said, "Will you go with me now?"

"We said you would, if you came back," Dad said.

"Go where?" I said.

Lucy counted on her fingers, "Sledding, art day, movies, roller-skating, nature walk."

"I will, every day. Rosie too?"

Lucy nodded. She stood close and handed the baby off to me.

That night we had a baguette sandwich cut in six – William's sweet, awkward girlfriend Tawny was with us. The fire still burned. We played board games and eventually settled into groups. Lucy lay on the floor coloring, and I lay beside her simply watching the colors go on. Mom and Dad put on a DVD and watched it with Jeffrey between them. William and Tawny tired of the movie and went upstairs, which made me look toward Mom.

"We couldn't have him 'out and about' too early in the mole-year, but now it's fine," Mom said.

Sleepily, Dad said, "No more little Jeffreys."

The two of them still fawned over their baby, even halfway through the year. I wanted to ask what would happen to him when they were gone, but it seemed unkind.

"Mom?" I said instead. "Why did we get the kitty right before Mole-Year's Eve?"

She smiled sadly. "So we'll have something to look forward to, when the sun rises on Mole-Year's Day."

That day was coming, after all. We'd greet the kitty, name her. Maybe we would throw out all the food we'd been eating for so long, or give it to someone else. Things would speed up again, the sun would rise and set, the weather become unpredictable once more. Maybe I would never vote or wish or pray in favor of this again. Maybe I would forget it all.

For now, I rolled back toward Lucy to provide an audience for what was becoming a virtuosic coloring performance. The pieces she'd done first had already faded to white.

THE GODS SHALL LAY SORE TROUBLE UPON THEM

The client tells Marie about how, in the fourth grade, his teacher stole his idea for a movie and sold it to Hollywood. His inventions were likewise stolen by employers over the years. Multiple million-dollar ideas, plagiarized.

They are in a corner of the office's private conversation rooms, which should be intimate, but Marie feels like she is watching a recording of a monologue rather than engaging in a conversation. She nods politely at first, makes an effort to sink back into her chair. As the client continues with examples, she begins to exaggerate signs of discomfort, looking up toward the clock, re-crossing her legs.

Finally she says, "Let's just exit the conversation for a moment and engage in some meta-talk, Mr. Weinke. How would you say this is going?"

Mr. Weinke leans back, says, "Why don't you tell me how it's going?"

He is blessed with sound teeth and regular, masculine features, but an excess of flesh enrobes his face. He has those deep-sunk eyes, unreachable in shadow, that are all too common among the clients. All expression obfuscated. She thinks sometimes that if their faces were only a little leaner, then they would be able to maintain eye contact and their conceits would melt away.

It is not her place to tell him what the conversational problem is. "First, let's review," she says.

"You asked me how I was doing, I told you."

"And what should follow from that?"

Mr. Weinke squints and purses his lips, leans forward. He begins again with the stories, taking an upsetting turn toward betrayals by siblings, past friends and ex-wives.

Again Marie stops him. He must be the one to recognize the problem. He closes his eyes and places a hand to his forehead. She feels for him then, so acutely. Goosebumps rise on her arms as he moves his hand up his forehead. He is pushing up his loose skin, holding his eyes wide open, and she sees for the first time that the eyes are a weak gray, striking against his ravaged skin.

He says, "I should ask how *you're* doing, Miss Marie. I should apologize for dominating the conversation."

With a surge of happiness, sweeping her hands to the side in a gesture to say that they are about to launch back into the actual conversation, she says, "No, it's been so interesting, but thank you. In fact, I was rather selfishly hoping you might ask about my wellbeing."

"How's that?" he asks.

"Well, you know that I have been lonely out here. I come from a large family, as we've discussed."

"I remember," he says. "Two brothers and two sisters."

"It's true, and you have such a good memory, Mr. Weinke. I am quite envious of your talents sometimes."

It hurts her to see that he does not acknowledge or even recognize the compliment, but still it is going well, and she continues. "Without my family, I *have* been lonely, and yet I'm in no position to have a pet or much social life. It wouldn't be fair to invite a poor helpless someone into my life, knowing how many hours I have to work. But all that is over. I'm having a roommate, starting today!"

"Now why would you want to share your room?" he says, which to Marie draws up thoughts of the sad barracks where he must sleep.

She thinks how intolerable these men must be to one another – and then catches herself. It's an ungenerous thought. Perhaps they are happy amongst themselves. Who knows?

"I've never not shared a room, to be honest," she says. She thinks of the orderliness of the girls' room at home, its three twin beds so often redecorated and rearranged over the years, the evenings she and her sisters shared there, then the camaraderie of college and the overcrowded Victorian in grad school.

She adds, "The woman – her name is Susan – is an exceptional match. She works all the time, too, some online work, writing or editing, and for leisure she likes to read, as I do, and she likes the same types of food as I do, and the same types of films."

"You will," he says. He is the one to glance at the clock now.

"I will? What, Mr. Weinke?"

"You will be very happy."

"I admire your talent again, Mr. Weinke."

"I thank you, but how's that?"

"You've read my mind. I was just thinking it now, that I was already so happy and that I might continue to be." She sweeps her hands to the sides to show the conversation's end. She says, "That was superb. I felt we were communicating on a fantastic level. What did you think?"

Mr. Weinke stands and gives her a warm handshake. He says, "I'm sorry I started off like that, but those kinds of things have been on my mind. Like, what'll people remember me for? When the guys think back on me, will they think of me as someone who was always getting cheated? Because that's the only *narrative* I see right now, to use your word."

As they walk out into the hall, she says, "These men may be talking about you when you're gone, Mr. Weinke, but it will be a long time in the future. And they will be talking about how long you've been gone from here, and what a life you've had. You are not going to be in rehabilitation much longer. I can feel it. And though the government might mark you a 'senior citizen', you are barely past midlife." She delivers this last with a fist of victory in the air as their paths diverge at the main hall.

He walks backward as they finish their goodbyes. Her flattery makes him move to a different rhythm. He says, "I would have thought we might talk about Roger today. Like, how we feel about it. But I guess I was mistaken."

Roger, of course. This mention of Roger crushes her – for it brings up many images of Roger in life and in death, as well as showing how

Mr. Weinke has been all the time working toward this as a punchline and knows it will come upon her like a blow. She vows to swallow the feeling, stay in her good mood.

She says something about it having been her plan to discuss Roger, or Mr. Harris, once people had some time to process their private grief, and she turns and walks and tries to will a bounce into her step.

By the time she's at the market, her Mr. Harris preoccupation and her Mr. Weinke preoccupation are so flourishing and intertwined that she's not noticed a thing on her walk. She hopes she obeyed the crossing signals but can't remember seeing any of them.

Mr. Weinke is going through a manipulative stage. It is natural to his development.

Mr. Harris was another matter. He simply died, on Monday during lunch hours, on the bench outside the cafeteria. He was elderly, and unwell, and a few had said that if he'd had to choose his death, he might have chosen just this one.

The sad part was that no one noticed him through lunch or during the clean-up rush. He leaned back against the wall, mouth open. It seemed that many clients and staff discovered him all at once. There was some attempt at CPR though the body was cooling by then, some outbursts about the failure of staff to pay attention. It was the worst thing that could have happened to the men, causing many setbacks that had driven Marie's entire exhausting work week.

And since then, Marie has been visualizing him. She's been dreading having to walk into dark corners because she fears she'll see his apparition. She fears the apparition though she does not believe that such things exist. All week she's missed sleep and grown jumpier. It is always this way after a death. In another week or two, she'll be back to normal and have an uneventful few months, unless of course there is another death.

Or, if there is another and then another quickly after, perhaps she will grow immune to the effect. She certainly doesn't hope for such a cure.

She moves through the market, carefully selecting items for dinner: tomatoes and lettuce, cilantro, tortillas, mild and sharp cheeses, butter.

She adds a white wine and a bar of good dark chocolate. This evening is going to be a treat.

She hasn't seen Susan in many months because after the roommate interviews, when Marie called back to offer the room, Susan cried and said that her landlord would not let her out of her lease after all, and so she was begging for Marie to hold the apartment for her.

When Marie called her mother, she was reminded again that she could not afford to live out west another few months without their help, and so she would have to take one of the other girls who had interviewed, either the daughter of a friend of Marie's father or the other girl, the one who had worked on one of his campaigns. Both of the girls had called Marie's father to ask her to give them the room, but he had forgotten to do so and so it was her mother's duty, and she wanted to say she really did think it would be best to take one of them – either one, that was Marie's choice.

Marie's mother barely let her talk during phone conversations. This was a bitter irony, as she always derided Marie's occupation, her 'calling'. What use was there to teach conversational skills to such a cohort? What good could it possibly do when all of them were so damned. (Not to mention her father's consistent votes against funding for the centers, which was part of the reason for Marie's own poverty, wasn't it?)

The resentment swells up again in the checkout line as Marie recalls her mother's parting, "Remember, honey, you can stay just as long as you can support yourself, and then you'll come home." Her reply, the comebacks all acknowledged but bracketed, was just a sigh, and then, "Thanks, Mom."

She didn't want those other girls in her rooms. She wanted Susan, and so she never called them and when they called, she blocked their numbers.

There isn't much left of the interview in memory, just the warm feeling Susan gave her. The woman was older than the other interviewees, perhaps a year or two on either side of forty, and the rapport between her and Marie fast and sharp.

Susan looked like a local but she entered into subtle code. She mentioned some books and made other types of references to show she came from a good family and was, like Marie, out west on a humanitarian mission, though she couldn't bear to work face-to-face with anyone anymore. She wrote articles from home and supposed she could do that back east just as well, though she said being out here in the middle of things made it all more immediate.

Susan cried when she had to delay. She was so ashamed to have to beg. There was no question that Marie would wait for her, and so she tightened her belt, and took much overtime, and made it through the six or seven months without the help of anyone, all the time assuring her mom how well she was doing, how well she was eating.

Still waiting at the checkout, Marie lets herself anticipate the next few hours. She visualizes walking home weighed down with bags but her energy renewing with each step through brightly lit and colorful streets, dicing cheese and vegetables and herbs, frying the quesadillas, savoring the wine and the chocolate, savoring the conversation in afghan-draped chairs, sighing happily before turning in for bed.

She is smiling when she fronts the line and the cashier seems to take it as aggression and bares her teeth in a rictus grin that drops the instant Marie takes her change.

The streets are dim and gray, dusk coming fast when she leaves the market. The word *crepuscular* springs to mind with all its associations of corpuscles and muscles, and mussels, and corpses. A tendrilled, tentacled dark heart stirs in the depth of each shadow.

She still fears the dark, old as she is. She still fears dreams, along with all her rational worries.

Too, her professional garb makes her stand out from the other walkers, and feels herself a target on the streets. She walks quickly, which raises her heartbeat, which only adds to the fear that, in any dark place where her eyes might rest will appear an image of Roger tilted back against the cafeteria wall, his open mouth.

* * *

When the doorbell rings, the apartment is tidy and quesadillas just beginning to brown on one side, the white cheese spilling and sizzling.

Susan is heavier, more haggard than Marie remembers, closer to fifty than forty. Her brows shade her eyes.

She and Marie embrace, and the taxi driver helps them bring in four suitcases and a large object with a light green cover that reminds Marie of a bird's cage. Marie almost asks about it, but then they are tipping the driver and seeing him out, and Susan is going on about the smell of the food, and so they make their way to the breakfast bar and begin the meal.

Susan asks Marie to remind her about what she does for work, and Marie speaks on this topic at some length. She has worked backward from today to the last two years and is discussing her master's degrees by the time she recognizes that they have almost finished eating.

"I'm so sorry," she says. "I've been living alone for so long I've come to believe I'm the only person on earth, apparently. Forgive me, and please, tell me how you are doing at work and otherwise."

Susan's eyes shift down and then up again to meet Marie's. She says, "I've been thinking what to say to that question."

"You've been all right, I hope," says Marie.

"Oh, yes. Work is fine. I've been so excited to move in."

"And I to have you."

"Yes. I've been imagining myself here, and I know we said that I would take the little bedroom, but whenever I've imagined myself here...."

"Yes?"

"Well, I've seen myself in the little nook. You know, I'll get up at night more often than you, I think. And you might need privacy, or anyway, it's right that you have privacy, since this is your place."

"I want you to have the bedroom," Marie says.

"And I really, really want the nook," Susan says. Marie can't see her eyes.

A sound comes from the nook, where the suitcases are standing. Marie feels a sharp increase in heart rate, feels she might faint off the stool and tries to stand. Susan is standing and crossing the dim room, bending toward the green cover that Marie sees now is a light blanket. She slides the blanket to the side, and Marie sees kicking feet. The baby announces itself in wails. Susan holds its tiny body to her chest and turns to begin her explanations.

"I need to stay in the nook because I need to get up in the night and, I don't know…. There's a little more room for him in the nook. Please, please don't put us out," she says. Her voice hitches, and Marie thinks she will cry, but she doesn't.

★   ★   ★

The drama is fleeting, and routine reestablishes soon. Marie sees little of the baby, in fact. He lives in a bassinet in the nook, which Susan has filled with futons covered with many blankets and quilts. A blanket curtains the wide entrance to the nook, but is always drawn open.

The baby sleeps each evening while Susan and Marie have dinner – lesser and lesser meals each night it seems, as though they are competing for who can eat the least – and then he wails on and off for a couple of hours, and then he sleeps again, and then he wakes. In the mornings while Marie prepares for work, baby and mother both sleep.

When Marie does catch a glimpse of him, she notes how his hairs come in white like the vellus hairs on the sides of her own face.

Routine is one thing, but Marie still hasn't shaken the unsettled feeling that began with Mr. Harris and intensified with the revelation of the baby. She begins to dream of a figure in Oshkosh overalls and a red-striped shirt, up at the top of a skyscraper. The wind is blowing hard and he's cartwheeling. She asks him to dance, and he dances, and then she asks him to freeze and he freezes, and then she can't get him to move again. His mouth is frozen open in a grin like a devil's, and in the dream she is pushing at the jaws to shut the mouth and then she freezes too. There is the paralysis, inability to speak, teeth locked tight – all those nightmare sensations – and then the dream bleeds into something else, a horrifying interview session at work or a long spelunking expedition through the endless maze of an underground house.

She wakes sweating and thinks it was in the first moment of waking that she'd put the chimp's face there. In the dream itself the figure was faceless, wasn't it? There's a jumbled mess of images: stubble on a man's jaw, the stairwell, the dark corners.

★　　★　　★

A client tells Marie about the dogs he had as a child and how, when he starts to feel hard against some of the older guys around here, he thinks of how fragile the dogs were when they grew old, how helpless, just like babies. The man is so young looking she can't bear to call him Mister, and so she breaks protocol and calls him Jeremy. He's so well socialized that she would never imagine why he's here if she hadn't read his file: outbursts, accusations, the usual paranoia noticed first by those closest to him.

He politely turns the conversation to pets she might have had, and she launches into a story she's told many times before: "I remember shopping for guinea pigs in a mall as a child. The window was filled with perhaps a hundred of them in every color and pattern. It must have taken an hour to choose the one with red spots on white. I remember feeling buyer's remorse in the car, suffering over the question of whether the one I'd got was the best of them, or even if I knew which one I *had* got since the creature had to stay in the box all the way home. And then, one morning just about a week later, I woke to see the red and white one I had come to love, and a calico one, and another like the original but with a more liver cast to the spots."

"I bet you were excited," he says. There is a turn to his lip. Something is wrong, but Marie continues.

"I was terrified. Despite having seen kittens being born, I was still shaky, or in denial, about the details of reproduction, or at least normal reproduction wasn't the first explanation that sprang to mind. I panicked. I wasn't sure if what I was seeing was real or a dream. I wanted my mom and dad to see it too and confirm that there were, in fact, three."

"You thought the guinea pig had divided. Or that someone had come in the night to place the extra ones there," he says.

"Or that my wish of having all of them was beginning to come true. Only I remember being afraid, not happy about a wish granted. Or not happy until my dad came and said something like, 'Well, of course, with all of them together like that, they'd be breeding.' He was angry. Like, we'd agreed to take one, not three."

"Just like your roommate," Jeremy says with a flat, cold edge to the words.

"Excuse me?"

"You agreed to take one, not two."

"Perhaps we should stop the conversation for a moment. Now, I meant nothing by that story, Jeremy."

"That's right. You never *mean* anything," he says. His face is still young but it is already vaguer than it was at the start of the conversation. The eyes are beginning to recede.

"Your roommate came, and there were two of them instead of one. That happened to me, too," he says.

"I haven't mentioned my roommate to you," she says.

"And have I mentioned to you about the time my mom bought me a guinea pig, about the time that guinea pig magically divided into three – have I told you that? – or have you got it from me some other way? I think you have. I think you must have found it out some other way."

He stands. He is transformed, that quickly. The eyes are cast in shadow now, the stubble showing along the jaw. He looks some years older to her, and Marie suddenly fears him.

"Now Jeremy, Mr. Walker I mean, you know that isn't true. Should we return to the conversation, or should we reschedule?"

"Are you starving yourself, Miss Marie? Why don't we talk about that?" he says.

"I have always been slender." She regrets saying this. Better to direct back toward politeness and try to end in a neutral way, but it is too late. The session must end now, and she is saying the words that end a session, which she could say in her sleep, and she is gathering her bag and coat.

"Have you seen Sam lately? Your Mr. Weinke?" Jeremy asks.

She is moving away from him, planning to go home early for once.

From the conversation room, he calls, "Do you ever even think about what's wrong with us?" and other things, as she walks down the hall toward the glass door into sunshine.

*   *   *

Susan is feeding the baby at the breakfast bar when Marie opens the door. She covers herself but not before Marie sees the wilted skin of her breast like the skin of a tomato forgotten on a windowsill. The baby might be almost a year old now, something like that, and the hair on his head has come in thick and soft and unmistakably gray. The broad streaks in it range from pewter through silver to white. Susan hides him most of the time, and that is what she is going to do now, but Marie says, "No, wait." She holds out her arms to take him.

Marie feels close to Susan now, though they rarely talk. They never talk about what is happening to Marie's body, which seems about to cease being, or the baby's hair, or Marie's dreams, or what is happening at Marie's work. The question of how Susan got the baby, too, is never raised. Yet today they fall into conversation on all these topics. Marie is invited to sit in the bright, well-cushioned nook. They sit cross-legged for all of the sunny afternoon and into the evening, the baby playing and then napping beside them.

Susan says, "Does your family want you back with them? Mine do."

Marie says, "They do. I'm never going back."

Susan says, "Neither am I."

Marie says, "The clients need me. They're always telling me bizarre stories, trying to make me believe their delusions, but if I can see their eyes, it's like they're begging me to disregard their words."

Susan says, "I'm beginning to see writing of my own in other people's articles. Is that strange? I catch half-sentences of mine all the time, but sometimes it's more, full paragraphs."

Marie says, "That's more common than you might think."

The baby rolls over onto his stomach, and Marie reaches out to stroke his hair. Susan watches her fingers for a while and tells how the baby reminds her of Hesiod's *Theogony* when he's talking about the extinct kinds of people and the ones to come. He says we will know the end of one or another of his races of men when they are born with their hair already gray.

Susan says, "I remember he says, 'The gods will lay sore trouble upon them,' and then there would be another kind of person to follow. There was some other story, too, the people made out of wood. They were okay at first, and then they froze up like wood, and the new people were made out of corn."

Marie nods. She read that too sometime, she thinks, or did she write it? She seems to remember writing in Jeremy's folder that the world would lay sore trouble upon him. She wrote that he froze just like wood.

Did Susan read that file? Well, that's all right if she did, for they are friends.

Susan launches into the story of the baby's origin, which is as unwholesome as Marie expected it might be.

Marie says, "Haven't you named him yet?"

Susan says, "I think I'm afraid to give him a name."

★ ★ ★

Mr. Weinke needs no visitors, but Marie visits every day in his private room. He's gone rigid and needs to be handled like an object. His mouth stands open just as Mr. Harris's did, and the only reason he was not carted out was that he was still so warm.

She is sure he will get over this, and she tells him so over and over. She calls him Sam now. She weeps and tells him about her dreams of the skyscraper and about the baby. She even speaks at some length on the topic of Roger – does he remember? – Roger, who died waiting for lunch that one day long ago, and how she started when looking into any dark place, for she'd see the specter of him, and how she feared the specter would look just like Sam looks now.

She's disgusted with herself each time she leaves the room, tells herself she will not go back.

She's breaking protocol time and again. The men – when they come, for they're often absent from sessions now – tell her the stories from her life, and she tells them the stories of theirs, and they are the same stories. Her eyes are hard to see when she looks in a mirror, which is rare.

And in the dream, she works backward night after night, from being rigid to playing with the figure in overalls, and farther back to the dark stairwell (flashes of stubble on a jaw), to the street level, to the frantic run. The dream is in black and white like an old photograph, the darkest parts of it alive with a metallic sheen.

★　　★　　★

Marie has a direct supervisor, but she has not seen them in years and does not remember anything about them because all communication is through email signed simply 'C'. She can never remember if she ever met C, maybe back in the first days of work. But then it had been a bustle – so many more men, so many other staff members rushing around and always a full schedule of conversation sessions. Now there are so few who come to sessions and no more coming in from the street, and the staff attendance is down. In the cafeteria now, a pair of servers meets the needs of the dozen or two dozen who are well enough to make their way in. When a man drops from attendance, he will be found later in a room like Mr. Weinke's, only now there are fewer staff members around to take care of his needs. Marie has taken to cleaning and spoon-feeding the men in her off hours, though this is not part of her job. If she doesn't do it, who will?

She no longer wears her dresses and skirts to work because they'll get so dirty, and by now they probably do not fit. She puts on scrubs from a supply closet and wears them home for washing because the laundry staff appear to have abandoned the center or been laid off. The room is empty and piled with laundry. She runs a load when she thinks of it, but often she forgets to dry it and finds it later, clumped and mildewed, and anyway the men rarely come to get clean clothes.

C emails every day now, asking if all is well, and Marie answers truthfully and in depth each time, but there is never a response, just another message the next morning. Going back through previous emails, she finds the same seven messages repeating in random order. She stops answering, and still they persist. She blocks the address.

She blocked her mother's phone number, too, after the last

conversations they had about what Marie ought to do. All she can think to do is keep working. Her meager paycheck keeps being deposited in her bank account, and the remaining men keep needing care, and so it would seem treacherous to stop working. What would happen to them?

One day Marie does not find Mr. Weinke in his room. She rushes about, asking everyone where he's gone, but no one can say. Her legs feel awfully stiff as she crosses the dead lawn behind the main building to the barracks. She passes empty room after empty room and then some rooms with men still sleeping in them, men reading on their bunks. Finally she sees Jeremy – Mr. Walker – in one of the bunk rooms toward the back, packing a duffel bag.

"Where is Mr. Weinke?" she asks.

"He's not in his room?" Mr. Walker says. He looks no different from the other clients now, but he is moving easily, and that is something to be grateful for.

"He's not," she says, and, "Listen, please help me. There are still men back in the main building and some staff, but not enough staff. You're well. You can help us with the feeding and the cleaning until we work out what the problem is. Please."

"Maybe Mr. Weinke walked away," he says. "That's all I'm about to do. Get some kind of living done while I still can, you know?"

"Please," she says. Her arm is beginning to tremble.

He turns his head fully toward her for the first time. He says, "I think you should sit down and rest, Miss Marie. You don't look well."

She refuses, and there is confusion around her. She turns to walk back to the main building and cannot. Mr. Walker is yelling, and then they are helping him lift her.

★   ★   ★

In the private room, many things come clear to Marie.

The staff. She always felt superior to them, but now she sees their dedication and their kindness. They clean her and feed her for many days.

She sees many ghosts, of Roger, of other men who passed before him – but they do not frighten her any longer. She does not suffer from the anticipation of them. They simply come and spend some time talking with her and leave. Roger looks good, his mouth no longer held open. He looks like he must have looked before all this mess. She sees that his eyes are brown.

When Mr. Weinke comes to sit with her and talk of the things he's seen out in the world, she thinks he too is a ghost. A staff member in filthy scrubs comes in when he's visiting, says she ought to be moved to the women's facility across the city.

"No, Miss Marie belongs here," he says.

In time, she decides that he is living. How else could he talk to the staff member? She does not ask the staff why they no longer come into the room to care for her; they must be busy.

She wishes she could ask him what happened, how he was cured, and as if she had spoken the words, he says, "Well, that's a long story," and proceeds to tell her all he's learned after falling into the illness – if that's what it was – and coming out again on the other end. He tries to advise her, but it is no different than before: he speaks of himself only, and there is no clear communication going on, only a monologue. She wishes he would leave, and he blinks his gray eyes, now clearly visible, gives his regrets for having once again been a bore, and backs out of the room.

It is some time before Susan visits with the little one. Walking now, he is perhaps two, perhaps three – Marie never knew many little children and so she is unsure. The brightness of him in his striped shirt and coveralls, the brightness of his silver hair against his mother's side tells her that she has been deluding herself. This child is living, and she is still just barely living, but all of the others that have entered the room have been only shadows. Susan is only a shadow now, too.

The child holds his nose when he enters. "I'm sorry, but no one has been around to take care of me in a while," she says, or she thinks. Her mouth, she believes, is stretched wide open. She can no longer feel the dryness of it.

"We don't mind," says Susan.

"We don't mind," says the boy with his voice muffled. He holds his hand tight over his mouth and nose.

They sit on the bench. It seems they intend to spend some time with Marie, for which she is grateful.

"I called your mother," Susan says. "I told her you were gone, not missing. I didn't know, and I thought that would be kinder."

"Very good," says Marie.

"So, the new generation," says Susan, looking toward the boy, who is standing, trying to pry the drain up out of the floor.

"He looks good. Did you ever name him?"

"I didn't think there was any need," she says.

"What brings you out?" says Marie.

"We're going to climb the stairs of the tallest building we can find," says Susan.

"I'm going to fly," says the boy with a grin.

Panic then – she didn't think she would ever feel it again. "No, oh no," she says. The dream, almost forgotten now, of the frantic climb and the figure gamboling at the top of a skyscraper, it comes to her. It takes up the last bit of panic she has left in her.

"Just kidding," says the boy. He must have somehow seen this silly dream of hers.

"I realized it was a joke," says Marie. "I did realize it, just not at the first second, you know?"

"No, we're going up there to see if we can see anyone still moving," says Susan.

"There could be others like me," says the boy. He seems very intelligent for his age.

"And if not?" says Marie.

"If not, we'll head east," says Susan.

"That's a good idea," says Marie.

"Should we wait for you, until you can join us?" says Susan.

"Oh, could you?" says Marie.

"Sure, I think there's plenty for the boy to eat here in the storeroom," says Susan.

"I'll be so grateful to have the chance to go with you," says Marie.

"Maybe I'll take him to stay in one of the rooms up front that's more aired out. No offense," says Susan.

"Oh yes, do that. I wouldn't want him to be uncomfortable," says Marie, and suddenly her prospects look bright. A mission for her and for Susan, which sounds like it could be exciting, and the promise of a bright future for the boy. Her panic is gone, her fear gone, and for the first time in years she feels the way of things makes sense again.

GINGERBREAD

My husband's calling again, so I bury the phone deep in my purse. What can I tell him? I never even told myself I was seeking this place, but as soon as I passed through this town, I guessed it. As soon as I stopped at the mom-and-pop store, I knew.

The witch's house lives around the corner at the end of a shaded street.

Now I stand outside its thicketed fence line. The cleared garden space is filled with sticks and chaff and deflated tomatoes from some past year.

Now I step onto its patchy lawn. The Realtor sign is blotched with age and half-hidden in morning glories. No one lives here. No one's supposed to but me.

My parents never knew what it was. They were here to 'flip' the place or some such. Not me – I was to keep out from underfoot as best I could, and so I strayed alone in different corners. The house repelled me at first, so messy and cold it was. It seemed we were always living in horrible places and leaving just as soon as they were habitable.

Alone and forgotten, I cut my foot on a piece of glass, bled into the floorboards. Everything changed then. As near as I can explain it, I became part of the house. And the house spoke to me. All its twisted parts transformed to something else.

It was so long ago, but I still remember glimpsing things through the colored-glass windows. I heard human voices, animals. Goats, I thought, horses. An old-timey life seemed to be happening back beyond the windows, but when I stepped outside it was only the lawn all filled with garbage and my dad and mom weary, cleaning up. My angry mom and dad painting, repairing, taking trips to the dump.

When they went off on those trips, that was when things would really come to life. It's all confused now, just flashes of texture and feeling.

When they finished their work, they dragged me away, and I was too young to know where the place was on a map. I tried to believe I'd imagined everything, but here it is.

I stand on the front step. The gingerbread trim is the same, the dark wooden door is the same, but the colors are different. I remember diamond panes like lemon suckers and red panes like cherry – but here are the stained-glass windows in raspberry, grape, and a deep peacock color that no candy should ever be. No light, no motion behind the panes. It's humid here on the step, an indoor feeling with the tree branches low and the vines enclosing. A smell of almost-clean hay. I stand patiently until the door creaks open.

My purse is vibrating when I set it down on the step, a sacrifice. I enter the tiny room alone, and the door drifts closed behind me. The smell reminds me of a health food store – sage and peppermint and fresher hay – with other odors underneath. Mildew, cat. My eyes adjust, but I see no cat. I see a large white dog on a basket-bed, smiling in greeting. A tidy room, jackets hung on pegs and gardening boots beneath them. All in my size, I'm sure.

I do not remember the dog, but I remember this feeling. It's a warm homey feeling tinged with mystery, expectation. The next door, leading deeper into the house, will not open. Not until I've given something to this room. I stoop down to pet the dog, who smiles more brightly and sways his lush tail. His collar is woven hemp, and the dangling tag is a coin pounded flat and inexpertly engraved: Chip. My husband's name.

"Are you Chip?" I say.

He closes his mouth briefly and smiles again, nudging up with his nose like I'm holding a treat, but I'm not. This is the kind of thing the house does, after all. If I want to leave of my own volition, I need to do it now – right now. I imagine a frantic flight, heart pounding, but I don't remember what my car looks like. I laid that all down at the door with… whatever I left on the step.

The real Chip's at work, worrying, trying to call again, but soon I won't remember that either. Soon this fine dog will be the only Chip I've ever met. Really, I'm almost there already. Chip is so silky to pet, his smile contagious. I sit, and he comes to me nosing and licking, tickling my nose with his long fur. I've given something – I no longer know just what.

The inner door opens with a startling click, and it's the kitchen on the other side. The gray kittens are wrestling on a rag rug under the table. I smell rich stew bubbling on the stove. Books and sketchpads arrayed on the table, a velvet robe draped on the back of a chair – and soft slippers too, just waiting.

I'm home.

Soft music, incense, a distant humming.

The witch. Will I find her this time? If I make each room my home, if I bleed into the house again and spend the time, take the time, will I see more than just a glimpse of her through the jewel-toned, water-textured glass?

This is where the sense of expectation comes in. Home but something more, too. The promise of a real family, finally. People who see me.

I strip off my clothes and ball them in a corner. One day I'll burn them outside – or in the fireplace if there is one. I think there is one, lighting itself now in the next room. Just now, I need to get into my robe and slippers. I need to stir the stew, water the houseplants, get back to my work.

★   ★   ★

The house is more abundant than I ever imagined. The fabrics are rich, both in texture and color. Silk and wool and velvet. Tiffany lamps, a dense tapestry on the chairs with those little nail-brads, too. Curves on everything.

It is my idea of a house coming more to life with each glance, with each touch of my hand. In the kitchen I find apples, eggs, milk. Never meat – never that – but plenty of cream and cheese, vegetables I have never seen before, dark-ripe forbidden berries.

There are dirty dishes, too, dishes that I haven't used. Trash to burn in the fireplace and unfamiliar clothes to scrub on the washboard and hang before the fire.

There is always so much to do, I can never seem to get to those books, that sketchbook, but I am content.

Each night the kittens and I lie down in the witch's bed and the blankets, no matter how often I wash them, are rank with her scent.

* * *

Some people came, a man and two girls with the kittens' names. I didn't know how they found this place, didn't understand most of what they said through the door, but I focused on those names and there was a little tickle in the back of my mind.

The man said he would make me come out. The door would not respond to him, and I felt safe. I stood for a long time and then sat. Chip laid his big head in my lap and smiled. He rolled onto his back so I could rub his belly, and I focused on his smile while the commotion heightened and then ceased outside.

I think the front door will never open again. Through the windows, the witch's world comes clearer and brighter every day. After my chores, Chip and the kittens and I spend long hours watching from the window seat.

They plant and harvest out there. They have their bonfires and bacchanals. They keep many animals, not just the goats, horses, and fowl. There are tall horned animals walking upright; there are flying things with long tufted tails and long creatures undulating between the blurred human forms.

The front door may never open again, but one day the back door will. I'll stagger out, dazed by light, or if it's night I'll step out terrified, ready to retreat into the safety of the house, but the house will not be there. This is what I dream each night as I toss and turn in the witch's bed: I step outside and there is no house. Just the old world with all its terrible forms in every direction. I'll find I was only pulled in for use as a servant, while my mind lasted, and now that my mind is gone, I must be used for something else.

The back door is coming to life somewhere close. I feel it tickle at the edges of my consciousness and keep expecting it to appear. Half-grown kittens circle at my ankles. Chip has gone somewhere else. Light explodes through the windows, brighter and brighter, the panes bleaching of color. It's soon, now. I know it.

LITTLE CAT, LITTLE HARE

Saturdays were the only days my boyfriend Grady and I had together, so I tried to be in the moment with him even though it was tough. I was in my last year of my grad program, teaching while working on my thesis. The weight of work was always preoccupying me – crushing me, really.

I expected to get impatient, but there at the flea market in the big Copse County fairgrounds building, between a set of antique canisters and a pile of ugly knit goods, I discovered a set of small paintings that pulled me in hard and, when I resolved to buy them, brought a bright, quick feeling of triumph.

The cat was what caught my eye first, such movement to it. The image first appeared to be made of brown static, and as I approached, I wondered if it was a textile or some sort of bas-relief. My focus went to the green hare, which was dimmer, *lesser* in some inexpressible way, but still had some of the same glimmery movement. The big thighs on the hare seemed to ripple; its whiskers seemed to twitch. My eyes went back to the cat, its long-nosed mysterious expression so familiar and yet so strange.

When I lifted the cat close, I saw the paint was not blended but applied in layers of lines like spiderwebs.

"Are these your own?" I asked the old woman who'd come to refold scarves beside me. The same person who did the paintings could not have done the orange and green knitted dish towel thingies, but it seemed polite to ask.

She started telling me about a poor little old woman named Helen who lived down the road a ways from her.

I said I was a student, that I wasn't studying art now but had in the past, and she said she was sure Helen hadn't gone to art school or anything like that. She didn't know if she could read, even, but wasn't she good? And as she took my money and made change, she rattled on about her granddaughter who I reminded her of and who would love to have a figure like mine, who ought to be in school like me. She complimented my tall boots, which made me point my toe and hold my leg out a little, and when I looked up was just when Grady caught my eye from across the aisle.

He'd been chatting with a guy selling blown glass, and they both paused, appreciating me. The other guy looked a little like Grady only less finished, somehow, and I took a moment just smiling at them before lifting up my purchases for them to see. Grady came and took my hand and kept hold of it until we got in the Jeep, and he drove straight to an old drive-in for fries that tasted like crispy fish batter and gave me an instant bellyache.

I hung my little hare and my little cat in the living room and stared at them while Grady watched TV. The darks of the cat painting were deep glossy brown like coffee; the lights speckled and swirled. Like when you look at your face in a mirror in a dim room – or sometimes a photo does it too – the lines seemed to shiver and shift, the cat angry, then pouting, then smiling to himself, the hare in my peripheral vision twitching for a jump.

On Sunday morning, sweet thoughtful Grady made me promise to stay on track while he was at work – I had housework and homework as well as much overdue grading. I put the grading off again because I could not bear it, settled on the worthy goal of drafting a chapter, then lost my urgency after an hour of fiddling with notes and staring comatose at the monitor.

I admired the little cat once more and this time took it down to feel the weight of it, to hold it closer. I turned the board over and saw, in light penciled cursive, a last name for Helen, an almost illegible address.

★　　★　　★

My gaze moved from my hands tensed on the wheel to the white sky rippling and crawling before me, the cars passing with children in the back staring after me, people eating in the front seat, all of them impossibly distant. I'd been too busy to think of doing anything on my own in months, and the fact of being on this trip – on a whim, on a lark – gave me a surge of terror, a surge of freedom. How had I gotten so pressed into my groove that just going for a stupid drive was such a big deal? What was wrong with me?

"Things are going to get easier," Grady had said before he left, tickling my face with his beard.

"Something has to change," I'd said, but I hadn't believed it could, not then. I didn't believe in change until I merged onto the freeway.

The truth was that the paintings had raised disturbing memories in me as though they came from my own mind, my own dreams or my past. Flickers of past homes and landscapes in the backgrounds of them – a swimming hole at the end of a pasture, an interior cold and smelling of mildew. The lines and evocations of the images seemed to play before me as I drove, and as the phone spoke out directions to the artist's house, it pinged too with messages, the first image saying *Hang in There!* with Grady's cartoon face on a kitten hanging from a clothesline.

I smiled, texted back that all was well. Another text came in as I was exiting the freeway, and I waited until I was stopped at a light to see it. *U finish ur paper?* it said. It made me think of when Grady was still in school, how he would go into the little office space he had in the guest bedroom and finish his work efficiently, as soon as it was assigned. I responded, texting *Almost…*and then sent a second one saying, *I can't. Went for a drive.* I turned off the phone and put it in my purse.

As I moved down the long dirt road, the sky went strange. Clouds came in quickly, but it was more than that. Shards of light came through, giving odd highlights to the distant trees and fences.

I parked in a rutted driveway just as the sun set and sat for a moment watching the sky. I rose and took the paintings out of my trunk, feeling faint and apprehensive as the boards vibrated in my hands. Helen's house hid behind vines and scraggly trees. At first a rough black mound against a brown field, it became a dark green tapestry glinted with gold and red as I approached.

I moved toward the little woman, not as old as I'd expected, who sat smoking on the porch. She cocked her head at me and lifted her upper lip to show dark pearlescent teeth. I told myself I would not go inside, would only stand and talk for a time, turn my phone back on and go home. Grady would be worrying.

"I'm so sorry. I know it's late," I said. "I found these. Bought, I mean. I hope…."

She only stamped out her cigarette, stood and opened the screen door to welcome me into a house smelling of breeze and soil.

"Electric's out," she said.

The cold came into me, soon as I entered, and the smell of mildew, smells of clay and turpentine, chicken and sour milk. The shadows developed into paintings on every surface, boards leaned against every wall, horses and people and dogs and many more creatures – many more cats. One fetal shape in plum and violet hung in the entry, a fawn or a faun nested in flowers, a grotesque little creature that seemed to pulse at the center of the composition, surrounded by vines and trees and tiny glimpses of smaller animals hiding in the vegetation.

I longed to go through the stacks and look at every image, but before I'd had my fill of the purple creature, Helen beckoned me around a corner into the kitchen and sat me at a flaking white table as she finished washing and drying her dishes. Ivy came through the wall near the baseboard, green glass bottles on the sill were filled with cuttings.

Helen's figure, her profile, were utterly average. "Have a good trip?" she said, and I muttered something about the traffic, but she wasn't listening.

The kitchen window already reflected her face. It was later than I'd thought.

Just before it fell dark, thunder sounded and the rains came. Helen needed to bring the chickens in, and I followed her through a long porch roofed in isinglass. Perhaps three dozen more paintings were stacked against damp walls. I stood in the mud just outside the porch door and watched her herd and lock up the chickens. The sky roiled.

On the way back inside, I thought to take off my shoes. I tried to push one off with the heel of my other foot, and it would not come off. I pulled, and it would not come off. I was shaking.

Helen put an arm around my shoulder and said, "Don't bother with that, dear."

"Something's wrong here," I said.

"Nothing's wrong," she said, and again she moved away from me, this time back to the front room. She lit candles on the mantel and moved around the room lighting more. The room was more opulent than I'd realized, with a fireplace and cut-velvet sofas, old speckled mirrors, barrister bookcases, dark stained-glass lamps, old books on the side tables, and all those paintings hung gallery style to the very ceiling and stacked against the lower walls – and there, a canopy bed tucked in the bay window. Helen leaned in to start a fire and said I could sit where I liked.

"Take the bed if you're cold," she said, and I was cold. I pulled back a brocade cover and slid between patterned flannel sheets. I tucked the covers around myself and sat until I got quite warm, and by then the fire was going, and I saw in the mirror above the fireplace that Helen had sat down in a chair with a book and angled the pages toward the candlelight.

"I need to be getting somewhere," I said.

"Oh, poo!" she said and pushed the book aside. She looked to the mirror and said, "Too dark for reading." She took a cup of brushes and a tray of watercolors out from the bottom of her table and opened a sketch pad. She dipped a brush in the glass of water she'd been drinking from.

"Too dark to read, but you can paint?" I said.

My voice was small in the big cluttered room with the rain on the roof and the rain hitting things all around the old windows, so I was not sure she heard me, but after a while she said, "Dark is best, you know, for finding the spirits in things."

She came to my bed and took the pillow beside me, shook it out of its case, and laid the case down on my knees. "Watch now," she said. She crumpled up the pillowcase and told me to tell her what I saw. The light was so dim, I barely made out folds and hollows.

"It's like looking at clouds," she said.

She did not go back to her chair right away. We looked until I said, "I know, it's like Grady."

"Your man?" she said.

I nodded. "See? Here's his cheekbone, and down here his beard, and here's his eyebrow." But I was shivering again. "Oh no," I said.

"Oh no, what?" she said. Her face was sinister. Something, I don't know, a mocking kind of expectation in it.

"I forgot my shoes," I said, and I gave the pillowcase over to her and lifted up the covers, dreading to see the dark mud all over the sheets, but there was nothing. My feet wore their little white ankle socks and nothing else.

"There's something wrong," I said.

"Something wrong?" said Helen. She paused to consider, added, "Could be," but then she just patted the covers back over me. She crumpled the pillowcase again and moved back to her chair.

"I need to be going somewhere," I said.

"Where?" she said, but I couldn't remember. I looked at the pillowcase until it became a rose, and I pulled on its edge. It was a roly-poly little dog.

"You're a student. Well, what do you study? Where do you study?" she said.

I couldn't say. Images of brick walls came to me, a glossy white floor and the smell of coffee, but I didn't trust that those were memories. Did I study something, or had that been a lie, and if a lie, was it mine or hers?

Figures leered and gestured everywhere in the room. Dim faces, purplish like bruises and dimmer, redder and greener figures behind them in the corners, a stream of rosy-gold horses moving in slow motion above the candles on the mantel. Helen's face in the mirror was no more real than any other.

And then I realized that she was looking up at me in the mirror, down at the block of paper. I was what she was sketching.

"And what were you meant to be doing today?" she said, but I didn't know that either. I realized the day was new. No more sound of rain, and now a rusty morning light from the window behind me fell on the mantel. My little cat and hare leaned on the mantel, and sun sparkled on something glassy that leaned in front of them.

Helen had traded her lap desk for an easel, and the scent of linseed oil came faint on a breeze. I struggled to sit up, to leave the bed, but my arms could not press down.

"It's all right," she said. "We're almost done."

Where was my purse? *My phone,* I tried to say, but my mouth would not open far enough.

And then it was strange, I saw the mantel and the mirror still, but I saw the other side of the room, too, the window and the bed. I saw myself lying in the bed with the covers pulled up. The covers sank and pulsed. Then there was no one in the bed, only Helen before me, running a soft brush over my face. She sighed and rose, stretched. She passed gas then, just as though there were no visitor, and I understood I was no longer a visitor. She moved toward the kitchen.

Something rustled up the path and then came a scratch and knock on the screen door, mumbling, and then Helen's impatient, "Come inside, then. Come see," and when she came back, it was in the company of a tall, bearded figure whose face did not make sense.

"She left these things here," said Helen with a broad gesture toward the mantel, and the man mumbled and paced a long time. I wished he would leave, and soon after he did, taking the phone but leaving the cat and hare behind with all the rest of Helen's creatures.

THE ENCAUSTING

I came to the seaside to find myself, to finally become the person I was meant to be.

I work mornings in a stuffy little gift shop just off the boardwalk and nights in the crafter's mall. It's scary to clean in there at night, but it feels good to be scared. I feel alive, like I just woke up.

Appetite's better than ever. The food court pumps out Thai food and fish and chips and thin-crust pizza. Indian food, Mexican, everything fresh and hot. There's a gelato stall, a stall that sells nothing but macarons.

I'd never eaten a macaron before I came here, not to mention tiramisu, sushi, crabmeat.

I'm making friends. Not at the gift shop but at the mall. They'll eat with me if I'm not too hidden away in a book. They'll persuade me to go to a bar and we'll complain about our lives. It's fun, I guess.

The Jeep's still running, still getting me through the tourist traffic. The cars make last-second turns and brake hard. Pedestrians cross like ducks in tie-dye, staring at their phones in the middle of the road.

But days off are what I live for. I lie on a blanket on the beach reading trashy used paperbacks and dozing in and out. I walk for hours, pick up my things on the way back.

I bought maroon sheets, and there are soapy flakes on them in the mornings, like when you peel a sunburn, only I haven't gotten a sunburn.

One morning Sam, the guy from the fish and chips stall, is in my bed with a sour look on his face.

"What is all of this?" he says.

"Sunburn," I say, but he must see it can't be.

Work soon, so I rush to the shower. I step out and begin drying, but the wax balls up, ropes up, sticks to the towel. I sigh, start a hot bath, dig under the sink for salt scrub and a loofah.

Sam comes to kiss me goodbye, and on impulse, I throw off my towel and back him into the bedroom. While it's going on, I feel the wax just flowing out of me. Sam doesn't ask, but he sees. He feels it on him. He won't be back here.

★   ★   ★

The crafter's mall ought to have been torn down long ago, but things seem to get left alone out here.

I stack the chairs and wash the main hall floor and do the first-floor bathrooms, which are a nightmare. Wind whistles through unseen cracks. The floor feels unsteady, upstairs and down. I work fast and come out into a dark, empty street, hoping the Jeep will start.

I have too much fear, and I think about what it might signify. I always expect something to jump out at me, but what? Am I guilty for being so selfish, coming out here? Expecting punishment?

It's a rush to get something to eat and some sleep, shower and find something decent to wear to the gift shop. It's exhausting to watch the shoppers put the little glass baubles back in place. It's exhausting to smile for four or five hours, and then the day feels ruined after that.

If I have the morning off, I sleep in and when I wake, all of my skin is tight and greasy. It creases and flakes. When I wrench myself into a sitting position, the surface of it breaks off my hips and knees. I take a piece of it in my fingers. The skin where it's broken off is red and mottled.

My pores are clogged, too. I get a magnifying mirror, hoping I can push out the plugs before I break out even more. I'm crying while I cake on my foundation.

It's getting worse, coming faster.

I learn to dissolve the wax in olive oil and scrape it off, as the Greek athletes used to do. They'd squeegee the oil off their bodies, and old ladies would use it because it was full of their youth and virility.

★   ★   ★

One morning it's thick enough to peel. The little vellus hairs on my jaw come off with a searing flash of pain, and my scalp is held in a tight wax cap. I pour olive oil on it and scrub like I'm shampooing, eye on the clock because I'm supposed to be at work. The oil and wax on my scalp make such a pulpy mess I cry.

I shampoo with the oil until I have no more oil. I follow up with dandruff shampoo, rinse, repeat. I make it to work with wet hair, but the next day I have to quit the gift shop. It's too hard to get presentable.

I keep cleaning for a while after that, holding my face as far back as I can in my sweatshirt hood. The wax is building up in the daytime now, and the people all avoid me – or I avoid them. I can't say which.

I can't say for sure that I raise my eyes to theirs, ever.

It takes a week to finally pry away from the crafter's mall. After they stop calling, I feel better again for a time. Three or four times a day I drive to the little apartment. I remove the greatest part of the wax, drive back out to the beach. And then I start bringing my bottle of oil and spatula to the beach. You can de-wax just as well in a bathroom stall.

And then I stop driving home to sleep.

And then I run out of oil.

The Jeep was ticketed sometime. It was towed sometime later while I wasn't watching. I'm not watching anything anymore. The wax has filled in around my eyes. It doesn't hurt. It feels safe. Like a wrapping. It feels right. I want to stop making it crack, and so I must be still. I lie on my blanket and let be what will be.

FALL INTO WATER, BECOME SOMEONE NEW

Lines after lines of picnic tables are set on the plain, and the men seated at them drink dark beer and swill cups of stew made from meat and fowl and fish and mollusks, tubers, and powdered milk. It's chalky stuff, but there's plenty to wash it down.

They like to sing, the men. A young-seeming one looks into the stew and tries to start, *Fish heads, rolling in the stew,* he sings, but his voice is high and thin and no one follows.

A man jumps on the table, a handsome one, though honestly they all look much the same with their wavy brown hair and large, wide ears.

He begins to stomp and to sing: *Oh, there's no one who knows you the way that we do.* The men begin to hum. The handsome one is standing tall, but the tank stands taller behind him. Apple-sized snails scrape the sides of it, their obscene mouths moving behind him, seeming to answer him in song.

Again he calls,

Oh, there's no one who knows you the way that we do.

And the men answer,

Fall into water, become someone new.

Fall into water, become someone new.

Fall into water, become someone new.

The man is stomping, dancing. He stops still, points into the distance where two others are taking the prisoner out of the shackles. The prisoner resists, digs his heels into the cracked earth, cries out until more men hurry over and grasp him under the knees.

The man on the table kicks and stomps and sings.

What is it coming? What's swallowing you?
And the men,
Fall into water, become someone new.
Fall into water, become someone new.
Fall into water, become someone new.
They're clomping tin cups on the table, stew and beer sloshing out. More of them climb up onto the tables. They dance and stomp and jump to click their heels. Some are so tipsy now that they slip in the stew and slide to the ground and crawl back up with the slime on their fronts to keep dancing and laughing.

The prisoner has been dragged all the way to the stairs now. He's not laughing; he's begging and screaming. He is hideous, with rough gray hair all over his head and his face, tiny ears. Four identical men are pushing him up the stairs, but he's struggling hard, and it's not enough. Others come down from the tables to help.

Calls the handsome one,
What does it feel like, becoming a stew?
And the men laugh. That's a line never heard before. He's only ribbing, but the prisoner doesn't know that.

The prisoner screams more lustily now; he's fighting them, but there are too many.

And the men, all off-key, off-time,
Fall into water, become someone new.
Fall into water, become someone new.
Fall into water, become someone new.
The prisoner balances on the tank's edge. Now he's fallen into the dark water. The men go silent, listening to the splashing, watching the flailing. A snail detaches and falls slowly to the bottom.

The murky thing at the back of the tank comes awake. It grasps out to the prisoner, who pushes away, presses his face to the glass. The face is gray and formless, bubbles streaming out of it. The men seem to hold their breath as the murky thing gently enfolds the prisoner. There are two pulses, and it's over. The thing falls away from him like a robe tossed aside, like a towel, and the man pushes off from the bottom and comes gasping to the top. His hands hold the tank's edge. His handsome face emerges. The water streams down over glorious new ears.

A cheer rises up from the men. A blanket is brought, a cup of stew, a cup of beer. Soon this new man will sing and stomp with the rest, and he will be the happiest among them.

SHE AIN'T STOPPIN'

Lewis woke from a dream, something about Carmine. All his dreams were about her now. He woke in that cellar-like space, another year's leaves blown in through the stairway, not many leaves since the wind rarely blew in that particular direction. All the other men still slept on the ground. Lewis stretched and came up into dappled forest light.

★   ★   ★

There had been a wedding. He and Carmine had walked along the hollow-way and under the wicker bower. Only in the dream had the sticks of the bower taken life around them, the vines coiling and pushing, flowers blooming. The ground seemed to grope and moan around their bare feet.

All of this space around them – the hollow wedding path ending in the bower, the cabins speckling the hills, the barn and the meadows filled with wildflowers and picnicking couples – all of it was the site not only of weddings but of Carmine's family's annual reunion.

In fact, the reunion was why they were there. He remembered that in idle moments, which were few. They were there for the reunion, and the wedding itself had been an impulse thing. (Well, the ring-box had been in his bag; he *had* intended to ask her soon.) Apparently several impulse weddings took place during each week-long reunion, but Lewis had no way of knowing that until after.

There were many things he learned, after.

There had been a wedding feast outside the barn and frenzied dancing inside. Every type of person numbered among Carmine's relatives, but mostly unsavory types. He was afraid of them.

At first, Lewis couldn't see anything of them in Carmine but then, as the night dragged on and her drinking spiked, suddenly he could see it. For an instant there in the barn-turned-ballroom, he *did* see it.

He shuddered, and then she turned in the light and all resemblance was gone. And anyway, he was likely just as grotesque as she at that moment, his face all flushed and stretched from smiling.

He carried her up the hill and over the threshold into the cabin – but slung on his shoulder rather than across his chest. He laid her down on the narrow bed. She still wore the same green romper she'd had on that morning when he picked her up at her off-campus apartment. The romper's tiny inseam was all damp.

Sweat, from the dancing.

★ ★ ★

Back in the barn, they did not tease Lewis much. Everyone knew that wedding nights were no longer what they used to be.

Lewis was thinking how he felt more comfortable among her kin now – *his* kin, he corrected himself. He sat at a card table nursing a tap beer and played for a while with a tavern puzzle while the place buzzed around him. There was a feeling of good-natured secret-keeping. He would catch one's eye, and though the man would smile warmly, he would always look away. Soon the only women were the two lovely ones making drinks and the few burly ones lingering around the tables. All the rest were men.

Lewis began to become aware of these little things they were handling and keeping from his direct view. Were they flashlights? They were the size and shape and had the diamond-plate texture of metal flashlight handles, but there were no flared ends to them.

There were the flashlight handles and there were little books, or scrolls? On the way out to the outhouse, he'd seen men turn away with these pages they held, or tuck them under tables – photographs? The paper was curved, though. The pages had come from the tubes.

Lewis was dog tired. He ought to have gone to bed hours ago, but he'd thought to make a good impression on these folk, and it was starting to work. He was flanked now by a big friendly lumberjack-looking man and a small old man with a Rip Van Winkle beard and deep wrinkles around lively eyes. Finally, Lewis was being joshed about his wedding night and given shots of old-timey stuff that burned his throat, lit up his head.

"That's *my* wife, right there," said the old-timer. He cocked his head at the supple young woman making drinks. "We wed at the last reunion."

The big man laughed heartily at this and then excused himself.

The little old one passed Lewis a metal tube under the bar. Lewis began to bring it up to examine it, but the old man pushed the object back down. His eyes went to the women keeping bar.

With vile breath, he whispered close to Lewis, "No, these are just for the menfolk, you know." He clapped Lewis on the back on his way out. "*You* know," he said, but Lewis surely did not.

He handled the thing under the table and found one end was a lid that swiveled out on metal hinges. He pushed his finger inside, and pressing against the tube's inner wall, brought out the scroll.

After that, he was acting as all the others did. He laughed at a joke, took a sip of his beer, looked down briefly, looked around to be sure no one had seen, took another peek.

It was not a scroll but a booklet curved for insertion in the tube. The paper was thick and slick as a high-quality magazine, but the content was nothing that Lewis could discern.

Black-printed symbols like letters or numbers in a language unknown to him. Cyrillic was the first thing he thought of, but it wasn't that; it was only that some of the symbols looked vaguely familiar. Long and sloshy as the day had been, he could not have focused on them long, even without the strange game the men were playing here. It felt like back in school, trying to hide the cell phone from the teacher.

The images took up most of the pages after the first few, and these were even stranger than the symbols. They first seemed to be only textures, snakelike diamond patterns and craggy expanses sometimes half-revealing a curve or a...fold.

They were pornographic images. His body knew it before he did. Blood rushed to his groin, and he was suddenly dizzy. He needed to get to the outhouse as well — all that beer.

And then his consciousness fractured. Someone was pounding on the outhouse door and on Lewis's forehead, which pressed hard against the other side.

Someone was tucking the tube into Lewis's front pocket. He was back in the barn, and the tube had gone rolling on the floor. The man next to him was saying, "Just for the menfolk. Don't you know that?"

Lewis thought the man was making a pass at him somehow. He crawled away from the man, mumbling nonsense, and flopped on the floor.

Sometime later, Lewis was seated on a rock, trying to see the booklet in moonlight. The images seemed even more sinister and alluring with the white of the paper glaring blue.

Finally two men came and helped him up the hill, one on either side, singing, "Here comes the groom" and something filthy after that. They did not get him all the way to his cabin. He wandered alone after they had gone, looking in windows until he found the one where Carmine slept. She had gotten up at some point to put on a bright white nightie. It glared blue in the moonlight like neon.

Only in his dream did he ravage her, seeing all that blue, thinking of the textures on the curved pages. In real life, he sprawled face-down beside her in his filthy clothes and blasted into sleep.

★   ★   ★

When Lewis woke, the moon shone still. His head hurt badly, and yet he felt quite sober and sane. Carmine was gone. Thinking she'd gone to the outhouse back behind the cabins, he waited a while. He brought out the tube and clicked on a flashlight for a closer look, but suddenly there was a sound, a distant sound of cheering as you might hear in the summertime in town, when sports are being played many blocks away. Lewis went to the window and he barely caught it, so far away and half-concealed by trees: another barn, larger and more rustic than the first, glowing gold from within.

Glowing gold around the gaps between the rough and weathered boards. Carmine had gone there. He knew she had.

★   ★   ★

In the dream, he was there in a blink.

In reality, it was a torturous slog. One path would end and Lewis would be lost in trees. He would have to wait for a cheer to come – the crowd was hushed between the cheers and shrieks, it seemed – and move in that direction. His pants tore on blackberry vines, and the mud was so deep and sucking in places, he thought he might be carried down in quicksand.

When Lewis arrived in the barnyard, they weren't cheering, but there was the murmur of keyed-up people in a close space, the light inside so bright it came through cracks like sun through window blinds.

He was afraid to go to the door alone. He waited until a man came hurrying back from the bushes and went in behind him. He need not have feared being noticed. In here were twice as many, three times as many as he'd seen at the wedding feast. All were dressed in their finest it seemed, though in many cases that wasn't very fine at all. A vague memory came of some catty thing his mother had said about one of Carmine's outfits. He did not linger on it.

Past the crowd there seemed to be a stage, brightly lit but set low. Most were still turned toward it, though it was empty for the moment.

Lewis did not know how he would find Carmine in the crowd. After all, many of the women had hair like hers, bodies not unlike hers – and he had no idea what she would be wearing. He edged his way past people, stopping to look into faces when he could, but everyone was tightening in on the stage now. He was caught. He could not see well past the people standing in front of him, but it seemed that someone led an animal out onto the stage. There was a flash of chain, a textured flash of scarred skin, or maybe it was a blanket.

The crowd murmured, expectant, and then there was a flicker of gilt fabric thrown, and he knew. His body knew what it was before he did. It was no animal up there. It was a goddess up there, though he couldn't see her clearly.

She was not on any chain, though there were chains involved somehow. He heard the links sliding on other links. He saw the glint of steel. The crowd pressed in closer. How could the crowd breathe now? Lewis felt himself a part of a large organism, a hive centered on the queen. He caught a glimpse of the line down her back. When the tall man before him bent in closer, he caught a half-second sight of her moving hips.

Her skin was like scales and like bark and dried-up riverbed. Her hips moved in circles. He could feel it. The crowd was writhing its own hips in close circles. Pulsing.

Some tension had built to its highest point. The cheering barely began and then something cut it off. Some still cheered and others panicked, shouted.

Lewis heard one thing clearly, one thing only: "Hold up. She ain't stoppin'."

The glints of skin he caught were moving faster than any large thing could move, shuddering like a hummingbird.

The air seemed to break. Everything pulled in closer and then exploded out. In slow motion, all blew out from the center.

There was no difference between this part and the dream of this part.

It was not even slow motion, was it? It was a complete stillness. The sides of the barn – the shattered wood – it all hung in the space around where the barn ought to have been.

The unsavory types blew out away from the barn, hung in the air. Their coarse women all hung in the air, their beautiful daughters – each one almost but not quite Carmine – well, the women hung in the air too. They had all been blown out from the barn in a great explosion. It seemed that any time now, they would break and bleed against trees and rocks and ground. Only they didn't, all was still, and Lewis seemed to float through it disembodied, seeing the air-scattered debris but unable to get to the center to see the goddess. At the center was only golden light.

His consciousness floated around the edges, through the suspended bodies, the planks and splinters, the loosed tubes and curved pages, then flasks and bottles and all the rest, looking for Carmine. He never did find her.

Dejected, his consciousness floated out into the forest. It wove through the other barn, where the wedding dance had gone on. The wedding dance still went on, but Carmine was not there either. Maybe this wedding dance was another day or another year.

His attention floated through the cabins one by one, through the stinking outhouses. It went on down the hill to weave through cars and campers in the vast graveled lot.

It wandered every inch of the grounds until it caught on a breeze and caught up in a gust of leaves, blew down into the little cellar. Bodies lay down there on the floor amongst leaves, though not so many leaves as one would think. The wind didn't come from this particular direction all the time.

Lewis's consciousness came back into his body, which woke him. For a moment he tried to go back inside the dream, for it had been a dream of Carmine.

This time another man woke up just near him. It was comical: each turned, and seeing the other's face, began to shriek. They caught themselves, held back the shrieks. They chuckled, reached for each other's faces. Eyes traveled the lengths of each other's beards.

"What happened to you, old-timer? You look like shit," they said.

A FARCE

Once a girl was so sure the world had gone farcical that she started taking a little something to help her see things true.

It wasn't anything much, just a trending topical all the girls at school applied from time to time. It came in a golden compact and went on with a puff. I applied mine mostly to the philtrum because scent was the sense that most often failed me – or was it the sense most often honest? I wasn't sure.

The lilacs around the gate smelled of fabric softening sheets, and fabric softening sheets smelled of stone. I wasn't entirely sure whether the topical had changed the smells or fixed them.

Sometimes I rubbed a little onto my eyelids and stared at the walls, the floor, saw through them to something more authentic. When studying got to be too much, I'd do that.

I'd look down on the lawn from my window and see what was about to come.

★   ★   ★

The girl was having a hard time, being neglected, being scapegoated for things around the house – all because of her sister's impending wedding.

Our whole family and all the people we know are well off – really quite well off, prominent even – but the fiancé is something else. He is shaped like a bear and soft like a bear, but his face is chiseled and airbrushed. He makes me think of the portrait of Henry VIII or a politician painted on the side of a building someplace even worse than this.

Once, when I sneaked down to Father's study late in the night, I found his computer unlocked and a shaky video taken inside a forbidden place, a speakeasy. Onto the stage stumbled a powdered actor, red circles of blush. He was playing the fiancé; I knew it instantly. Saying the very things the fiancé had said in a recent speech, screeching them in a high-pitched voice and all the crowd laughing, roaring.

I think of it sometimes now, replay it in my mind.

I'm trying to piece together what brought me here, but it is hard to set things straight. I was a careless girl and then I was thrown away.

★   ★   ★

The girl was locked in the tower.

The girl was locked in a cellar.

The girl was disappeared.

It was lucky my friend Chelsea visited the day before. We sat in the gazebo while Mother pruned roses. She was watching us closely, but Chelsea had just enough time to press a new compact into my hand. Chelsea was tight and formal. I tried to read her eyes but could not.

"What is it?" I whispered when Mother's back was to us again, but she shook her head slowly. Her face was red.

When she'd gone, I was there with Mother for a half hour more. She stopped pruning, took off her gloves. A maid brought cold water and little pink cakes.

Mother gave no hint what was coming. We talked about nothing of importance. Weather, a disagreement I'd had with a girlfriend. I was smug and happy to have her attention on me so long with no criticism and no mention of the wedding.

Mother went inside just before the long car pulled into the driveway.

Two young men in shirtsleeves came out of the back. I was curious at first, and then I fought them. Scratched. If Father had not been watching from the window, if he had not nodded and turned away, I'd have thought I was being kidnapped for ransom.

I am not entirely sure where I am now. The walls are brick and the floor a damp slate. It is dark and terrible at night, but I am cared for. I have my meals, a bed and toilet. Sometimes they bring in magazines or a stack of romantic novels. They would take the compact from me if they could, so I keep it hidden.

If I touch the puff to my eyelids, I can still look down to the view of the lawn as it was from my bedroom window. I imagine it is the wedding day, all the white tables and servers in black, the guests in so many colors. I should have been a bridesmaid.

Without my compact, I would be afraid, but I have the compact. I keep it tucked in my bra and draw it out only when I can't bear any more of the dark loneliness.

I only hope it will last.

I touch the puff to my eyelids, and the actor comes out dressed like a marionette in his suit matched to the fiancé's suit. He's no older than I am, just a boy in white pancake makeup, pink rouge circles on his cheeks, strings attached to his arms and legs, and at first you can't see the X-shaped wooden structure at the top, but then it drops, and on the boards' surface is the name of the corporation or lobbyist or whatever that the fiancé is said to work for in secret, and the little boy playing the marionette starts squealing the fiancé's speech. And then he starts pissing himself.

The crowd roars.

Sometime later, perhaps six months after I saw that video, my fiancé's fiercest political opponent disappeared.

I saw the video, and so now I am disappeared.

My fiancé? I think maybe that is so.

Maybe he saw me and changed his choice. I am an appealing little thing and livelier than my sister.

★　★　★

The girl made a false move and found herself in danger.

I remember school so fondly now. All the girls, all the little fads and obsessions we had, all the gossip. I was so happy and didn't know it. Always complaining about how daunting the reading was, complaining about my strict and critical parents, pushing out the world with the powder.

And it was a private school, my home a vast mansion.

I was lucky once.

Now, looking back, it seems that I *was* one of the many bridesmaids in the lawn wedding. I laughed and floated over the plush green grass in a long lavender gown.

It seems I was the bride at the table hearing speeches in my honor.

I caught the bouquet.

I threw the bouquet.

Or has it even happened? I'm not sure.

I keep dreaming that the door creaks open and the bear-man is silhouetted in light. It is only a dream. No one comes, only a burly maid with a tray of food atop a stack of clean linens and pajamas. I never try to fight her. I try to talk to her, but she looks away. Her face looks red and hot.

The food is nicer than we ever had at home. I am becoming very fat here.

She makes me stand at the far wall while she changes my linens. I draw back my arms, and the compact pops out of my top. I flinch to catch it, but it smacks open on the ground. The maid looks up. We see the powder cast across the damp slate floor.

I pause and then start to bend for it.

"Leave it," she says, but she is not commanding. Not much older than myself though she's terribly muscle-bound. What a coarse life this girl must lead, but she's vain of her hands. She gloves them carefully before any cleaning, and so in that instant her eye moves to her stack of linens, I'm already throwing myself onto the powder. She's heavy on me, pulling me back, but she cannot stop my desperate grasp for it. She cannot stop me bringing my palms up to my open eyes and pressing them closed full of powder.

It is like a film, or like two films:

In one, from above, I watch the large girl curse herself and bring a rag to the beautiful girl who is crouched and shivering, touching her own throat and face, soiling her pajama top with hands still covered in powder.

"What is it? What have you done?" the large one says. Her eyes go to the cell's closed door.

Does she think some bear will come in soon?

The beautiful girl can't respond, or she won't. She goes on rocking and shivering and begins making sounds. I can't say if she's laughing or crying.

That's the one film, but there is another I see at the same time: the same room, the same girls, but the view is from the opposite side and now the girls sit on the bed, knees turned together like the closest of friends.

The beautiful girl holds her eyes closed but eyebrows raised. She thinks she sees through her eyelids! She smiles falsely, seeming to gaze into the large girl's face. They seem to gaze into each other's faces. A close-up, then, and I see the little bit of powder on the maid's lashes, the glassiness in her eyes. Her red flush is gone.

She is a beautiful one, too; I see it now.

For a moment I wonder if this one is me. I hope she is because this one's body is going slack. She looks so peaceful slumping sideways on the clean bed.

"I can't," she drones. They've had some conversation that I've missed.

The girl in pajamas whispers, "You can. You already have. Don't you see?"

She squeezes the maid's knee and rises. The ring of keys she holds close for silence. She crosses the room, unlocks the door, and walks out onto a balcony high above a bright lawn. The light would stun her if her eyes were open.

She rushes down the stone staircase, spiraling around and around and around the tower. At the bottom she stumbles, so dizzy she is from the turning. The camera work is shaky and at first I cannot see the place except to say it is hot and bright. Flagstones, ivy, and flowering trees. Sudden rumbling as of people moving quickly over a wooden bridge.

The girl flinches and crouches down. Maybe she senses the cool; maybe that's how she knows what direction. She crouches low and crawls into shade.

She slips onto her belly in leaf mold and rises to hurry until she comes to a brick wall. Eyes closed, still she stops before making contact. She turns her back to it, slides down panting.

Zoom out from her now past trees, past crenellated rooflines, long gardens, hundreds of acres of grass. Zoom out to see the size of the wall and gasp.

Men in shirtsleeves move like chickens on the grass. A bear-man looms on a high balcony.

*   *   *

The girl lived for some days as a woodland creature.

For a long time I'm sure I am watching a film, an endless, idiotic film filled with chases and low physical comedy. Men run into walls, into each other, they fall into the water features when they jump to catch me.

Sometimes it's a girl and sometimes a wily creature who leads the chase. Dashing across the lawns and through formal gardens, around and around the inside of the wall, she morphs into fox, raccoon, rabbit.

She never finds a gate.

She perches in trees some nights, her long cat's tale twitching irritably. Other nights, she digs nests in untended corners and curls to sleep under last year's leaves. Days, she filches pies from windowsills, hot bread from the cooling racks. She laughs silently, eats – and watches the lawn.

But films end, and powder wears off too soon. I cry it out of my eyes and sweat it out of my face. There is residue around my collar to suck for a while, and then it's entirely gone. I'm mourning the end of a long, long friendship.

I hide my body in the leaves again, but this time I feel every sharpness. Even the air is harsh. Even the dirt on my knuckles seems to cut.

My belly lurches. Maybe I never had any pies. I start to doubt if I left that room so peacefully after all.

I remember the tower fondly now. The able maid and clean bed, the meals, even the toilet. I was so happy and didn't know.

I was lucky once.

*   *   *

The wedding comes – and the gate.

Morning. White tents are rising on the lawn, and fairy lights, torches, long tables. The sky's full of helicopters full of guests.

"Here, kitty, kitty," someone calls close by my nest. I know this voice from speeches.

"*Here,* kitty, kitty, kitty, kitty, kitty." That one is my father. They are just past a thin row of trees.

They have me, and for a moment I'm glad.

I catch my mother and sister in a distant window. Mother's updo and her beaded rose dress move aside like a human curtain to reveal my sister's nervous face in a long mirror. I am glad it is not my face at all; I'd thought at one time it might be.

I am glad now that the powder wore off. Everything's so precise now.

Father says I have nothing to fear. Nothing has happened and nothing will, only I need to come out and see my dress. There's still time for a nap if I come out soon. There will be food and presents, music. It all sounds fortunate.

My fiancé asks, "Isn't there a saucer of milk for poor kitty?"

Father says, "Oh, yes, Chelsea brought your things, your *compact.*"

Oh, even that?

But when I look back up to the window, my sister stands tall in a lavender dress.

I smell stone and lilac and something else – iron? Copper?

Their hands will be on me soon, the grip always just above the elbows. I can't really move like a fox or even a bunny, but I tense and take one long deep breath.

I think I smell a gate.

THE APARTMENT

The city itself was horror enough to me. I'd dreamed of a smoking, stinking yellow-gray blot on the horizon and myself a train barreling toward it. I never reached the city in dreams, only in life.

I arrived fearing all the stereotypical things that you're shown to fear in movies – cold-eyed strangers, the indifferent rich, the muggings and all possible assaults on your body and property. I had little enough property. My body was stocky and strong; people never seemed able to violate it. If someone shoved me, I shoved back harder. I did not mind their blank stares. I understood them.

People are the same all over. It was the spaces of the city that unnerved me. More than once, standing in the suck of air between two skyscrapers, I looked up and was caught in a rush of vertigo much like the fear of heights.

I walked past a park early on and noticed the shrubs all covered with greasy dust, caught little glimpses of grass inside as I hurried past, and it looked to me like Astroturf covered in lint and litter like the filthy carpet of the trailer where I grew up.

The tunnels were the worst. They seemed to have come out of me, a manifestation of my own nightmares. Suffocating, claustrophobic dread – and at the same time a little thrill, like looking at a mannequin made in your image.

And though I was unsettled from the very beginning, I thought it would lessen.

There were reasons I had come. I tried to focus on them: classes to take, difficult ones, and a part-time job that could lead to connections in the field I'd always dreamed of working in. I could build a reputation in the city and then move anywhere I liked. It was the job more than anything else that brought me here – something I had competed for and won, something I'd wanted badly despite its being in the city.

I even had an aunt a few dozen blocks away who had often lamented the fact that no one visited. I spent long afternoons in her cold apartment, which stank of garlic and copper. Nauseated by the deep brown wall-to-wall and the many-eyed paisley on the closed drapes, I held focus on her face and tried to remember her from back at family reunions and such, which made me think of green trees and burbling streams and breezes.

"I suppose it's just that everything feels like it's indoors," I told her. "You never get outside, really. You're always inside."

"You'll get used to it," she said.

"And the garbage smell," I said. I couldn't remember the scent of clean nature anymore; I only remembered being able to open the door of whatever hovel and walk out into something better.

"You get used to anything," Aunt Ruth said.

★   ★   ★

You do, to a point. I began to find myself immersing more and more into my work and my readings for class. I would become aware of the city like coming awake in a strange room and then lose awareness again. I forgot I was here, or maybe forgot I had not always been here.

A girl at work became a friend. We adventured together, eating and drinking so much we had to take up running. A friend of a friend we met running became my neglectful lover. Good connections followed from the part-time job, and on the same week I was to graduate, a very decent offer came through. I thought some of my people from home might come to celebrate. They said they would but backed out one by one.

"They always say they'll come," said Ruth. I was forbidden to call her Aunt Ruth because it made her feel so old. Her hair was dyed the mocha brown of her carpet but below she had the crinkled face of an apple-doll.

I'd been sharing a room, but now friends were keeping eyes out for apartments. Ruth looked harder than anyone – and she found one, right in this very building where even the halls smelled of garlic and copper.

Or like shit, I realized just then. Old people shit.

But we were already on our way to see the space. Ruth turned and locked her door. The halls were scuffed, with dark peeling paint just like apartment building halls in all the movies you see about worn-out cities. The halls were nonsensical, just as you'd imagine, because of how these apartments had been sectioned off from larger spaces.

We walked past many doors in a long hall that seemed to dead-end, only to make a right-hand turn at the last minute.

"I thought we'd be going to the stairs," I said. This new hall was narrower with no doors on it.

"It's just a little farther," Ruth said.

"You're not saying it's on the same floor," I said, but it was. The hall seemed to end again and veered to the right at the last minute, and at the end of another doorless hall a door stood open, an impatient-looking lady waiting in a white-painted, wood-floored space inside.

It was just like in the movie scenes of young people viewing apartments in the city. The tiny space seemed large to us, those floors a marvel. The fireplace could not be used but would add atmosphere. The window looked out on horrors but brought in buckets of cheerful light.

This is someone else's dream, I thought.

"Are you sure?" I said just as scripted. "All this, for this price?"

It didn't seem fair. These were someone else's hopes coming true (and this was a trap, too, a way for the city to keep me close), but still I flushed and stammered as I signed the papers. I mirrored back the real estate lady's broad, wet, desperate smile.

Ruth looked on, triumphant.

★　　★　　★

A rush of years, a wall of work shot through with little glints of drama and glamour. I saw some of the city's finer sides and sampled of its terrors.

I no longer felt unsettled all the time, but I did sometimes float outside of myself. In the midst of a party, bringing out hors d'oeuvres, I might feel I was watching a movie. A ridiculous movie, actually, based on an outdated fantasy of city life. The work lunches and dinners were just like that, too. I heard the charming repartee and smelled the wine, but nothing was real.

In bed I might wonder if sex ever happened or if the room had just dimmed to black and then faded back in to morning. Ruth would land one knock on the wall behind my bed when she fixed her breakfast, and I would knock back.

I found myself on the street more than once, pulse pounding, a stranger far back but gaining on me, all the windows dim, all the doors locked. I'd start out feeling the fear in my body and then hover back over my shoulder judging, thinking how stupid it was to be in a scene so cliché. I'd hover on ahead into something else, some other scene.

A wolfish person at work would corner me, and again I'd only hover ahead to another better scene where morning faded back in through the window and Ruth gave her collegial knock.

★   ★   ★

The gathering at the lawyer's office was yet another cliché. *So they finally visited*, some part of me thought, but a truer part knew these weren't my people anymore. We all gasped on cue – oh, no one had thought it would be *that* much – and then they directed disgust and accusations at me.

A windfall. Everyone's dream.

I'd never realized Ruth owned her place. The savings she'd left would buy mine as well, just barely. For the first time in my life, I had so many options. I could go and be wealthy somewhere else. I could even retire, but not here, or probably not here. Some part of me struggled over the decisions, brought out an actual calculator and a pad, but I hovered away from that scene because it was settled: I would buy my place and knock down the wall between it and Ruth's. I'd need to keep earning well to get the permits and start the renovations.

I would never get away.

★   ★   ★

I was lacking sleep and much dragged down by bureaucracy over the next few months. When I finally had the chance to open those paisley drapes, I nearly took them down with me in a faint to the floor. The scene outside was incomprehensible – bright clouds floating in an aqua sky, rolling hills and trees, a burbling stream and a clutch of small shoddy homes. I knelt and pushed the window up as far as it would go, perhaps two inches, and though the sounds of cars and the sights of the city faded back in immediately, the scent lingered strange and green with catches of catalpa or maybe honeysuckle, damp earth, woodfire.

I shut the window, brought those drapes quite tight again, and turned back to the room to breathe deeply of the closer air, which had no smell and no taste.

I'd get used to it, Ruth once said, and I had.

The carpet had been pulled up, revealing floors much like my own but more stained. There'd been a cat here sometime. There'd been a lot of life here, everywhere, and all around. Ruth's life was still here.

She stood before me for an instant, featureless except for the glossy dyed hair. She faded out and what faded in was an image of the space far in the future when all the renovations were done. It was bright and sophisticated, the decor all eclectic and witty like something from a magazine. Maybe it would *be* in a magazine; certainly I had the connections to make that happen.

A place like this would make me more important, too, wouldn't it? I would rise in my profession even more quickly than I already had.

This is someone else's dream, I thought, and then, *No, this is my dream. This is what I have always wanted.*

But I couldn't convince myself, not even for a moment. It was such a small and pathetic dream, and it *wasn't* mine. It wasn't even Ruth's. She'd been content to sit on her money in a closed-up room and complain about the family.

It was the city's dream, I realized. It was what the city wanted, to build and rebuild, to go forward and then back. I was simply a hand in the city's great project.

And I tried to hover into the future, to a time when it was done, when I could at least enjoy the fruits of the labor, but I'd lost that power. I had to suffer through every decision, every argument on the phone. I had to watch and worry over the workers and then make myself, somehow, fit for work. The knock would come with the morning light, and I would not have slept. I would reach to knock back and find no wall there anymore.

THE BOOK OF BRATS

Val's mother, in lieu of a sex talk, had marched her to Waldenbooks to select a paperback book on puberty. Before letting Val have it, she'd stapled together the pages on boys and intercourse, leaving Val free to read or not read the rest of the book. Val had absorbed herself in it and found a lot of the images memorable (including, of course, those forbidden sections with all their diagrams, first peeked at between staples and then hastily un-stapled and re-stapled), but though Val was a writer and not an artist at all, only a few of the lines had stood out. One was a supposedly common chant girls used to do while performing calisthenics:

We must, we must, we must increase our bust
It's better, it's better, it's better for the sweater
We might, we may, we might get big someday

The other part that she remembered (or almost remembered) was a chapter title, something like 'Tits, Titties, Boobs, Jugs, Tatas, and Melons: Your Breasts', which many years later inspired the title and subtitle of *The Book of Brats*.

Val had tried and failed many times over the years to find the puberty book. Perhaps no surprise that the chapter title didn't bring up the book since the term was inexact. (It brought up porn, actually.) Even stranger was that nothing came up for the chant.

Gaps in the internet made Val feel like she was losing it. Well, she *was* losing it in certain ways. For example, she was having a harder and harder time with vocabulary. She'd never had perfect access to the good old word *horde*, but Jesus Christ how she'd declined! Just the other day she'd forgotten her phone at home and spent a good half hour trying to bring up the word *gargoyle*. Looking at an actual gargoyle on one of the crumbling buildings around the park, she still failed to recall the word.

Along the walk she had gasped, seeing a brown-orange rubber draped among leaves and fast-food litter. This brought up a joke her countrified mother once told her:

One kid says, "I found a condom on the patio."

Other kid: "What's a patio?"

What's a patio, indeed. No kids in the park, and why was nearly everyone behind closed doors these days? Had they come to fear their neighbors? Was there something in the air? She'd seen the rubber's equal or worse on every walk she'd taken in this park, but still they shocked her from time to time, this one looking a cousin to the dappled banana slugs of her long-ago childhood in the suburbs of a wetter place than this.

She was losing it, oh yes.

The word *gargoyle* came up in two shakes once she could search. She'd blanked on the movie title but googled the name of an actress who'd played a gargoyle-monster in a movie she remembered.

This word was needed for a little something she had in mind for their winter's occupation, just a little picture book about a girl in a neighborhood like the one where Val lived with her husband, Stan. All the kids in their picture books lived in a neighborhood like their own; that was part of Val and Stan's identity in the marketplace.

"This little girl makes friends with a gargoyle on the building across the street and gets awakened to the twilight world of living statues," she told Stan, passing her notes across the table that afternoon.

"Why did we retire? Can you tell me that?" he said.

Had they retired? Their cramped dining room was still set up to double as an office. Stan chose a mechanical pencil from one of the cups on the lazy Susan, rubbed his forehead and looked down at her mess of papers.

Val often mimicked his nasal voice and his exasperated sighs but not now, not when she wanted something. "Just a sketch, and we'll think about it," she said.

He sipped his tea and didn't move his eyes from her notes and half-assed stick people sketches for a good five minutes. Finally he sighed, saying, "I could see something with that mermaid fountain sculpture over by the women's shelter. Maybe the girl-hero kind of looks like the sculpture, only she's chubbier." He'd already started to draw shapes on the back of one of Val's notes. He wouldn't be looking up again for an hour.

"Don't wear yourself out on that. I've thought of another brat, too," she said on her way to get dinner started.

His smile was soft and pure. "All right, dear."

★   ★   ★

The *Book of Brats* had begun just as their picture books were breaking through. In the first, a little boy-hero finds a secret door in his room leading to a nightmare city. They'd been awfully proud of that one, but they didn't start really selling until after the second one, with its hero-pairing of a spunky girl and her super-intelligent Saint Bernedoodle. They'd already finished the third and were on track to birth book number four by the second year. Those were heady times.

They hadn't had setbacks or morbid thoughts, and so how had *The Book of Brats* even come up? It would have seemed the kind of thing to conceive itself after they'd gotten jaded (which they never, ever did).

The catalyst must have been when Stan's mother started whining about grandchildren. "Fuck, no," was Val's response the first time she heard this idea, and Stan heartily agreed. Neither of them had dreamed of having any children – or pets, for that matter. Their own hero-pairing was all they'd needed, along with their books and their half-livable apartment just off the city's heart. That was one part of it, their self-containment. Another part was the well-founded feeling that parents in general were terrible and that they would have been more terrible than average. Atheists, moody workaholics, grim, forgetful, uninterested in sports. What monsters they would have created!

The full title was *Rug Rats, Ankle Biters, Snotnoses, Crumb Catchers, Curtain Climbers, and Failed Abortions: The Book of Brats.* Val brought her blackest humor to the crooked rhymes, and Stan, much influenced by *The Gashlycrumb Tinies*, brought his sharp and wicked pen-and-wash to these evil twins of the heroic boys and girls and anthropomorphic animals from their commercial books.

But this book was so much more than an Edward Gorey homage. Over the years it had attracted and collected...things, corroborations? Postcards, magazine and news clippings, photos, receipts, ticket stubs. Whenever something in the world reflected one of their brats, they tucked it into the file-folder pages behind that brat's story. The book became a documentary of monsters. The book made these creatures feel real.

★   ★   ★

"I love it," said Val.

He'd drawn a roly-poly girl posing to match the statue by the women's shelter. Far in the background stood the silhouette of the gargoyle who was to be this girl's friend.

"I thought you might love it," said Stan.

"You're in?"

"All in, never fear," he said. He kissed the back of her head on the way to the dresser where they kept their brats. He pushed aside sketches and dinner plates to make space for the book, thick and precious as an old family Bible. He opened to its empty back pages.

Pencil poised, he said, "You've met another brat?"

"Met?" she said. They did this sometimes, pretended they were not so far gone as they really were. She couldn't recall the word for what it was, but then she thought of *wolf*, then *coyote*. *Coy* – sometimes they played coy.

"You've thought up another brat?" he said because he was kind.

"No, *met* is right," she said. She put her hand on his and then in his still-thick hair. She'd lifted herself slightly, so he knew to pull her chair closer to his. They liked it better if their legs touched while they worked.

"I'm sorry," she said as she pressed her shoulder into his.

"Don't be sorry," he said. He gave her a soft, sweet kiss.

"I have a piece of...."

"Ephemera?" he said. He paged through to the next folder.

"You can scrapbook this one," she said, passing him the snack-size zipper baggie with its slippery brown-orange contents.

"Oh, honey," he said. He reached for the hand sanitizer.

"I already—" she said, rubbing her hands.

He rubbed the sanitizer into his hands and, frowning, smeared it all over the outside of the baggie, then dried it with a tissue. He selected an X-Acto knife and scrapbook tape from the lazy Susan. He set the baggie into the page and wrote a caption with date and place, then flipped back several pages to sketch as she spoke:

"I met...not just a brat but the...." Pinnacle? Apotheosis? Antithesis? All her better words had left her. This happened sometimes in the evenings.

"The Ur-brat?" Stan suggested.

"Oh, this makes me tired," she said. But she didn't feel tired; she felt scared. Her heart raced. She wished to turn away from Stan, pick out the narrow route to their bed, start again another day. She wouldn't sleep – her skin all hot and goose-pimpled. Didn't he notice? She wouldn't sleep, but she could hide.

Something was happening now. Something called out to her, tickling the edges of her mind like a forgotten word.

"You met a Very Important Brat, in any case," Stan said, nodding. He was already sketching a little child.

"Big," she said, and more emphatically, "*old.*"

"Grown?" He erased nothing, only adjusted the edges to draw the figure out leaner, then he looked at her a long while.

There was suddenly so much to say and no way to say it. Each of the children in their bookstore books had a doppelgänger brat – each of them except that first heroic boy, the one who entered the nightmare city. The nightmare city – it was here, had always been here. They'd only been too in love with each other and with their little life to see it. The boy had never been here because—

Stan had one hand over her hot, quavering hand. He was trying to get the pencil between her fingers. "Please," he said, "just draw, just try."

—because there was only one of that boy.

She tried, and maybe it was Stan's hand on hers that did it: she drew.

Stan had cartoonified the two of them many times, himself as a delicate milquetoast, Val big and sexy with mountains of curls. *She* drew them now, here as they sat at the table, drew them around Stan's sketch so that the figure seemed to emerge from the book. She added on to the boy, making him as they had always secretly known him, taller than they were and blessed with the best each had to pass down.

Violently, she turned the page, began another sketch. Again and again.

Backward, she sketched out the whole of their life – a life so cyclical it was hard to know what direction things went. Just book after book, after all. One might as well have come before another. She grew thinner and Stan's hair darker. That was all to say it was backward.

In the pictures, she drew and Stan wrote the stories, which may as well have been the way it was. It certainly seemed so now.

And at the end, the sheet facing the one where her piece of 'ephemera' sat bordered and captioned, in the last image, they were naked and frail, slumped cross-legged in the center of a bed. Between them a banana slug lay wet and broken.

The Book of Brats became the book of *a* brat, their brat. Joey or something. Her hand held no pencil but a glass of weak white wine. Their mouths were smiling as Stan paged through the many photographs of this celebrated son, seeking the end.

Behind them, drafted out of thin air, their boy loomed.

IN DARK TABITTREE

They entered a gently winding road canopied by trees, and the temperature dropped in the car. The children sighed with relief.

"Lovely," said Rena, half awake. In her half-dream, the road was a bed and the bright green tree cover a snarl of silk and lace.

The house impressed them, tall on its hill above the quaint little town. Rena's fantasy had been to change every single thing in the house. She'd picked out the colors and all, but after they'd stood looking up at it with the car engine ticking behind it, after the children had run upstairs to claim their rooms and Tomás had toured her around, guiding with a hand at her hip, she realized nothing needed changing. The inside was perfect just as it was, with its worn floors and woodwork, its frayed wallpaper richer than anything she might have bought. Clawfoot tubs, deep closets, an earthy musk that would build until they opened windows in the evenings and let in the cleansing scents of honeysuckle and rain and the sounds of birds.

The things they had sent ahead with movers were settled in among the things left behind so perfectly, it was as though everything they owned had always been there.

They only needed to dust. Or she did, with Teddie and Gully for helpers. Tomás went into his book-filled study and closed the door.

★   ★   ★

The children's negotiations involved rock, paper, scissors. Teddie won the entire third floor, and with much grace Gully accepted the vast attic floor with its fancy stained-glass window and shaky little balcony. They had been skeptical about parting – had stayed in one bedroom back in the city – but there was just so much space here, they felt obliged to spread out.

The children were entering their teens now, each an only child who had long wished for a sibling and, oh, sometimes wishes come true! Sometimes something your father or mother says will be a gift actually is a gift, and unlike in movies and books, you make friends with your step-sibling and find, really, a soul-mate who looks like you and is the same age. Sometimes you make believe you have always been together or even that you are twins.

They had felt this way for five years now. It was time to separate just slightly, and all was well and good.

They busied themselves arranging their items in their separate spaces but always saw each other first thing in the morning and last thing before sleeping. The final days of summer rolled out happily, the last happy days they would have together as a family.

*　　*　　*

Tomás had moved back to Tabittree with a sense of pride and a sense of failure strangely mixed. As a child he had often looked up at this fancy house on the hill with desperate longing, so there was that, and yet leaving the city was giving up a fight.

On registration day he had ushered the kids out of the public school red in the face. It had never been like that here, or did he misremember? Everyone so vapid and slow, everything so poor and dreary.

A woman was waiting by his car with a brochure about a new progressive arts-based school. She was a teacher at that school and wore that certain mix of bohemian and upscale recreation-store clothing that made a woman instantly trustworthy.

The kids whispered together in the back seat, not listening, and so Tomás said to this woman, "My Gully..." and did not know what else to say. He thought Rena's daughter, Teddie, just might be all right in the dismal public school, but not Gully. They were too sensitive.

"Just follow me," said the teacher, gesturing toward a silver Outback. "Just see."

After they had all toured the four-room schoolhouse, after the children were once more whispering in the back seat, the teacher said something strange.

"You're starting to remember some things, aren't you? I'm returning to Tabittree too. It takes time. Relax."

Tomás didn't press her on the meaning of that. God, he never even asked if the school was accredited.

★　　★　　★

Tomás and Rena sat in Adirondack chairs looking out from the front porch, out at the dark little town.

"It reminds me of…" she said.

"What?" said Tomás after a moment.

She ran her thumbnail along her lower lip. He didn't like that tic. "It reminds me of something," she said.

It reminded her of Breughel – or Bosch, even – the town and the people rushing and trudging in tall trees and little glints of sky. Felt like a god's-eye view.

The air was damp and close. It announced itself over and over, like the longing for some addictive thing she was trying to quit.

★　　★　　★

Rena, Gully, and Teddie sat in a porch swing looking out from the back porch at the acres of natural land, tall trees and complicated undergrowth in many shades of green, brown, and violet with the blue hills beyond. It was not jungle – not in this place, which was the South or the Midwest, depending on whom you asked – but it felt like jungle, vast and close at once. Nothing but nature.

The scene before them occurred to Teddie as a pattern, as though it were printed or, no – woven into fabric.

The scene felt close like the air felt close and tugged at her mind the same way. An addictive thing that kept announcing itself, though, for the longest time, she did not venture outside in that direction. When she and Gully left the house, which was seldom, it was over the front porch and down the many steps into town.

No need to drive here, which was a blessing. Since arriving, no one had felt like driving at all.

★ ★ ★

Gully and Teddie cooked breakfast on the first day of school. Rena was not up to it, and Tomás was nowhere to be seen.

Rena sat in the breakfast nook looking out to the back jungle. There were many steps leading down to it, just as there were in front, but she had never taken those steps. Maybe the children had.

She said, "I've been asking around, because I was interested, you know..." and she trailed off.

Gully slid the final pancake onto the stack. Teddie gave the scrambled eggs one last turn and ground ample coarse pepper onto them. So smoothly they worked together. Teddie gathered three napkins, three forks, and they sat beside Rena.

The food was so good, they all fell silent for a while, thinking their own thoughts.

Suddenly Rena said, "Interested in local history, and the name is so strange, don't you think? And I asked at the library – have you been there? – it's terrible, damp and claustrophobic. But I suppose no one would want books, living out here. Why would you need to escape into books when you can escape into the..."

"Mom, are you all right?" said Teddie. She eased the plate from under her mother's hand and stacked it with the other plates for rinsing.

"I went to the library, and the woman there was so old, you know, and well I'm sure she's not a librarian really, but she was the one they had set up as the librarian, and so I thought this was because she knew things. Wouldn't you think so, a little place like this? But she didn't seem to know much of anything at all."

"Mom," said Teddie, grasping Rena's hand, "we have to go. We have to go to school."

"Oh, have a nice day, sweetie," she said and then she stared into Gully's eyes with a soft, serene expression, adding, "Sweeties."

The children hurried off through the hall, over the porch and down the many steps toward school. Rena sat sipping on orange juice.

"The name came from Tibbetts' Tree," the old lady had said. The lady in the library. She'd said, "An old man founded the town, name of Tibbetts, and the town was named for a tree he planeted near to the center of town."

Planeted, she had said, not planted. Rena made note of that because it brought the strangest image to mind, a sprawling broad tree like the tree of life in the middle of town, a spaceship's beam sizzling down.

"Or Talbot," the old woman said a moment later while Rena was browsing.

"Or maybe it was Tabbott," she said, just as Rena was going out the library door, with the door-bells tinkling.

★   ★   ★

The Fancy House, Tomás had thought of it, as a little boy on his way to fish in the ponds on the weekends and on his way to school in the afternoons – and it had not been nearly so fancy back then, had been somewhat decrepit in fact. And now it was just perfect.

He spent his days walking through the town and beyond. Sometimes he stopped and took an ingenious folding fishing rod from his satchel.

"I'm not looking for work right now," Tomás had several occasions to say. Saying it warmed him. He had never imagined to be in the position, at so young an age, to take a few years off to think and plan. He had expected to work every day, bleary eyed and desperate with need. But the luck had come, because houses in the city were worth so much more than houses in Tabittree.

As though life were dearer there, when in fact it was dearer here than anywhere. Oh, how could he have ever left? He supposed that was what you were supposed to do, if you were smart, flee, but why? A half-ring of hills cupped the north side of town while the south spilled out into fertile fields and pastures. A lazy stream ran through, pooling into ponds loud with birds and, in the evening, frogs. The old folks had liked to eat those frogs, but there didn't seem to be any of that sort of distasteful back-woods business anymore. It seemed now that people drove into the town of Barber for groceries and they probably ordered a great deal of things online as well. No place was an island, after all. Not anymore.

"You will remember things," the teacher had said. Something like that, and he was beginning to, especially with the fishing rod in hand, leaned back against a tree with a blade of stiff grass in his mouth. Beginning to remember.

★   ★   ★

The two of them stood in front of the class, as they'd anticipated doing. They had not expected the room to be so crowded. Someone had brought in more desks since the tour they'd taken with their father.

Their teacher was the very one they had met with Tomás. She introduced them as siblings. Though Gully was darker-skinned, they were both about the same build, with short black hair and wide black eyes. It occurred to them, as they squeezed along narrow paths to assigned desks, that no one here suspected they were stepsiblings.

They had not expected the classmates to favor Gully, but that was what happened, so that all through the many interactions that long first day, Gully kept having to pull Teddie into conversations, kept having to look toward her so that other people might follow the look and see her. If this had ever happened at their last school, Teddie had been the one to do it. Something had shifted.

Gully wondered if, without these efforts, their sister might simply disappear.

★   ★   ★

"I'm worried. I mean the school is fun and all, but we do need to get into college someday," Teddie said over their dinner of fresh-caught fish. "We had like ten recesses today."

"It was five," said Gully, whose body had tensed. The school had been such an unexpected pleasure, and they worried Teddie might ruin things.

"It's better than the public school, I promise," said Tomás, who had graced them with his presence in honor of this first day of school. "Unless you want to be home-schooled," he added, looking to Rena.

She had pulled one of the parlor's brocade wing chairs up to the dining table for her greater comfort and sat there cross-legged with a very full glass of wine in hand. Whatever else was going on with her, this new happiness was something all of them savored and felt grateful for.

She said, "In my humble opinion, a little relaxation is not the worst thing."

They did agree.

*　　*　　*

Rena and Tomás sat in a porch swing looking out at the acres of jungle with the purple-brown mountains beyond. The day was more humid than any so far, and more than ever it felt that the scene before them was printed or embroidered onto fabric. The closer the air, the closer the scene.

"It's so lovely, it doesn't seem real," Rena said.

"It doesn't seem real because you haven't walked out that way, have you?" said Tomás.

She'd set herself a new, firm limit on wine and so she was quite sober. If she'd had a couple of glasses, it might have felt more normal to take Tomás's hand and then drop it to hold the stair rail, but as things were it felt overstimulating, the light too stark and the printed scene looming judgmentally.

They moved single-file down the steps and onto a vague path with ferns at its edges, little wildflowers, wood-litter and rocks. The path disappeared in undergrowth, but he kept them going straight, stooping under trees and rounding bushes from time to time. Things were blurred as in mid-distance, even up close. It was the air.

They walked a long time and heard many birds but saw no crawling animals.

Tears came to Tomás's eyes for no clear reason. He felt he needed to speak before he lost control of his voice. "It's all right," he said. "You can do this every day if you like. Not all day, maybe, but every day walk out here and have a good soak. The path will make itself if you do it. I think it would be good."

"A soak?"

But she already heard the warm water flowing out of rock ahead and smelled the hint of sulfur. It might have been a natural hot spring pool at one time, but rocks had been laid in patterns around the edges later on so she knew people had soaked here for a long while.

Tomás felt close with her, but he felt far away, too. It made him want to walk ahead, maybe loop around toward his fishing hole, and in fact he should have walked away, but instead he took the things from his satchel. He spread the blanket on the damp grasses. He laid out the towels, loosened his tie.

After that, it was all a rush: stripping, entering the pool, kissing her deeply like he had when the marriage was young. The kissing went on a long time like sucking hard candy so slowly. He brought them out of the pool onto the blanket. He knew what he was doing and kept himself deep inside, which she loved, but when the time came to pull out, he plowed deeper still, and her spasms were harder than ever before. Like clenching fists. She started to push away and then she pulled him hard against her so that he knew.

"That was not smart," she said, after. "You know you need to be a full year past your last period before you're safe."

But this is what would make her safe. He felt it.

Somehow, he knew not how, this was what had already made her safe.

* * *

After lunch and the third recess, they started a mural on the side of the school, a lovely forest scene that, when it was done, if it was good, would make the school almost invisible. The teacher insisted that when they did the low parts, they did not stoop but instead maintained a flat-footed squat. Their teacher's husband hung around just going off about "P.E. and art at the same time, kiddos. Looking good, looking good." He came around a lot, always sort of cheerleading the teacher's efforts. Gully thought it quite sweet, but it was one of the many things that bothered Teddie.

"Art, well *sure* it's art. What else would you call it?" the teacher's husband said, like someone had challenged his point. Gully watched the teacher walking out towards the woods. She liked everyone to pee outside when they could – something about the septic system – but Teddie took the opportunity to sneak inside.

"Art, you know, *art*," said the teacher's husband. He didn't make note of Teddie leaving, but the teacher did just as soon as she came back and caught Gully, for once, alone. She squatted down next to them. This teacher was always beaming, and now she beamed a little more brightly than usual. "You're doing *great*," she said, though Gully hadn't done much besides a tentative stippling of green.

"Teddie just needed something from, uh, inside," said Gully.

"*Great*," said the teacher, offering Gully a hand up. "I've been meaning to see how you're doing."

"Great," said Gully, making an effort to beam too because it really was true. Everything felt right here. There was none of the stress and pull of the city, and everyone so welcoming, and this schoolwork like nothing they had encountered before, so fitting to Gully's propensities.

"Let's stretch those legs a bit," the teacher said, and Gully turned away from the school doors so they'd not catch Teddie coming out. Protecting Teddie was one of Gully's strongest impulses.

They walked a long while in a prairie-like clearing and into the woods. The teacher talked, and Gully answered, feeling only half awake.

"And so how are you feeling, really?"

"You'll remember things – if you haven't already…"

And Gully had one firm, clear image: their hand stroking a mountain, grasping a mountain and feeling it give.

"Your sister, what can you tell me…"

"Well, she'll remember soon enough, too."

★   ★   ★

Gully and Tomás sat in the porch swing looking out at the acres of greenery while Rena, unconscious of being watched, skipped along her path toward the hot spring pool. She wore a sagging fuchsia one-piece. Her trail was already walked quite clear.

"It's a fantastic school," said Tomás.

"It is, truly," said Gully, who had never in life been so solemn or felt so familiar with Tomás. He was a good father, generally, as far as that went, and yet there had never been all that much between them. Now it felt like there was something unspoken.

"I hear that Teddie's not getting on quite as well," said Tomás and then more softly, "Are you remembering anything yet?"

Gully didn't answer but watched Rena laying out her blanket. It seemed wrong that, as long and as far as she must have walked, they still saw her clearly.

"Little animals, both of them," Tomás said. "That teacher of yours thought Teddie was mine all this time. I corrected that misconception, of course."

Teddie was up in her room where she stayed so often now. She read and drew, but Gully thought the bulk of her time was spent reconnecting with friends online. Probably complaining about Tabittree and their little school she hated and that Gully found so dear.

Rena was lying back on the blanket now, easing her shoulder-straps down. Gully felt uncomfortable watching and turned to Tomás. "I haven't ever been here before, have I? Before we moved in, I mean."

"My God, she seems so close, doesn't she? Like a tiny little figure on a curtain pattern, like you could reach out and touch her." Tomás winked at Gully.

"I don't think she knows we're watching. We ought to...you know, privacy."

"You wouldn't blush, you wouldn't walk away, if you saw a beautiful horse prancing around in the yard. Not that I'm saying she's so beautiful anymore."

"I'm feeling uncomfortable right now," said Gully. Oh, they were terribly uncomfortable. Skin cold and crawling.

"Maybe not a beautiful horse. Maybe an old nag. I mean, she nags, a *lot*. Weren't you the one to point that out, actually?"

And Gully's cheeks grew hot. They had talked about that early on. Years ago, Gully had spoken against Rena and was ashamed of it now.

Firmly, Tomás said, "Reach out and touch her."

Gully smiled, looked down. Tomás gripped Gully's hand and brought it partway up, leaving his child to raise it the rest of the way of their own volition. Still the uncomfortable smile, but Gully raised the hand to eye level and lined up the fingertip with one of her pale, bare, distant kneecaps.

Deep in the forest, Rena's shrieks rang out.

★ ★ ★

"I think you better stay home sick tomorrow," Gully said one long afternoon near equinox. They were curled at either end of Teddie's window seat watching the town bustle along below them. Some of the trees had turned gold, orange, and pink.

"They *have* been saying I don't look well," said Teddie. "'Are you all right? You look pale,' and things like that."

"You seem fine."

Teddie squinted. "I seem fine, but I should stay home sick tomorrow?"

Oh, she was like a little animal, wasn't she? Dear and sweet as ever, but lacking some ability to make her fully—

No, Gully decided. That was a terrible thing to think. They would not think it.

"You better be sick for the rest of the year, actually," they said.

Teddie's lip quivered, and she pushed her foot against Gully's. "Why? What is it?"

"It's nothing," said Gully.

"I don't want to be like *she* is." A glance down. She meant Rena. "I don't want to lose my mind."

"Then stay home tomorrow."

"Why?"

Because tomorrow we will sit in a circle and try to imagine we are moving outside of time.

"Because you look pale."

*   *   *

"Something touched me, out there," Rena said as they drifted toward sleep.

Tomás rubbed her shoulder and shushed her. He pulled her close, stroked her bare, rounding belly.

*   *   *

"I'm not, but if I were, you and I would be going on a trip, don't doubt that," Rena said in the kitchen. Teddie heard it because the walls were not so thick as everyone thought.

"Don't say that," said Tomás.

"Of course I'll say that. I'll say what I want." She whispered, "You know I never wanted…I only wanted Teddie. That's it and that's all."

"I said don't say things like that."

"Surely the old women around here have herbs and things. I know what these people are like. I know. But that's not even what I want. I want to take the car, and you can stay here and look after the kids."

"Herbs and things? Sweetheart, you're not making sense."

"Oh, you know what I mean. What was that in *Hamlet*?"

"What?"

"Oh, Ophelia lists off all these flowers. I could have sworn I'd memorized it. My head is all fizzy."

"It is. *Fuzzy*, though."

"What?"

"Fuzzy. You shouldn't be making any decisions in this state of mind."

* * *

Tomás and Gully sat in Adirondack chairs looking out from the front porch, down at Teddie and Rena planting bulbs around the base of a tree.

"They look the same, but the one is a vessel for something greater. Mine is precious and the other is just—"

"I'm not going to listen to this," said Gully, standing.

"You'll understand. It takes time. There's nothing you can do to rush it. Just go to school. Those are good folks. Like us."

"Okay," said Gully with a little of the edge they used to always have before coming to Tabittree.

"Like us," Tomás said again, but Gully had gone inside.

* * *

They were curled at either end of Teddie's window seat watching trick-or-treaters hustling along amongst the purple and orange lights and the gold and pink trees.

"I think you should leave here," said Gully.

Teddie's eyes went wide. "I have nowhere to go."

"Take your mother and leave here. She'll get better once you're gone."

Teddie scooted closer, whispering, "Can't you tell me?" but Rena had come up the stairs, was peering through the railing.

"Something touched me," Rena said. "When I was out having my soak. Not just today, the last few times. I'm afraid to go out there now."

"Go lie down, Mom," Teddie said. "I'll bring you tea."

Rena stood for a moment and turned back down the stairs.

"Tell me," said Teddie, and Gully did try. Rushed and confused, Gully tried:

The school wasn't pretending to be a regular school now that Teddie was gone, now that all the kids were starting to remember things. Gully was slow to remember, maybe the slowest, but there were still little hints of things. The mountain – they'd held a mountain in their hand and crushed it once, in some other life. They'd sewn or woven something once. It had to do with time and space, finding a way to see past them. It wasn't easy for anyone, not even the teachers. They were all beginners, really. All they did was try to find the ways to make it happen. Sitting in a circle either out in the forest or on the classroom floor, they did that a lot now. The desks had been moved out. Sometimes the forest would start to lean in on them, like it was inhaling, and things far away became close. Sometimes they would touch things far away, or speak – that was another thing they tried – one would stand many yards away and the other try to whisper in their ear. They would do other things, things that were hard to remember.

They would try talking about their progress, but the talk was all empty. "Are you doing well? Are you remembering?"

And so there wasn't anything much to tell. But there was a sense of something greater coming, something real.

And, yes, something had touched Rena in the forest. Gully had touched her but only once and was so sorry. Telling this, Gully started to cry. The other times, it must have been Tomás or someone else. And Tomás was the one who had lost his mind. Not Rena. Oh, Teddie really ought to take Rena and go while they still could.

"I can't really even drive," Teddie said, the tears streaming down her cheeks too now.

"You're going to have to try," said Gully. "Now go and get Mom some tea."

Gully had never called her Mom before.

*   *   *

Rena whispered, "Tabby Street was what the old woman at the grocery store said."

"What's that mean?" said Teddie, though she guessed. It would be like a red light district, wouldn't it, like a whorehouse was a cat house?

★   ★   ★

"Tonight your parents will be here," said the teacher. "Or, some of them might not be, but each of you will have someone here, that's the thing. And we'll do this like we have been, only the adults will be there too. It will be much more powerful that way, can't you imagine? We'll go all the way."

"We'll have a breakthrough," said the teacher's husband.

"What about my mom?" said Gully.

The teacher smiled and nodded. She touched her belly.

"What about Teddie?"

They turned their eyes down to the grass.

The teacher said, "Tapestry was the original name for the town because that's what the landscape looks like, a lush dark tapestry. But it was always more than that. This was a place that flattened, or could flatten, so that the space before you shortened, so that it looked like figures embroidered or woven into fabric. Everyone senses that, even people like your mom and Teddie can sense that, all the people in the public school and all the rest. But we are special. We don't just see this place. We navigate it."

"And who is 'we'?" said Gully. "What's different about us?'

"We don't know that just yet," said the teacher.

"We're all just beginners," said one of the younger children. It was something they had all been saying.

"I think we're fairies," said a girl who reminded Gully of Teddie. How was it this girl could stay and their dear Teddie had to leave?

"I think we're gods," said a boy and the others thought it too. Gully saw that in their quiet attention. No one had spoken so brazenly before. It was the night coming up, making them careless and bold.

"My dad says the people of Tabbitree, the important ones anyway, were all called back together," said another child.

The teacher's husband nodded; the teacher nodded. They were about to move off toward separate spaces to read, to comb their hair, to nap and otherwise save their energy for the night ahead.

They were just about to rest when the parents began arriving, Tomás among the first of them.

Gully felt the tug toward their father's power, the wish to be allied with such a force. Nothing of the old Tomás remained now, or was that right? It remained, perhaps but was only held off, as Gully held off so much now.

Their work was not supposed to happen until night, but here it was not yet dusk and the forest already shuddered and gasped around them. A thunderous feeling in the guts and some turned away from the circle to vomit, and some who were stronger moved away from the group to heave, returning more eager than before.

A great discomfort fell over Gully. Was this feeling something to overcome, or was it a guiding hand?

They looked at the father beside them and felt he was so massive, so distant, it would take hours to run to his side. Tomás's eyes burned orange. Gully's guts twisted, and they moved away from the circle.

*　　*　　*

Rena and Teddie sat in the porch swing looking out at the near-winter jungle. They thought that Tomás would be coming home soon, and Teddie had already packed some things into Rena's trunk. All to do now was the convincing.

"I think Tabittree must come from tapestry," said Teddie.

"Yes, that's exactly right," said Rena. "Exactly that." The trees were drawn in silvery floss on a deep green velvet, the ground-cover leaves were tiny little stitches and the pebbles were loops of thicker thread.

"Because sometimes something comes to the forefront that you wouldn't know was there," said Teddie.

"It's so lovely here," said Rena with a pained smile.

"It is," sighed Teddie.

"But we have to go, don't we?"

"We do, and now," said Teddie. "Can you drive at all?"

"I'll do it," said Gully.

They turned.

Gully wore a heavy backpack. They reached out and took their mom's hand, saying, "I'll drive."

Teddie hugged them, Rena too, but quickly. They didn't lock or even shut the doors as they hurried through the hall, across the porch, down the steps.

"Tomás will be here," Rena said.

"He won't. They started early," said Gully. They were already getting in the car, anyway.

Gully drove down the steep drive. A couple of turns and they were out of town. They watched the rearview windows for a while, watched the fabric of Tabittree seem to pull and fold, and after the fires started, they didn't watch. They looked forward.

A moment more and they were under the snarled-lace canopy, all brilliant orange now.

"Last night I dreamed I went to Tabittree again," said Rena with a bitter laugh.

And Gully said, "Fuck that."

CHICORY

My first time running out of gas, I don't explode or even cuss. No rescue coming; the phone's already dead. That's why I ran out of gas in the first place – no maps. Always terrible with direction, I ought to be grateful this is the first time.

The high desert highway mesmerizes, you see. Hours roll out under the scorching sky. Hills scattered with the same sagebrush and bleached grasses. You go up a rise, and there's a roadcut of russet-black stone shaped like an eyebrow window, maybe a dark table shape in the distance, and you go down the hill until you can't see the distance anymore. From time to time you pass an abandoned structure, a broken fence, an exit for a town. Mirages stop appearing, and the sky begins to pink. You realize you're off track and turn back. You run out of gas.

It's a dry hundred-degree day, the sun at three or four, light movement in the air. Could be worse. I cross my purse over my chest, roll up the windows, and lock the doors. I think of my sneakers' white bubblegum soles and imagine plucking out all the rocks and goat-heads at the end of this mess. Maybe I'll just throw them away.

The first time I came out this way, I thought everything so alien. Deep winter, sun bright on snow that melted the next day to reveal green-gray expanses and those sinister roadcuts.

I walk level for a time, and then down very gently, then up. I know I'm headed up only because the fronts of my legs burn. Nothing changes, just sagebrush and dead grass and the reddish-black masses of rock. Faded blacktop and soil at the sides like light-brown sugar mixed with ashes.

The sagebrush smells sharp and then fades. Insects lift out of the grass and then lizards poke in from the road's edges. The sky dims, but as I focus on the horizon, it whitens. I just know I left my sunglasses back at the diner but grope through the purse one more time. The crunching at my feet makes me think of those lunchtime nachos. It has to be close to suppertime now.

The road is gravel. It happened so gradually I kept saying that it was not happening, but there's no denying it now. I'm sweating, dry as it is. Pissed at myself, as I so often am.

I think of the first time I rode through the desert, Mom and Dad murmuring in the front seat and the word *mirage* catching my attention.

I'm hot now, but I feel such a shiver. Arm hairs rise and, well, my nipples tighten.

Because the mirage pointed out that day in the car – the watery shimmer that disappears as you approach – that was what I'd been seeing *all* day, but this one up ahead kept getting closer and clearer. Actual water with something living at its edges, which as I approach reveals itself to be a spindly wildflower with a purple spire. Two months ago, they might have bloomed here, but now?

I stand at the puddle for a time. It's mostly seeped into the gravel, and the sun will take care of the rest. A small lizard gets its drink before I turn away, and when I look back, there's just a dark stain.

My thighs burn as the road angles up. When it levels again, many purple and yellow flowers speckle a valley. A lone Russian olive stands a driveway's length from the road. The next rise is edged in brutal rock. Then a spray of blue dots. When I reach them, my stomach drops.

Chicory. It should grow on abandoned lots in Midwestern cities. It is very wrong here. I grasp the stem. Too soft. I know I'll feel guilty, but I jerk up the plant and toss it as far as I can. A breeze comes, wafting the first hints of honeysuckle down from the rise.

★   ★   ★

Maybe I should turn back, but I don't. I climb. Scraggly trees grow in a line below – a creek or a river, even – and too soon the road leads through them. The air grows humid.

I walk faster. Honeysuckle strangles a broken-off fence; a single fern sprawls in the Y of the road. I smell tree blossoms but can't look up (dogwood?); I don't want to know. I take the left – always do – and soon I have to lean back to keep from stumbling ahead too fast. Ferns and moss-covered wood line the road, which I can't deny is just rutted earth. No sign of gravel.

Trees intrude, some robed in moss. One holds out a red bundle of seed. If I stop and take it in my hand, I'll see it's something like millet, powdery on the skin and tart in the mouth, but I don't stop. I don't slow. My shoes feel damp inside. I don't look down.

A dark salamander flicks from a puddle onto thick blue-green grass. I hurry, holding myself stiff to keep from sprawling down. The sweat on my arms, like oil now, doesn't cool me.

The road turns sharply right and levels, revealing a broad driveway, muddy like the road. A cabin crouches at its end behind cherries, wild roses, creeping vine. As I approach, green claws reach out of the driveway. I run breathless to the porch, knock at the door. I look back to catch bulbs coming up in the yard. The forest spills out for miles, green now but going orange.

I knock again, press my forehead to the window to see nothing but an orange back wall, the dark edges of a cluttered room.

I turn in time to catch red and yellow tulips pushing out of their green spikes. Violets and forget-me-nots follow, buttercups, dandelions. Through the trees, I catch flashes of silver and glass from a vehicle barreling down the road. I lean back into the door, and when it gives, I turn inside.

THE CHILDREN OF ROBBIE

The house was moved to this street a few years ago when they widened
Falls. Oh yeah, they moved it at night. I sat out on my front porch and
watched it come down Maple. It was a big production, closed the road.
The people who owned the house at the time had most of their lawn in
the easement. They would have had sidewalk just a couple of feet from
the door, and so they moved the house down to this corner and sold the
lot. The lot eventually became a Stinker gas station, but it stood empty
a while.

I'm telling about Robbie's children, but in order to see it, you need to
see the house where Robbie and his human family lived.

It didn't seem like the house would ever look right. Most of the
houses around here are ranches. A couple of the old ones are the original
clapboard bungalows from the twenties, but this is a full-sized farmhouse,
must have five bedrooms, screen porch on the bottom, gabled roof. I
never have gone inside it yet. It stood there just a week or two before they
were planting bare-root roses and bearded irises all around it, throwing
handfuls of wildflower mix all over. Planting trees. It's real pretty now,
like having a bed and breakfast right on the street. The family working on
it moved in. They had kids of all ages, like an old-time farm family.

Sweet, fearless kids, fit and healthy – like farm kids. Not like the kids
that get brought up in the city.

One day, about a year from the time they moved in, the biggest
teenage boy comes running out of the house in his swim trunks, no shoes,
chasing after the dog. They have an above-ground pool in the back.

"Robbie, Robbie," he's calling. At first it's stern, "Robbie, you get
back here," like he's commanding the dog. Then he's pleading, whining.
The dog's headed toward Springfield, which is busy in the morning.

It was a weekday morning, summer. The kids were off but everybody else was still working.

A dog that age would have been neutered, usually, in the city. Maybe they were in violation of something, I don't know. He must have been a year and a half, maybe two. The kid was out half the day looking for him.

Apparently they didn't have the missing dog up on the neighborhood app. My wife thought that was funny, a house with teenagers like that. I told her it was just because they were country kids. She didn't buy that.

★   ★   ★

Robbie, meanwhile, had not risked crossing Springfield. He *knew* that was a busy street. What he did was veer left. He tucked butt – and it was glorious. Imagine never having run when you weren't on the leash or in the fenced backyard, and then you're finally out in what you think is nature. People wouldn't be able to do it like that. They'd get winded. But a dog has instinct. It's the same reason they can swim first time they try.

He flew on a residential street parallel to Springfield, headed toward the five-lane road that everyone takes to get on the connector. Holy shit! He's halfway across before he realizes where he is, and there are cars bearing down on him, easing on the brakes because they don't want to get rear-ended. He's a big dog, some kind of Lab mix. They don't want to hit him, but it's close. He just keeps going. He makes it.

Imagine the terror, halfway across. He's a brave dog, but he's a smart dog. By the time he's crossed, he's no longer thinking about the freedom. He's thinking about his big comfortable house and all the pretty boys and girls who feed him under the table. Or no, not yet. He'll be thinking about that soon but not yet, because he's just caught a scent.

It's the best thing he's ever smelled. It's that favorite dinner you smell when you've come home from a hard day, the smell of whatever perfume gets you titillated, some person you've desperately missed and come back to. If you haven't guessed, it's the smell of a lady dog. He's never in his life smelled this smell.

He's got a good nose, but it takes a while. He gets in a yard where there are chickens. A lady there thinks he's after the chickens and starts growling to scare him, picks up a stick. He flees down an alley and through a shed to a wet, shaded space. He smells her close. She's here, somewhere.

It could not be more romantic. There are all these sweet, delicate flowers like bleeding hearts and forget-me-nots, columbine, lily of the valley, with a lot of grass coming up between them. Robbie doesn't know the names of the flowers, but he gets the overall atmosphere. This was someone's sacred space, but now they're gone, they're dead or maybe inside the house, depressed, watching the Netflick.

Robbie's adrenaline is pumping, blood is pumping hard, and before you know it, *he's* pumping into the softest, sweetest bitch anyone ever heard of. He's never pumped into any sentient creature before. She's tan-gold, fluffy, large. It's all over before he can take in her features. The feeling coursing through him is the sweetest feeling he's ever had, all through his body. He can no longer smell her so strong. He's contented, elated. They are still connected. They pant together until it is safe to separate, and then she lies down and begins to lick herself. He follows suit.

Robbie sleeps the rest of the day. When he gets up to water the flowers, she's gone. Sometime late in the night, the traffic on the five-lane road dies down enough so he can begin the march home. He's bobbing along, thinking, *Is my family where I left them? Do they still love me?* All those things you'd think, coming home like that.

He scratches on the front door, someone comes, and there are cheers a minute later.

★   ★   ★

Robbie doesn't think about the lady dog again. He sometimes thinks about the running. They take him to the vet, and he thinks about that a little less.

Summer is all it's meant to be. The kids – there must be five or six of them. I never can tell who all belongs there and which ones might be friends or cousins – they swim in the morning, they go for walks up to the grocery store for their parents, mow the lawn. They're always moving. They're happy.

My wife thinks their parents shouldn't let them get so tan. They're an anachronistic family, all around. The dad lets them ride in the bed of the truck sometimes. I'm pretty sure that's illegal. They don't wear seatbelts. The dad smokes, even smokes inside the house, I'm told.

I don't think it's so bad to grow up like that. I loved riding in the back of a truck when I was a kid. I can't think of a lot of things I'd give that up for.

Summer lingers, summer flies. The mom takes them all to get clothes. I see them, each with their bags, and I know what's in them are sensible clothes to keep them looking well-cared for, no designer shit, and not too much of it. I think they're a model family all around. I tell my wife this, and she sighs like it's something against her. I'm in the doghouse.

Meanwhile, Robbie hasn't even spared a thought for the lady dog. He's been caught up in the best summer of his life. The most eventful summer, anyway. There was the run and the mating, the surgery, but he's also been swimming every time the kids do, guarding the house at night, digging in the lawn, walks. It's been busy.

One evening on a walk at the end of the summer, he and the teenage boy happen to take that street parallel to Springfield, the one that comes out unexpectedly onto the big five-lane road. The dog's scared as hell, but there's a crosswalk on the next block, and the boy takes it no problem, and when they get to the other side, Robbie sees her.

She's not in the road, but she's not far from it. She's been struck and crawled over to here, he thinks, but it isn't clear that's what happened. I think something else must have gotten her. I can't imagine she would have walked into the road, no way.

Whatever happened, she's at the back of a weedy parking lot close to a red-painted fence, close to a dumpster. Her fluffy tan-gold fur blows around in a breeze.

He sees the pink belly with the teats swelled like fingers.

He's been walked past the scene before he can register what it means to him, but he's a smart dog. He gets there right away: Robbie's children are out there somewhere in the night, whimpering, starving.

I'd like to say he got loose right then and was smart enough to lead the kid straight to them, but it didn't happen like that. He bawled and tried to pull away. He played a mule and just sat there. He tried, but what can a dog, even a big dog, do against a boy the size of a grown man, one that has him around the throat? He wasn't going to bite the kid. He couldn't do anything, and he knew it. They went home.

How he fretted. He wouldn't let them – nor us – sleep that night. He cried to go out, each time pacing to all the places he had at one time or another thought might be an escape route, but the backyard was tight. It wasn't going to happen.

His chance comes when the dad goes out to get the paper – they still had the paper delivered, which my wife had remarked upon, I assure you. The dad opens the door in his underwear and an open robe. The dad isn't the kid. He shouts at the running-away dog to F himself and goes back inside.

Robbie takes it slow. He's their only hope, he knows. He finds a backyard near the crossing and lies there waiting for rush hour to die down. Then when he crosses, he does it where he and the boy crossed. He makes his way to the alley no problem after that. It's brunchtime when he gets there.

The hidden garden has not been watered all summer. The flowers are going to seed, grasses high and browning at the tips. It's too hot for puppies. He goes to the corner where he and the lady dog had lain down to lick themselves, and there is nothing. The grass isn't even trampled. It's like they were never there.

Flies circle something in the corner, but it's just a dark, dry poo. He knew what it was before checking, but he still felt the dread of it deep inside him.

He catches their scent just then. He moves toward a wall with flaking paint at the end of the garden. He hears a small, weak something moan in its sleep.

The babies were in the shed, far back in a corner behind a stack of potting soil, on an old dog bed with a towel on it. Three small human babies and one big boy puppy that looked a little bit like Robbie when he was a puppy. They slept fitfully, all curled together. It would have been dangerously hot in the shed except for a box fan running in the window.

Robbie tried to hold his breath, to keep himself from whimpering. The scene felt wrong to him, like the lady dog had been set up in this place and the human who set her up there might be somewhere near. Deep fright, then. He went and peeked out the door. He saw the run-down pink house just past a weedy stretch of yard.

If he had thought about the lady dog even a little bit, he'd thought of her as a stray. Could this be her home, her human family? What kind of a human family might leave four babies on the floor of a shed?

Robbie hadn't thought about his next move, but he'd have guessed the next move to be to find any decent-looking human and cry to them about the puppies, and trust them to check his tags and take him and his puppies back to his human family. Now this would be impossible.

If he cried out now, couldn't it happen that a sadistic person might come out of that house and take all of the puppies inside? Or simply shut the door of the shed, kick him away from there? No, he had to move them himself.

He picked up the boy puppy. Don't be too hard on Robbie for his choice. It wasn't because this puppy was so clearly his own boy. It was more that he sensed it would not hurt this puppy to be taken by the scruff.

Robbie stalked slowly out of the shed, through the forgotten garden, out to the alley. All the time he was carrying the puppy (who ended up being named Robinson because apparently Robbie's real name was Robin), he felt crushing guilt over the puppies left behind, and a real urgency to get home. He felt that he would never be able to cross the street carrying Robinson, let alone get out again afterward and somehow shuttle the others across. It was an impossible task. He thought if he could only just get Robinson home, that would be enough. He could die in the road as long as that was done first. And then, of course, after that thought the guilt came crushing down again because all of the puppies needed him, not just this one who looked like him.

It was a miracle, then, when he saw, on the other side of the busy road, a lanky figure striding.

Robbie set his son in the dirt and howled out to the boy. The boy heard him.

★   ★   ★

My wife says this is a tall tale, but I swear I saw it. It was noon, sun blazing, everyone inside with the air conditioners running. I was the only one sitting out on a front porch. I don't know why, guess I never got used to sitting inside on a beautiful day.

They came down Maple, the boy's end of the leash loose in his elbow-crook because the dog wasn't pulling. He was just walking along with that happy look dogs have when there isn't much wrong with the world. Held tight against the boy's chest were the puppy that would be named Robinson and three little baby girls. They were smaller than babies ought to be. One of them had a little orangey down on her head. They all went straight into the house, and no one came out again for the rest of the day. The little kids didn't even come back out for a swim in the evening.

For a long time, I would say things to my wife, like, "Those three youngest of theirs are not like the rest," but now I'm not so sure. The babies are toddlers now, and Robinson is a half-grown pup. He's naughty. I think he's smarter than anyone realizes.

The toddlers do look a little weird. They're skinnier than they ought to be, which was my evidence when I used to make the point about them being different from the rest. But every day they're a little less skinny. In a year or two I think they might be as robust as the rest of the family.

No one seems to have asked how the house one day had five or six kids and the next day had eight or nine. They say people can't count so well over a certain number, which I don't know about. They say people don't know their neighbors anymore, and I can attest to that.

They have plenty of room for them all. They keep the place up. I don't know why I care.

It's only when Robinson comes around, I start to wonder. They can't seem to keep him fenced, and when he gets out, he always seems to find me. I'll sit down with him and tell him a story. He'll tell me one.

Most of his stories aren't the sort of thing I can put into words. I've tried to do that with the story of his origin and his rescue. He made that one so simple that even a dummy like me could follow, and he made sure it was sweet and sad so I would like it. Or maybe it's because it was a story his dad told him, is why it's so simple. I don't know. I think Robbie's surely no smarter than I am, but who can say?

Robinson's fur is deep auburn, fluffy. The tips of hairs lighter so that in the sun he has an aura around him. I crave him, hope all day that he'll visit. While he's here with me, I feel fulfilled. Only after he's gone, I'll feel frightened and lonely. I'll feel guilty, like I shouldn't have done it, shouldn't have touched him again.

The biggest boy will cross the street and say, "Is he bothering you again?" and call Robinson back. "I don't know why you always bother that nice man," he'll say, and he'll ruffle the fur on the top of Robinson's head just like he does with the kids.

The story of his origin is one thing. Robinson's other stories are intricate, psychedelic stuff. I pet his back and the shapes and colors and smells come at me. It's like being a little kid again, riding in the bed of the truck, standing up and closing your eyes as you speed along a country road with the light strobing through trees above you. It's like that but more than that. I can't explain. Sometimes I think he's telling me things he can't tell his family, that he's entrusting me with something. Other times, I think he's toying with me just to show how small and helpless and dumb I really am.

I don't argue anymore when the wife says something underhanded about the family. She's wrong, but she's right. She smells something and can't say what it is. One day, I think, I will go inside that house and see something that proves what they are. Until then, how can I say anything against a nice family like that?

THE PACK

I should never have let Lee move us out here. All that time we were hooked into Zillow, I secretly prayed she'd fixate on one with a smaller lot and higher square footage. Instead, we opted for acreage bordering public land, the house little more than an afterthought: one room for living, one for sleeping, one bathroom with the washer and dryer wrenched in, and a sloping lean-to added on to serve as workshop, guest room, storage for dog supplies and yes, kitchen. It was Lee's choice; I couldn't deny her.

Oh, but the outside made up for it those first few years. We were happy. Though there was nothing to see in town, Lee would drive in whenever we wanted and then, this: the thriving garden, the new puppy, the picnics and hikes. Lee trained all three dogs to be safe off-leash, which I'd never thought could happen. I planted flowers everywhere and trained morning glories, wistaria and orange-flowering trumpet vines up the walls to cover the ugly lean-to. We brought a tree guy out to prune the little orchard. The trees thanked us with so much fruit we had to take up canning.

Our bodies changed shape. We grew fatter from all the home cooking while our legs narrowed and toned from hiking and our arms grew brawny from woodcutting and gardening.

The truth was we both felt awfully fit up until Lee started getting the breaks. First was the fractured arm – a yellowjacket stung while she was high on a ladder picking apples. That one could have happened to anyone. It healed up right on schedule and then things just seemed to snowball: a fall on a hike and the ankle was screwed up, and it healed, and then a slip in the bathroom shattered her wrist, then the dogs didn't see Lee while they were running. She took a terrible crash to her ribs. We spent weeks in the city running up bills, not just for the treatments and hospital room but also hotels, food, gas, dog boarding. Osteoporosis, the likely cause, was ruled out early. There didn't seem to be anything wrong with Lee's bones. What was making the accidents happen, then? It seemed like they investigated every little thing, her brain and inner ear to her toe joints. In the end, the experts agreed that the series of breaks had been all coincidence.

Only now, between the lingering pain and the fear, Lee just about couldn't move. I didn't like to focus on it, but the bills would send me back to work. Not just a job (if indeed I could find one) but a commute. Little traffic, one would hope, but bad roads in the winter and deer shooting into the road.

The place was paid for, but I feared we'd lose it if the debt got too bad. Sometimes I felt we had already lost everything and just didn't know it yet. Other times I felt that fear was silly, something that could never happen, a sign of my losing it. We were both getting squirrely, but I tried to hide my own irrationality, tried to be strong for Lee.

Nothing got taken care of all that time. Vegetables froze in the garden, and with the thaw, the vines went wild. New ones with white-and-celadon blossoms joined and then overtook the rest. The trees went unpruned, fruit falling onto the ground, drawing wildlife, freezing and thawing to stink.

The dogs were distressed from being boarded and then neglected at home. I felt I didn't know these creatures who lost their cool chasing things off the property, sending me out into the forest with a flashlight, so helpless and small – scared of falling and breaking something myself, or being shot by a hunter. Even more, I feared that the dogs might be shot or break their legs.

I was always living through worst-case scenarios, it seemed.

I hadn't been afraid of the woods with Lee, but it was different now. The first few times the dogs ran off in the night, I hyperventilated and bawled the whole time I searched. I resolved to chain them, which broke my heart all over again. They sat quietly indoors but would jump up and beg to go out whenever I made a move. They hated the chains but hated more to be inside with us.

Lee stayed in bed sweating and thrashing in terrible nightmares. I slept thinly on the bed's outer edge until Lee begged me to go elsewhere in case I might break her in my sleep. I carried my pillow into the lean-to and headed for the futon where we'd hoped some wandering relative or old friend might sleep one day. I stopped, gasped.

The vines had come inside the lean-to and made themselves at home, coiling around the futon frame, threading into the stove burners, groping into the bag of dog food with their spiny fingers. I'd heated up something or other on the stove not too long ago, so that infestation was new, but the other encroachments might not have been so new. Who'd been paying attention?

Lee hadn't come into this room in a while, either. I recalled that just the other day, she'd said she could not stand to be in the lean-to anymore. Maybe it was too cold?

Certainly drafts swirled in the room. The vines must have compromised the windows. I investigated. Yes, and they'd compromised the floor. The dog food was gone, and I had the strange thought that the vines had eaten it. Up close, their veiny green blossoms were formed like the propeller-seeds of maples – or like dragonfly wings. They had that pearly, iridescent sheen. Just now these blossoms riffled in the breeze inside the lean-to.

I stepped outside and hauled the dogs in by their chains. I stoked the fire, layered their beds and all the couch blankets onto the floor and set about bonding with them, stroking their fur and cooing to them. Dogs forgive. Soon we were a pack again, just the four of us. I regretted Lee being apart from this reconciliation, but I was weary. I coiled into the blankets, and we slept into the afternoon. I would not piece it all together until it was too late, but the vine had already invaded us.

All this time, Lee had one arm hanging off the side of the bed. Something hadn't healed just right, and it eased the pain to get some extra blood into her wrist. The whole arm dangled, tempting the new vines that were just then exploring that space between bed and wall. The vines reached out with grasping tendrils thick as fingers. Lee might have held on to a wiry hand, squeezed it in half-sleep thinking it was me. The hand squeezed back. The hand raked through her sweaty hair on its way to her shoulder. I was puttering around by then, and my feet hit a creaky spot on the floor. Lee moaned, and the hand slipped back to its protected spot between the bed and wall.

"Dogs are out of food," I said from the bedroom doorway. I barely saw Lee in the darkened room and caught no hint of the vine. "I've got to go to town."

I didn't want to drive, didn't want to leave Lee.

"Can you get ginger ale?" she said.

I nodded. Yes, ginger ale, soup, and ice cream. All the foods for sick folks, though Lee wasn't sick. Just aching and scared. And heartsick, same as me.

It was sunny with scattered rain. The dogs enjoyed the ride. I did too. While we sped toward town, the vine repeated its travel up Lee's arm and through her hair, onto her shoulder, over her ribs. Only this time, Lee was awake and staring in awe. Lee's blood moved faster. Maybe the vine heard that or felt it. Felt it, most probably. A pulsing. The vine pulsed back.

While I trudged through the grocery store, the dogs were good. They paced, protecting the car, barking at shoppers who came close to the windows.

While they paced, the vine pushed against certain parts of Lee's body, the places where the breaks had been.

While I stood in the checkout line, a strange shiver went through me. *Lee – Lee's in danger.* Suddenly I needed to hurry home. I fumbled the change the cashier passed to me and left it scattered on the floor.

Another break, that's what I feared.

While the dogs pushed their noses out into speeding air, the vine began entry into the bone. Had it gotten a taste for marrow from the dog food? Or did it already know what it needed to form its fruit and its swarms?

This vine that had infiltrated so much else now plowed its slow way into its first human body. Not *victim.* No one thought of Lee as the victim, neither the vine nor Lee herself. This new thing she hadn't known to fear had come, and it was gentle. It burrowed deep and laid a seed into a crevice of unmended bone. Another seed, another.

While a Miata tailgated so hard I could barely breathe, the first seed sprouted – or egg hatched. It wasn't clear which. Lee felt a thrill. New layered blossoms like corsages opened rapidly from her wrist, from her ribs and leg and arm. She tore off her nightgown to see the wonder of them, celadon green but bordered in rose and gold and a hundred different blues, all rainbow-pearly as oil in puddles. They opened so powerfully that she heard another break. She felt nothing.

The convertible kept veering to pass and then tucking back in behind me. Now, finally, a stretch of empty road opened up. I slowed. It came up alongside – just as a truck entered the road. Someone laid on the horn and I veered, praying. *The dogs, oh, the dogs.*

But we were safe, all of us. We leveled out, slowed onto the shoulder. The red car was far in the distance now. I cried just briefly in relief, the dogs whimpering and licking my neck and face. Dogs have extra senses at times like this.

They felt it, saw it maybe: the anxiety that had held me so long was now dissipated.

While we had our moment on the shoulder, the blossoms grew larger. They grew firm with a lacy coral-like bone. Lee thought of flowers formed of porcelain. The vines that had held her retreated, making her slump and shatter in places. She felt nothing but was aware, watching. Her hand was farther from her body than it had ever been. The wrist was, it seemed, a deep pile of pollen – but animated. Crawling.

Lee was no longer the focus. Whatever happened, on and in her body, was beside the point. One sinewy vine lashed around her mouth, holding her fast to the bedframe, but the rest had moved on, lurking all around the bedroom door, just waiting for the four of us to walk into the room. Maybe the dogs were what it wanted all along, or maybe it would do something novel with my unbroken body. Lee would wait. She would see.

She would speak, soon enough. That last vine would loosen and move on to other entertainments. Later, as I dangled from the ceiling, as the dogs grew their beautiful, terrible wings, as the larval things filled up the air, we would be able to speak, to share notes. What had gone on while I was in town, what would happen next, what did it all mean, how would it end? There was no pain, and so what looked like destruction did not feel like destruction. It felt like a new beginning.

Yes, we would come back together, all five of us now, to share not regret but only wonder.

A WHITE FILIGREE

I ride through dark woods to Grandmother's house as always, but when I arrive, an acre or more of trees have been torn from the ground. Where her house should be, there is nothing but a leaf like that of a philodendron. It is three hundred feet wide, still green and lusty.

My horse wants to shy away home. I force him back to the tree line, tie him. He whinnies as I cross the dry yard.

"I know how you loved the trees, but it needed more sun," Grandma says when she crawls from under the leaf. She touches its tip and it quivers upward, revealing the house cuddled beneath.

She hugs me, saying, "Come see what I've been doing." How svelte she is now!

The house is snug as always though it swims in bright green light instead of skulking under forest shadows. She shows me to the kitchen window where tiny plants are nurtured, says one of them will be mine. They cock their heads at this like puppies. They push back against her hand when she strokes them. I move to touch, but she swats me away.

"Come see the downstairs," she says. I don't remember a downstairs. We move toward her little bedroom where pine walls still stand. Where her little bed was, a hole opens into the earth. She smiles, leads me down steps made of roots. Roots push out of the walls, stroke our shoulders as we descend. When we reach the bottom, the cozy chamber pulses with them.

"Plants want to please us just as much as dogs do," she says, "only I didn't know how to tell them what I wanted until now." She strokes at young white roots in the wall; they push out to cradle her. She shows how they will make a hammock for her, a rocking chair, how they will weave together to make a rustic dining table and benches, how they will push rabbits out of the ground.

Supper is rabbit stew with carrots and potatoes at the table of white filigree. We eat heartily.

"Where did the trees go?" I say.

Grandma places her index and middle fingers on the table in a kneeling position, raises them to standing, walks them away.

"You made them walk away?"

A root unweaves itself from the table and strokes Grandma in a questioning way. "No, not you!" she says. She strokes it urgently until it weaves itself back into the tabletop and falls to rest.

"It thought I was asking it to go away just now," she says to me. And to the root, she says, "I would never, ever do that."

Grandma is soon sleepy. She strokes the roots to make a hammock for her and one for me. I see hers fasten onto her, see it clamp down. She is so comfortable, she says. A thin root snakes into her mouth. She giggles. It tickles so.

I cannot make myself get into my hammock, tempting as it looks. As soon as she sleeps, I make my way out to my horse. I will not come back for a month or two. She'll need nothing more from me until later in autumn, and we'll see then if this thing is evergreen. I think not, but I can't say for sure.

THE SECOND ATTEMPT

A glance after dinner at the tree line and at you, and I know we're going back. I move the swaddled figure from the bottom of my pack into my front pocket. The shape is porcine, ursine, canine? Four-footed, anyway, weighted forward as though moving with leisurely power.

We walk away from camp unseen, or if seen, uncalled for. We are unpopular workmates, you so quick to anger and me your silent goon.

We keep a straight line until we're thick in trees, search another hour for the clearing. We walk over a low hill and down toward this home, this hateful place. In twilight it looks sketched in pen and dark water wash.

"You remember where?" you say. I nod. "Then get to it." You're off to gather wood.

I find the rusted shovel in what was the garden, find the place, bury the thing. You build the fire just off the front steps. Though we planned to see about finding something like a bed, we stretch out on the porch and fall asleep in the firelight.

The thing is still emerging when my eyes open. The fire blazes four feet, higher. The thing is well lit on the other side, but I'm uncertain of its shape. It is birthed now, standing, stretching, coming down with a spring in its joints. It is weighted forward and moving slowly around the fire.

The rest is a confusion of sparks and coarse, strong-smelling fur. We dance with the gentle bear, caress it. Then, its body gone, we feel its force in our muscles. You and I hold hands and dance into the fire. We kick coals onto the porch where they catch. You kick a log through what used to be a window.

Flames rise higher than the stars. When it's all down to shimmering coals, I let my hot eyes fall closed. When I open them, I'm cold on the porch step, the little figure gripped in my hand now a different shape. I wake you with my crying. You comfort me. You promise we can try again.

NIGHT, WHEN WINDOWS TURN TO MIRROR

The wheelchair sat abandoned in the living room beside the coffee table, but that shouldn't have bothered Maxine. Father could walk well enough. He could climb the half-flight of stairs when they visited her brother's split-level, for goodness' sake. He just needed some time, and she needed to stay close in case he faltered.

Maxine knew he was all right, wherever he was. She started his favorite supper, spaghetti with meat sauce. There was powdery parmesan for the garlic bread, only when she checked, there wasn't any bread on the counter. She remembered carrying it into the kitchen, still soft and warm in its paper wrapper.

The air-conditioning whirred, television cackled in the living room, water boiled, the microwave made its grinding noise. All of this going, and still she heard her father say, "Maxine." It wasn't harsh, like a command. If anything, he sounded amused. She went into the living room, and he was not there.

Maxine crossed back through the kitchen to the garage, looked inside, and he was not in the dark back seat of the car, or behind the car. All the time, the television blared from the living room, a game show of some kind with leering, deriding laughter. She crossed back through the living room toward the hall and called, "Father?" in the direction of the bedrooms. He did not respond.

When she finally flicked off the television, all was so quiet that she heard water foam over onto the electric burner. She paced back into the kitchen and heard him call again, just as she touched the hot handle of the saucepan. The call was almost certainly from his bedroom. She took up a towel to move the saucepan off the heat and moved back through the living room, moved down the hall.

Father's bed was made up with the blue quilt, his nightstands cluttered but clean, his recliner empty, television off – all was in order. "Father?" she called. "Are we having a game, then? Should I check the closet?"

She went into the bathroom at the end of the hall. All was in order here, as well as in her bedroom. She barely had to glance inside the rooms to know.

She crossed back through the living room to the kitchen, set the water back on the glowing burner, and found her gaze stopping on the pantry door. She'd forgotten to check the pantry earlier! If this was a game, he would be hiding in the pantry, wouldn't he? She switched on the lights from outside the door and swung the door open to reveal golden pine shelves stocked with brightly colored boxes and cans. No Father, but she said, "Oh, there you are!" to the grocery sack, which had gotten misplaced on the pantry shelf. Inside were the wedge of parmesan, the lovely baguette, the olives and soft butter – all the things she'd meant to use to make the meal. Happily, she brought out the board and knife to cut the bread.

She could not recall buying this slim baguette or placing it in the bag, and the parmesan was not the kind she regularly bought, but they were nice, weren't they? She thought of how good the supper would be. Supper. She smiled about some long-ago campaign she and her brother had been on to modernize the old man's vocabulary, and all the times he teased them saying folksy things in public.

As Maxine sprinkled a mix of herbs and parmesan over the buttered bread, Father called, this time from much farther away. She couldn't make out the words, but he said something longer and this time seemed to laugh or perhaps cough at the end of it. She was annoyed to have to keep cutting off her meal preparations, but the water wasn't about to boil, and so she set off again to find him. When she returned to his room, this time she remembered the closet doors led not to a closet but to a proper dressing room. His dressing table was orderly, shirts and suits hanging all blue and black and gray. Stacks of earth-tone sweaters. He was not behind the dressing table, not stacked in the trunk of summer things.

She could have kicked herself, though, when her eyes focused past his bed to the French doors to his sitting room. How could she have forgotten to check his sitting room? She opened the doors. His leather sofa and armchair stood empty. The tables were clear, just a crystal decanter on one of the end tables. The gas fireplace was on, but she turned it off with the switch on the wall. It was stupid to have the fire running alongside the air-conditioning.

Maxine crossed back to her bedroom, with a quick check in the hall bathroom, which was still clean and empty. She was beginning to get a little worried that Father might not be playing a game. Where could he be? She checked her bedroom again and paced through to her own sitting room, stopping to appreciate the lovely tapestries and the rich wool rugs inside, the little collections of figurines, the glossy plants.

Stroking the fine white leather of her loveseat on her way out of the room, she left a long brown smear – spaghetti sauce! Her sweatshirt cuff was saturated, the skin beneath it cold and slimy, and her hands, now that she noticed, reeked of cheese and garlic. She moved slowly back through her bedroom to her dressing room, just as beautifully decadent as Father's was austere. Fine shoes and dresses lay all out of order, every-colored, a riot of different patterns and sheens.

Maxine pulled off her sweatshirt and tossed it on the floor beside a silk gown, then crossed back out to the hall bathroom to wash and dry her hands before returning for a light-red cashmere sweater. She pulled it on, stroked the shoulders and down the sides, the fabric so soft and warm, and as she did this, her eyes settled on a door.

She moved deeper into her closet and opened the door to her private bathroom. It was all luxurious clothes and bath products strewn across the marble floor and vanity top. The sunken tub was half full of cooling lavender-scented water. As she reached in to take the washcloth out of the drain, it occurred to Maxine that she had not done a thorough search of Father's rooms.

Annoyed with herself for overlooking things, Maxine went back through the hall, bedroom, and dressing room to the door of his private bathroom. She knocked quietly, called, "Anyone in there?" and rolled up her sleeves before opening the door. His toilet, shower stall, and sink stood bare and blank. His own deep bathtub was filled with fragrant, milky water into which she reached and, dreading something, swept through with her hand before pulling the plug. Bending over made the blood pulse in her ears, and the cold water on her arm made her feel strange. She dried her arm and pulled the sweater over it, hoping she'd not stretched the sleeve out of shape.

Maxine crossed out into the hall and through the living room, but this time instead of going directly into the kitchen, she stepped down into the sunken family room. The pillows on the red leather sectional were tidy, coffee table dusted, rugs clean. There was some space behind the sectional, so she leaned over the seat to check that area. She saw a three-foot-deep stretch of oak floor behind it, glossy and bare. Maxine was getting to be perplexed and a little queasy now.

She went back to the kitchen. This time, the water boiled hard. She finally put in the spaghetti and salt, set the timer. She wanted to start the broiler for the bread but was afraid he might call out again. She didn't want to burn the bread. For that matter, she thought, she should take the spaghetti off the burner. But then she wouldn't be able to time it correctly. The spaghetti would overcook.

She tried to remember when and where she had last seen Father, but that was difficult to say. She wanted to say they had just been watching television in the living room, she on the sofa with an afghan on her legs and he in the wheelchair beside the coffee table. That seemed likely because it was what they generally did before supper, but if it were true, then wouldn't she remember the program? She couldn't remember it for the life of her. She tried to recall what had been so annoying about it that she'd needed to turn it off.

She searched her mind for what other part of the house she might need to check, when from very far away she heard him. This time, there *was* urgency in his voice. A sentence or two, something he needed her to know. She could not make out words except her name at the very end.

She laughed at herself then, because back when he used to call to her brother Steve, she would always come running, the 'seen' in Maxine sounding like the word 'Steve' when yelled in that way, from far away. She would arrive before Father and see she hadn't been the one he beckoned.

Her name came again, so far away but insistent. There were still five minutes left on the spaghetti, so she moved once more toward his bedroom. This direction called to her more than the others. She moved through the bedroom to the sitting room again, and then she could have kicked herself. She hadn't bothered to move past his sittingroom chair and sofa to the second set of double doors that led into his study. She grasped their handles, swung them wide – feeling triumphant – and saw his desk was orderly, computer on and running a screensaver, nets of rainbow color like string art, but he was not there. Maxine turned off the computer by holding down the power button. She sighed.

It seemed to her that Father had always been in this room, and that this was the room in which he should be hiding if he were playing a game. She peeked under the desk. She pulled out a filing cabinet drawer. The wood was a hard, lustrous brown, the motion of the drawer so smooth. *What a beautiful piece,* she thought.

In the kitchen, the oven timer made its weak trill; she hadn't heard it. Spaghetti strands bubbled up in over-thick water. She was so hungry, and now she had to see if there was any more pasta. She went into the pantry. The food was all orderly but the pantry so deep and so dark that she had to spend some time checking. When she came to the back wall of the pantry, she opened the door to the freezer room. An immense freezer on one wall, shelves on the other with big boxes of toilet paper, kitty litter, detergent. On seeing the litter, she called, "Here kitty, kitty," in a halfhearted way.

A headache was starting, and a slick cool sweat along her back. She wasn't comfortable here in this room. Its distance from the kitchen suggested it must lie at the outside edge of the house, but it felt like the narrow bowels of the house, close and dank as a basement. Maxine stopped and took three deep, slow breaths to calm herself. This was the kind of room she might have bolted from without reason as a child, but she was an adult. She opened the freezer and took her time selecting a sack of ravioli, a package of sausage, a pound of ground beef wrapped in white paper.

In the kitchen, she set the things out on the counter. When she went to thaw the meat, she saw that the microwave held a glass dish full of lukewarm sauce. When she lifted the lid, the smell reminded her of the brown-red smear she'd made on the loveseat. She didn't think it was still all right, and besides, she'd seen better sauces in the pantry, or in the freezer there were perhaps tubs of even better sauce. She moved back through the pantry to the freezer room, but this time, before she could open the freezer, she thought of wine. She opened the door leading from the freezer room to the wine cellar and carefully moved down its steps. She glanced around the small space just in case Father might be there, then selected something to drink as well as something to splash into the sauce. She brought a lovely jar of sauce from the pantry and sat down in the kitchen to have just one glass of the wine meant for cooking. She had poured it and touched the glass to her lips when he spoke, this time from even farther away and with an echo. "I can't find you," she called. She laughed to herself. She raised the glass again, and this time he called out in an angry shout. She walked slowly into the living room, paused to decide which way to turn. She tended to make right turns, all things being equal, so that sent her into the family room. This time she walked behind the couch and pulled aside the velvet drapes that covered the doors to the indoor pool.

Maxine felt like crying now. She was so very hungry, she was growing so very tired, and she was filled with stress from all the starts she had taken. She told herself she did not worry about Father's well-being, only his location. There was nothing to do but open the French doors. Bright motion-sensor lights came on. The combination of white light and pool chemicals hit her eyes and throat like chopped onions, and the tears came tumbling down.

She cried, too, for the beauty of the pool that lay bright blue before her. The room was so stunning: pure white walls, high ceilings carved with scrollwork and leaves, big potted plants standing here and there. Blue-lit niches in the walls suggested windows, and on the floor, green and blue tiles with arabesque patterns echoed the designs in the ceiling. She walked the pool's perimeter, checking behind each of the fluted columns. A stack of thick towels sat on a white chaise. A white table held a pot of pink succulents.

Maxine must have forgotten how stunning this space was. How was it she did not spend all her time in here? She looked up to the skylights where the sky pressed against the glass like thick black velvet.

She moved to the back wall and noticed between two niches a discreet little door, which she opened to see a modest white one-piece hanging on a wooden hanger from a wooden peg above a wooden slat bench. Maxine imagined between the other niches, other doors. Perhaps a weight room, a dry sauna, a steam sauna. Perhaps a laundry room to provide the fluffy towels. A powder room, a shower or a set of showers. She moved quickly, opening the doors one by one, and it was all as she imagined. And all the rooms empty.

Nothing would be more soothing than to put on the swimsuit and swim, or lie back in a float, but even if Maxine could have stopped thinking about Father for ten minutes – even if she could do that – she was so hungry. She set off back to the kitchen. Make the meal, finally have a drink, relax. Father could be anywhere, and he was really very good at walking.

On the way to the kitchen, however, Maxine realized she had not checked the theater. She moved straight from the family room across the living room and pulled open its dark doors. The theater was so black she couldn't see a thing until she'd twisted up the dimmer switch. The soft light revealed the movie screen and the double rows of tufted tapestry benches, the deeply carpeted steps between them. She wondered at how she and Father had decided to always watch television in the small living room instead of lounging here in greater comfort.

There was movement, then, in the corner of her eye. She moved her head to the left and saw nothing, just a black wall, but she suddenly felt afraid of what might be in or past the theater.

Maxine was afraid but still so tired, so hungry – so overcome with stress – that when she returned to the kitchen, she decided to cook the ravioli and eat it plain with the powdered parmesan and have done with it. She set the water back on the burner and turned it on, just as Father called out – clearly from the direction of the theater!

She rushed back to the doors, and on opening them, from the opposite wall she caught a slip of light, a door closing. She ran through the darkened theater to the door, and opened it, and found herself in a vast hall, low-lit with deco sconces and a wildly patterned carpet. *It's only the lobby*, she told herself, but the thought felt wrong to her. She turned to the right; the hall ran on into darkness. She turned right again and caught the figure – just the back of a leg, a heel – going around a corner. She ran for it, but by the time she'd come to the corner, the person must have rounded another corner. The hall ran on for miles, it seemed, all with the foliage-figured green-and-purple carpet writhing around underneath. An actual labyrinth, like things from movies and dreams.

Maxine was not sure how far she was from the kitchen, but the panic subsided somewhat. She walked more slowly now; a figure moving so quickly could not be Father, and it was beginning to seem as though the movement might be a trick of the carpet pattern. The more slowly she walked, the more the edges of all things seemed to snake and move, though it was clearly only a clean, bare hallway.

She came to the concessions stand, which had been emptied of supplies long ago. The machines all stood in place, the soda fountains and popcorn makers and coffee makers, but they were cleaned, the sign-screens all blank. A cleaning rag and a fountain soda had been forgotten on the counter. The paper cup had disintegrated at the bottom, a circle of long-dried leakage around it. The rag had been squeezed tightly and dried and mildewed in place.

Sadness overwhelmed Maxine as she made her way back through the halls. The feeling was all about guilt and lost chances at something wonderful. How could she have forgotten the theater so thoroughly, and how had they stopped using it, and why had they wasted the money on it if they weren't going to use it? Really, she had no memory of ever having built or abandoned it, though it was so undeniably familiar, so much a part of her home. The endless hall and the doors to other rooms, she could not search all of these, and Father was not in the theater. There were no films playing, and she had called loudly at every turn. She remembered standing on the glass counter of the concessions area and screaming to him, over and over. It was why her throat hurt so badly. She had done all she could.

In the kitchen, the bottom of the pan had scorched black and was smoking and stinking. She threw the damned thing against the wall. She turned off the burner.

Suddenly, a fantasy of gnawing a frozen ravioli came to her. It would be so soothing, like a baby's teething ring. She took up the bag and tried to pull or pop it open like a bag of chips, but the seal would not break.

She remembered the meat in the microwave, opened the door. The smell was so rich and ripe she gagged. Fat and blood pooled around the edge of the lazy Susan.

She started at Father's call and was soon crying and running through all the rooms again. In his study, this time she remembered to check the door opening out into a vast office suite. Though she could not believe she had forgotten this place, she wasn't hopeful to find him here. She stalked through the empty cubicles at the heart of the workspace and went in and out of the executive offices along its perimeter. There was no one.

She went back to the garage and opened the large door at the back of it, which led to the storage garage with Father's rows of automobiles, each one less used and more outdated than the last. She walked past these many cars with the same feeling of guilt she'd had in the theater. Each vehicle wasted, each one a forgotten treasure. A tiny convertible with burl-wood interior, tires rotting; a glossy blue Wrangler and then a green one of the same year; a limousine with nowhere to go. At the end of the row, she opened the larger garage door and walked down a slope into a vast, empty, low-ceilinged parking garage, and she wandered through it for a half hour, hearing her hoarse calls echo.

When she came back into the kitchen, Father's voice came through clearly for the first time. "Upstairs!" he called. There was something in his voice that suggested all of this had been very silly.

She rushed through the living room toward the corner between the hall and the theater doors where a wrought-iron staircase spiraled. How had she forgotten to check upstairs? How could she have ever forgotten this beautiful staircase, the organic curves of its filigree, black with bright copper embellishments? She climbed and noticed that the copper ornaments at the top, the little grapes and grape leaves and faces, were all aged to thick verdigris.

Her heart, her lungs, her legs felt hot from the strain of the stairs. Her knees and perhaps her hips, too, made creaking noises as she climbed.

"Father?" she called as she walked into a pleasant white sitting room with irregular curved dimensions. There were a few pieces of modern white furniture, dust, and nothing else, no windows.

"All the way up," he called back.

She followed the curved wall on her right, which led up a few steps to another ill-defined white room. This one had just a step stool with a long-dead potted fern on it.

She was beginning to remember how the upstairs section of the house was shaped like a nautilus shell curving up, little room after little room, a half-flight of wide wooden stairs between each, and she regretted never doing much with any of the rooms. The next room held two tall bookshelves filled with forgotten books. The next room was another sitting room barely large enough for its two dusty cut-velvet sofas. She squeezed between them and into the last room. Here,

Father sat on the floor leaning against a bench covered with books, all of them coated in dust and cobwebs, as was the floor. He was still.

This was the last room, the one she always forgot was here, the room no one ever got around to finishing that had so much potential. Father was there on the floor, books stacked around him.

"I was calling and calling," he said. His voice cracked. He was in pain.

The floor was so thick with dust it felt like she was wading through sand, and now she saw how the dust distorted his features. His eyelids lost their shape in it, but his eyes glittered through.

"What's wrong?" she said. "What can I do?"

"Nothing," he said. "I was reading, and this...."

All went to white as he said it. The books were white, her father white, and it all began to blow away around her into blackness. It was as though the whole scene around her were a sculpture made of parmesan, and someone blew it and revealed a black plate beneath.

There wasn't any thought of saving him; the top of his head blew away in the first gust, and the rest of the room was following close upon that. She turned and stumbled back through the rooms of the snail shell, each of them disappearing behind her perhaps, or perhaps not. She did not look back.

Heart pumping, limbs all vibrating, Maxine sat back in her place on the living room sofa. She pulled her afghan over her knees and tucked in her feet, all the time thinking what a strange thing this was to do. She did not look back toward the spiral staircase to see if the rest of the house was going to blow away. She knew, somehow, this was not going to happen. She did not begin to grieve for her father, and yet she knew that the vision upstairs was not exactly her father, not fully her father.

She thought, *I am about to tell myself that there is no upstairs.* There was no staircase in that corner. The hall just kept curving around to the right like a shell getting narrower and narrower. Nothing stands in that hall but a series of identical mirrors and mirror tables, only the mirrors, if you look closely, are just windows with black felt behind them. You run until you're crushed between the walls. It was a dream she'd had.

Maxine decided to say she'd woken up from that dream, but it wasn't so. Still, she practiced thinking she'd woken up here on the sofa just now. Her hand came from under the afghan, grasped the remote control from the sofa arm, turned on the set, and quickly pressed the volume down. She closed her eyes and forced her tense body back into a lounging position. Her abdominal muscles burned, legs burned. Her throat was so sore.

On the television, a man mumbled in tones that reminded her of Steve. It was a soothing sound, like having someone here in the room. She breathed deeply, willing her heart to slow. Of course she could not will herself into sleep, but she no longer felt such keen panic.

Her eyes jerked back to the corner, expecting the staircase might be gone, but it stood solid and steady. Slowly, she stood and approached it.

Behind her, Steve spoke to a reporter. He stood in front of this very house. The front door was visible. Maxine caught this image in the one glance she took. She glanced at the staircase, glanced back at the television as part of a general sweep, and before she registered what it was on the screen, she had her eyes back on the staircase, which stood there the same as ever. The copper faces, copper leaves, the thick black iron steps. She approached it, looked up. No black sky loomed at the top. She felt that if she climbed it again, she would climb through the same rooms, all the way to the top, and her father would not be there. She called, "Father?" and there was no answer.

As she listened, she caught a bit more mumbling from the television, but when she turned to look, it was a commercial for heavy-duty trucks.

She looked down. Behind the staircase, low windows looked out onto rocks close to the glass. Past the rocks, she thought, was a slope of scrubby lawn and then a swimming hole and beyond that the ocean. She could not see any of it because the night was black, but in the morning....

"I said *down*stairs!" Father called, and she looked in that direction. Her right hand lay on the rail to the upstairs staircase, but her left hand rested on the warmer wooden rail of the staircase leading to the basement.

A feeling of dread came to her as the air rose up, earthy and humid. Basement air.

She walked away slowly, back to the kitchen to eat, but she could not. Shaking, she tried to open a sack of cookies, but it would not open. The bread would not move under her teeth. And was the kitchen more beautiful than ever? Cleaner, surfaces glossier and more luxe. She thought it was.

She could sit down at the table, but she couldn't rest. It came to Maxine that she had never sat still, never eaten, never slept. She had never taken pleasure, not once in her entire life. She had only paced and checked and fetched and come when beckoned.

Shaking, she came back to the wooden stairs. He was still calling from somewhere far down. She descended carefully, found the basement not so very dark. The stairs opened onto a small room, but she saw darker stairs leading to a subbasement, rocky, mousehole-shaped openings to the caves, a set of plain double doors that might lead to a cabinet or to another room. A cat made a small sound somewhere deep inside this new labyrinth. Water dripped somewhere.

Terrified, starving, beginning to worry about Father's safety now, Maxine found a flashlight on a shelf at the base of the stairs. She set off.

FULL PUBLICATION HISTORY

'Playmate' is original to this collection.

'Every Day's a Party (With You)'. *Mixtape: 1986* from *The Dread Machine*, 2022 and *Tales to Terrify*, 2023.

'Waterfall'. *Diet Riot: A Fatterpunk Anthology*, 2022.

'One Eye Opened in That Other Place'. *Three-Lobed Burning Eye*, 2023.

'The Portrait of Basil Hallward'. *Tales to Terrify*, 2020 and *long con magazine*, 2022.

'Threads Like Wire, Like Vine'. *Handmade Horror Stories*, 2021 and *Tales to Terrify*, 2022.

'An Education' is original to this collection.

'The Maiden in Robes', *Dark Recesses Press*, 2023.

'Smaller Still Than Me'. *The Arcanist*, 2020.

'The Glass Owl'. *From the Ashes: An Anthology of Elemental Urban Fantasy (for Burn Survivors)*, 2023.

'A Chronicle of the Mole-Year', *Strange Horizons*, 2023.

'The Gods Shall Lay Sore Trouble Upon Them'. *Nightscript*, 2020 and *Boneyard Soup*, 2021.

'Gingerbread' is original to this collection.

'Little Cat, Little Hare' is original to this collection.

'The Encausting'. *Seaside Gothic*, 2022.

'Fall Into Water, Become Someone New'. *The Antihumanist*, 2022.

'She Ain't Stoppin''. *Vastarien*, 2021.

'A Farce'. *Pumpernickel House*, 2022.

'The Apartment'. *Horror Library 7*, 2022.

'The Book of Brats'. *Chthonic Matter, 2023*.

'In Dark Tabittree'. *Cosmic Horror Monthly*, 2023.

'Chicory' is original to this collection.

'The Children of Robbie'. *Black Dandy*, 2017.

'The Pack'. *Underland Arcana*, 2022.

'A White Filigree'. *Three Drops from a Cauldron*, 2018.

'The Second Attempt'. *Land Luck Review*, 2022.

'Night, When Windows Turn to Mirror'. *Mooncalves*, 2023.

CONTENT NOTES

Notes are provided here in hopes of helping readers navigate any difficult content in this collection:

- 'Every Day's a Party (With You)': blood and gore.
- 'Waterfall': indirect references to fatphobia/body shaming.
- 'The Portrait of Basil Hallward': violence, murder.
- 'Blue in the Streets' and 'The Children of Robbie': (off-page) animal deaths.
- 'The Children of Robbie': infants in distress.
- 'A Farce' and 'In Dark Tabittree': sexist ideas.
- 'One Eye Opened in That Other Place', 'The Maiden in Robes', 'The Gods Shall Lay Sore Trouble Upon Them', 'The Encausting', 'Fall Into Water, Become Someone New', and 'The Pack': body horror. I would consider it mild.

ACKNOWLEDGMENTS

This collection is dedicated to the editors and staff of the magazines, journals, small presses, and podcasts that make up our thriving literary scene. These folks have my admiration and gratitude for all they do. There is so much beautiful writing available that would have gone nowhere without their love and attention.

It is fitting to single out Don D'Auria for special thanks, since he took on the project of editing and publishing all three volumes of my short fiction written from 2016 to 2022 in beautiful volumes such as the one you are holding (or screen-reading) right now. I have said this many times, but thank you, Don! I often have grandiose project ideas that do not come to fruition, but this three-volume set of collections was one dream that did come true, with much work and care from you. With *One Eye Opened in that Other Place*, the entire trilogy is now complete! I hope that anyone reading this will consider picking up *The Best of Our Past, the Worst of Our Future: A Collection of Horror Short Stories* and *Promise: A Collection of Weird Science Fiction Short Stories*. Heartfelt thanks to Mike Valsted, Sarah Miniaci, and the entire Flame Tree Press team as well!

I also want to thank the editors of the reprints in this collection: Alin Walker, Monica Louzon, and the team of *The Dread Machine*; Drew Sebesteny, Seth Williams, Meredith Morgenstern and the team of *Tales to Terrify*; Nico Bell and Sonora Taylor, the editors of *Diet Riot: A Fatterpunk Anthology*; Andrew S. Fuller of *Three-Lobed Burning Eye*; Andy Verboom and the team of *long con magazine*; M.M. Macleod, the editor of *Handmade Horror Stories;* Bailey Hunter and the team of *Dark Recesses Press;* Josh Hrala and the team of *The Arcanist;* Zelda Knight of Aurelia Leo; Hebe Stanton and the entire team at *Strange Horizons*; C.M. Muller of Chthonic Matter; T.L. Spezia of *Boneyard Soup;* Seb Reilly of *Seaside Gothic;* Tim Dubber of *The Antihumanist*; Jon Padgett and the wonderful team at

Grimscribe Press; Couri Johnson of *Pumpernickel House;* Charles Tyra and Carson Winter of *Cosmic Horror Monthly*; H. Andrew Lynch of *Black Dandy;* Kate Garrett and the team at *Three Drops from a Cauldron;* Utahna Faith of *Land Luck Review;* and John W.M. Thompson of NO Press. It's wonderful to see many of these venues thriving, but a few others have run their course. All have done astounding work.

While I am at it, a few editors who have not worked on stories in this collection but who are special nonetheless: editors of many of the works that have inspired me over the years include the legendary Ellen Datlow, Andy Cox of TTA Press, Wendy N. Wagner of *Nightmare Magazine*, and Michael Kelly of Undertow Press. I also want to recognize Joe Sullivan of Cemetery Gates Media, who published my Bram Stoker Award®-winning first novel *Beulah*; Alex Hofelich and the entire team at *PseudoPod*, where I work as an Associate Editor; Ai Jiang, with whom I co-edited *Wilted Pages: An Anthology of Dark Academia*, and Alan Lastufka of Shortwave Publishing, who published that book; Willow Dawn Becker, with whom I co-edited *Mother: Tales of Love and Terror* for her Press Weird Little Worlds; Samuel M. Moss, a great writing friend and editor of *ergot*; and writing friends who are also editors such as Alexis Dubon, TJ Price, Jolie S. Toomajan, Sofia Ajram, Christopher O'Halloran, and so many more.

Thanks are also in order to writing groups, critique partners, and so on, but space runs short. They are mentioned in the acknowledgments pages of *The Best of Our Past, the Worst of Our Future* and *Promise: A Collection of Weird Science Fiction Short Stories*.

FLAME TREE PRESS
FICTION WITHOUT FRONTIERS
Award-Winning Authors & Original Voices

Flame Tree Press is the trade fiction imprint of Flame Tree
Publishing, focusing on excellent writing in horror and the
supernatural, crime and mystery, science fiction and fantasy.
Our aim is to explore beyond the boundaries of the everyday,
with tales from both award-winning authors and original voices.

•

Also by Christi Nogle:
Promise
The Best of Our Past, the Worst of Our Future

You may also enjoy:
Think Yourself Lucky by Ramsey Campbell
The Hungry Moon by Ramsey Campbell
The Influence by Ramsey Campbell
The Wise Friend by Ramsey Campbell
Somebody's Voice by Ramsey Campbell
Fellstones by Ramsey Campbell
The Lonely Lands by Ramsey Campbell
The Haunting of Henderson Close by Catherine Cavendish
The Garden of Bewitchment by Catherine Cavendish
In Darkness, Shadows Breathe by Catherine Cavendish
Dark Observation by Catherine Cavendish
The After-Death of Caroline Rand by Catherine Cavendish
Dead Ends by Marc E. Fitch
The Toy Thief by D.W. Gillespie
One By One by D.W. Gillespie
Black Wings by Megan Hart
Silent Key by Laurel Hightower
Will Haunt You by Brian Kirk
We Are Monsters by Brian Kirk
Those Who Came Before by J.H. Moncrieff
Stoker's Wilde by Steven Hopstaken & Melissa Prusi
Stoker's Wilde West by Steven Hopstaken & Melissa Prusi
Land of the Dead by Steven Hopstaken & Melissa Prusi
Whisperwood by Alex Woodroe

•

Join our mailing list for free short stories, new release details,
news about our authors and special promotions:

flametreepress.com